Sindbad the Sailor & other stories from the Arabian Nights

Sindbad the Sailor entertains Sindbad the Landsman.   Page 7

Sindbad the Sailor & other stories from the Arabian Nights

OMEGA BOOKS

First published in 1914 by Hodder and Stoughton

This edition published 1986 by Omega Books Ltd,
1 West Street, Ware, Hertfordshire, under licence
from the proprietor.

Illustrations by Edmund Dulac copyright M.G. Anderson

ISBN 1-85007-062-8
Printed and bound in Hong Kong by South China Printing Co.

ILLUSTRATIONS

SINDBAD THE SAILOR

iii

ILLUSTRATIONS

ALADDIN AND THE WONDERFUL LAMP

iv

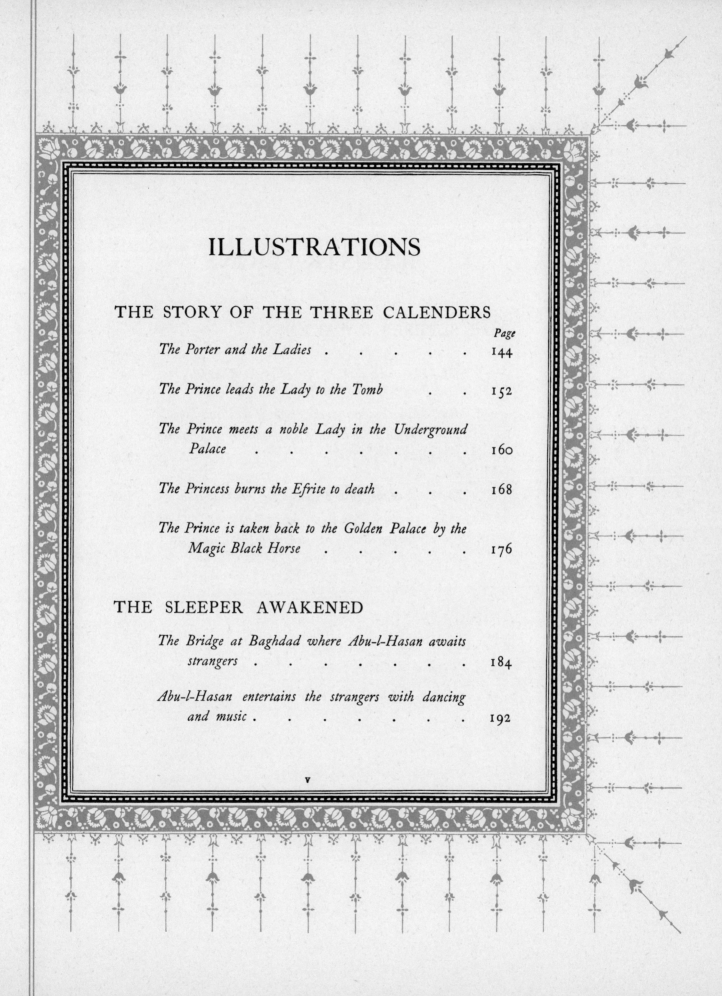

ILLUSTRATIONS

THE STORY OF THE THREE CALENDERS

THE SLEEPER AWAKENED

ILLUSTRATIONS

THE SLEEPER AWAKENED

SINDBAD THE SAILOR

IN the time of Harun-er-Rashid there was, in Baghdad,
a rich merchant named Sindbad the Sailor, the source
of whose wealth was a mystery. It seemed to be
inexhaustible. For long seasons he kept open house, and
his entertainments were the most magnificent of all save
only those of Er-Rashid himself. All that riches could buy
seemed at his disposal, and he lavished the good things of
this life upon his guests. Pages, slaves and attendants there
were in great number ; his garden was spacious and beautiful,
and his house was filled with every costly luxury.

This Sindbad the Sailor has a story to tell—the story of
his life—but he never told it to any until, one day, there
came to him one Sindbad the Landsman, a man of poor and
humble birth. This man pleased him greatly with an apt
recitation dealing with the widely different lots dispensed by
God to men, and, being pleased, he was struck with the
happy conceit that, now Sindbad the Sailor was at last confronted with Sindbad the Landsman, it would be no bad
thing were he to narrate the story of his life so that all might
know his strange adventures and conjecture no longer as to
the source of his fabulous wealth.

Accordingly Sindbad the Sailor held seven receptions
on seven different days, and, although on each occasion a
multitude of guests was assembled to listen, he failed not to
address his words from first to last to his simple listener,

7

Sindbad the Landsman.   Following is his narration of the strange and wonderful adventures he experienced in his seven voyages :—

THE FIRST VOYAGE OF SINDBAD THE SAILOR

MY father was a merchant of high rank and rich possessions.   He died when I was but a child, leaving me all his wealth.   When I reached manhood's estate I used my inheritance with no thought for the morrow, living in a sumptuous manner and consorting with the richest young men of Baghdad.   I continued this life for many years until, at last, when reason prevailed with me to mend my plan, I found with dismay that I had sunk to poverty.   And then it was that I arose and sold what goods remained to me for three thousand pieces of silver, and girded myself, resolving to travel to other lands and rebuild my fortune by the wit of my mind and the labour of my hands.

With a part of my hoard I bought merchandise for exchange in far lands, and also such things as I should require in my travels.   Thus prepared I set sail with a company of merchants in a ship bound for the city of El-Basrah.   For many days and nights we sailed upon the sea, visiting islands and passing thence to other islands ; and everywhere we bartered, and bought and sold.   At length we came to an island unlike the others.   It seemed like a garden that had floated from off the sides of Paradise and established itself in the sea.   And here our ship cast anchor and we landed.   Then fires were lighted, and, while some cooked, others washed in the cool stream, and yet others amused themselves admiring the beauties of the place.

8

When all had eaten of the food prepared the shore became a gay scene of sport and play, in which I engaged to the full. But, suddenly, a cry from the master of the ship put an end to our gaiety. Standing at the side of the vessel he called loudly, "Hear me, and may God preserve you! Hasten back and leave everything; save yourselves from sudden death, for this that ye think is an island is not such. It is a mighty fish lying entranced in sleep on the surface of the sea since times of old, and trees have grown upon it; but your fires and your frolicking have awakened it, and lo! it moves; and, if it sink into the sea, ye will assuredly be drowned. Hasten then, and save yourselves!"

At this we all, with one accord, left everything and fled for the ship, hoping to escape with our lives. While we were making for safety the island moved with a great turmoil and sank behind us in the sea, and the waves leapt against each other above it. For a time I gave myself up as lost, for I was drawn down fathoms deep; but, by God's grace, I rose again to the surface, and to my hand was one of the large wooden bowls which some of the passengers had taken on shore for the purpose of washing. This I seized, and established myself in it, and thus combated the leaping waves, steadying myself with my hands and feet. In vain I called on the master of the ship. He heard me not. He had spread his sails and pursued his way, thinking that none beside those who had been taken up were left alive.

Astride my wooden bowl I gazed longingly at the ship until it was out of sight. Then I prepared for death as the night was closing around me. Perchance I swooned, for I remembered naught else until I found myself stranded upon a mountainous island. There were trees overhanging, and I grasped a drooping bough and drew myself up from the fretting wave. My limbs were benumbed, and, on looking at my legs, I saw the marks made by the nibbling teeth of fish, and marvelled at my salvation from death.

Staggering forward, I flung myself high on the beach like one dead, and so I remained until the dawn of the next day, when the sun, rising upon me, woke me to a sense of such a condition as I had never known before. Long—long it was before I could rise to a sitting posture, and longer still before I could crawl on my hands and knees to a space of grass that was shielded from the sun. Thence, in time, I staggered till I came to a brook, of which I drank; and strength returned to me. I found luscious fruits and ate of them, and drank again of the clear waters of the brook. And so I continued many days roaming the island and wondering at its beauties until I was strong again as before.

And it chanced, as I took my way to and fro in the island, revelling in the sight of things that God had set there, that on a day when the sea was sounding loudly on the shore I beheld something in the distance which excited my curiosity. It seemed like a wild animal of gigantic size, and, as I approached, I feared it was some fabulous beast of the sea. But, as I drew still nearer, I was overcome with amazement to see a beautiful mare standing high, with mane and tail floating on the breeze. She was tethered to a stake on the shore, and, at sight of me, she screamed loudly and stamped her fore-feet on the sand; but, ere I turned to flee, I beheld a man come forth from a cave near by, and he ran after me, calling on me to give an account of myself and my presence in that place. Thereupon I laid my story before him, sparing no detail, even to the wooden bowl by means of which and the grace of God I had come thither.

Gladness seized him at my recital, and he took my hand. Saying, "Come with me!" he led me into his cave and set food before me. I ate until I was satisfied; and, being at my ease, I repeated my story more minutely, and he wondered thereat. Then I said, "Thou hast the truth of my adventures upon the sea; now I pray thee, O my master, tell me who *thou* art, that thou dwellest hidden in a cave while thy mare is tethered on the shore." He was in no way displeased at my curiosity, but answered me in plain words. "I am one of the grooms of the King El-Mihraj," he said, "and the others are scattered about the island. For, look you, friend, it is the time of the new moon, when the sea-horse cometh up out of the sea; and it is our plan to bring our best mares hither and tether them by the shore so that they may lure the sea-horses into our hands."

While I was wondering at the manner of this cunning device a magnificent sea-horse rose from the waves, shaking the foam from its crest and neighing loudly. As it approached, my companion drew me into the cave and placed himself at the opening with a long coil of thick cord in his hand. Presently by means of this he leashed the sea-horse with great dexterity, and fettered him, and subdued him. Then, with the mare and the sea-horse, he led me to his companions, who, when they had heard my story, were all of one mind that I should accompany them to the city of the King. So they mounted me on one of the mares and I rode with them to the King's palace.

As soon as we had arrived at the palace gates they went in to the King and informed him of my strange adventures; whereupon he sent for me, and they led me before him. He greeted me very courteously and bade me tell him my story, which, when he had heard it, filled him with amazement, so that he cried, "By Allah! my son, of a truth thou art favoured by fate; for how else could'st thou escape so great a peril? Praise God for thy deliverance!" And he made much of me and caused me to be treated with honour; and he appointed me master of the harbour and comptroller of the shipping.

My condition then was no longer that of a wayfarer. I rose day by day to a higher and a higher place in the King's favour, and he took me into his council in all affairs of State. For a long time I served him well, and he ceased not to recompense me with a liberal hand. Yet my thoughts turned ever to Baghdad, the Abode of Peace; but, when I enquired of merchants and travellers and masters of ships, in which direction it lay, and how one might come at it, they one and all shook their heads at the name of a strange city of which they had never heard. At last, weary of the wonders of that island and the sea around it—wonders the which, if I had time to tell you, would cause you the greatest amazement,— wearied, too, with my arduous duties, but most of all with my prolonged absence from my own land, I stood one day on the sea shore when a great ship drew near and a number of merchants landed from it.

The sailors brought forth their merchandise, and, when I had made an account of it, I enquired of the master of the ship if that were the whole of his cargo. "All, O my master," he replied; "all save some bales whose owner was drowned on our voyage hither; but even these, being in my charge, I desire to sell on behalf of his family in Baghdad." "Sayest thou so?" I cried. "Tell me, I pray thee, the name of the owner of these goods." And he replied, "His name was Sindbad the Sailor, and he was drowned on our way hither."

When I heard this I regarded him more closely and recognised him. Then I cried out, "O my master, I am he; and they are my goods that are in thy hold." But he neither recognised me nor believed my words; whereupon I narrated to him the history of my supposed death; but he shook his head and called upon Allah to witness that there was neither faith nor conscience in any. "Look you!" he said. "Thou heardst me say the owner was dead, and therefore thou desirest the goods for thyself free of price. I tell thee we saw him sink into the sea with many others." "O my master," I answered, "hear me and then judge of my veracity." With this I narrated to him many trivial things which happened before we reached the great-fish island, and which could never be known to me had I not been on the ship. And then it was that he and many of the merchants regarded me with fixed looks and recognised me. "By Allah!" said they one and all, "we truly believed thee drowned, but here we find thee alive." And they pressed upon me and congratulated me, and the master of the ship gave me my goods, at sight of which I was overjoyed; and they all rejoiced with me.

Mindful of the King I served, I at once opened my bales, and, selecting the most costly articles, went in to him and laid them at his feet, telling him how I had regained the goods of which they were a part. And the King wondered greatly at my good fortune and graciously accepted my gifts. He also showed me great favour and honour in that he bestowed upon me gifts in return for mine.

Then, having sold my remaining goods at a profit, I

13

bought largely of the merchandise of the city, and, when the ship was about to sail, I approached the King and thanked him for his great kindness to me, and humbly begged his leave to depart to my own city and family. So he gave me his blessing and a great wealth of merchandise and rare commodities, and bade me farewell. And soon thereafter, having stowed all my goods in the hold of the ship, I set sail with the others for Baghdad.

Our voyage was fortunate, and, with the aid of favourable winds, we reached the city of El-Basrah in safety. Thence I repaired to Baghdad, and my family and my friends gave me a joyous welcome. And when I had sold my merchandise I set up a large establishment, sparing no cost. And I bought land and houses, and gathered round me wealthy companions, in whose society I soon forgot the dangers and terrors I had suffered in other lands. Such is the story of my first voyage; and, to-morrow, by God's grace, I will narrate to you the strange adventures of my second voyage.

THE SECOND VOYAGE OF SINDBAD THE SAILOR

AS I related yesterday, I was living here in Baghdad in the midst of every delight, surrounded by companions after my own heart. But a time came when the wandering spirit seized me again and I longed for the sight, even for the perils, of other and unknown lands. This, and the fact that I had decreased my substance by large expenditure, led me to adventure a second journey, at once to relieve the monotony of life and to replenish my exhausted store.

The step was quickly taken. Having collected suitable merchandise I repaired to the river, and, without a word to anyone, embarked on a new ship finely rigged and manned by a large crew. Together with a goodly party of merchants I sailed away, and we passed over the deep from island to island and from sea to sea, with fair winds filling the sails. And at every place at which we cast anchor we bought and sold and bartered. So we continued until we came to an uninhabited island of great beauty. The trees hung with ripe fruits; birds of bright plumage flew hither and thither over the shining foliage, and their songs were heard in the topmost branches; rare flowers laid their scent upon the breeze, and pure clear streams coursed everywhere. When we landed we fell to extolling these master touches of the Creator's hand, for, indeed, the place was, as it were, born of fragrant musk—so fresh and beautiful and full of all delights not made by man. Selecting a rare spot on the bank of a stream, I sat apart, meditating upon the wonderful works of the Omnipotent One. There the soft zephyrs singing in the trees, and the stream murmuring at my feet, lulled me to slumber; and, when I awoke later, I looked forth upon the sea and lo, the ship was far out on the wall of the ocean sloping to the sky. They had forgotten me and I was left alone upon the island.

Despair fell upon me as I gazed around and realised that I was desolate. And I said within myself, "What if I escaped from dangers in the past when all seemed lost—it still remains that here at least there is no escape." Then I blamed myself for leaving my comfortable life in Baghdad to undertake this voyage; for here there was neither strong food nor strong drink; nor rich apparel, nor gold, nor goods. As I pondered to the point of madness on these things a restless spirit came upon me, and I ran to and fro in the island, retracing my steps and crossing them; but I found naught to lessen my despair.

At last I climbed to the top of a high tree, and, looking forth in every direction, saw only sky and sea and trees and watercourses. As I gazed, however, my eye reverted again and again to an object in a distant part of the island. It was round and white, and of enormous size. This aroused my curiosity and I resolved to find out what it was. Having marked its position I descended from the tree and made my way towards it. When I reached it I found to my astonishment that it was a gigantic dome, white and shining. My first thought was to walk round it to ascertain if there were some door or opening, but none could I find in its whole circumference, which was about fifty paces.

While I was meditating on some means to gain an entrance to this strange structure, behold, the sky darkened; and on looking towards the sinking sun, I saw it was hidden by a great black cloud,—an unwonted thing, as it was the summer season. While I continued to gaze the object drew rapidly nearer, and now I could discern in it the shape of a monstrous bird approaching swiftly through the air; and this it was that blotted out the sun.

Marvelling greatly I recalled a story told by travellers about certain islands where was found a bird of immense size called the rukh, which fed its young on elephants. It was then I knew that the great white dome I had discovered was one of this bird's eggs,—at which, not the least of the Creator's works, I wondered greatly. Then, while I so wondered, the giant bird alighted over the egg, and, crouching down, spread its wings and brooded over it, and composed itself to sleep.

The Episode of the Whale.   Page 9

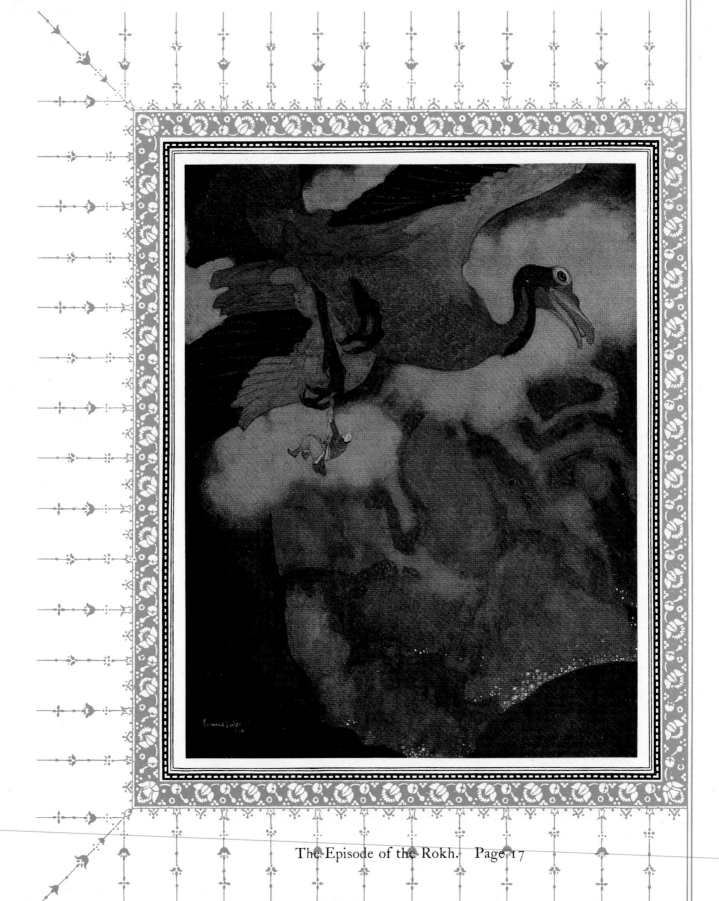

The Episode of the Rokh.   Page 17

Here, thought I, was a chance of escaping from the island. Unfolding my turban I twisted it into a rope, and bound one end of it tightly about my waist; then I approached the great bird cautiously, and fastened the other end securely to one of its feet; for thus, when it flew away, it might perchance bear me through the air to some inhabited region.

The whole night long I lay awake thinking of my projected flight, but it was not until morning that the bird awoke, and, with a loud cry, rose from the egg, bearing me aloft. Higher and higher it soared, until I thought it must reach the stars; then, gradually, in vast circles, it descended, and finally came to earth on a high table-land. In great fear lest the bird should discover my presence I made haste to loose the turban from its foot, and, having done so, I crept away, trembling in every limb. Then, as I watched the bird from a distance, I observed it pick something from the ground and soar away with it clutched in its talons; and I looked again and saw that it was an enormous serpent twisting and writhing in the grasp of the bird as it flew swiftly towards the sea. And at this strange thing I wondered greatly as I folded my turban.

But what desert place had I come to by this daring misadventure? On the one side of the table-land was a deep valley, and, on the other, a steep mountain which no foot of man could climb. Had I only remained in the island I should at least have had fruit to eat and water to drink, but here was nothing but desolation, from which I had no hope of escape. There was no course but to descend into the valley; and this I did, little caring whither I went.

Now, I had not walked therein but a few furlongs when I observed that the ground I trod was strewn with diamonds

of large size, but—and this gave me cause for wild alarm—
coiled here and there amongst the stones were gigantic
serpents such as the one I had seen the bird bear away in its
talons.   As soon as I was aware of these sleeping serpents,
which were of the same hue as the ground whereon they lay,
I stept warily lest I should awaken them and be devoured.

In this way was I proceeding down that valley, my flesh
quaking and my knees a-tremble, when suddenly the flayed
carcase of a slaughtered beast fell with a great noise before
me.   This aroused great wonder in my mind and also called
to my recollection a story I had heard in my youth from a
merchant traveller who had visited lands whence none else had
ever come to deny the truth of it—a story confirmed by others
who claimed a reputation for wide knowledge, and feared to
lose it.   It was this—that in a far land, where diamonds are
as thickly strewn as the venomous serpents and other deadly
perils which render it difficult to come at them, the daring
merchants who seek these precious stones employ a cunning
stratagem.   They take a beast and slaughter it on the heights
above the valley, and, having skinned it and lacerated the
flesh, they throw it down.   And, when it reaches the bottom
of the valley whereon the diamonds lie, the stones adhere to
the moist flesh.   From the depths of the sky descends the
watching vulture of the giant kind, and this bird, seizing the
carcase in its talons, soars with it to the mountain tops;
whereupon the merchants spring out and frighten the bird
away with loud cries, and then take the stones adhering to
the meat and bear them to their own country.   I had my
whole life long regarded this story with a half-shut eye, but
now, beholding the slaughtered beast before me, and guessing full well the meaning of its presence there, I said within

18

myself, "By Allah! no marvel is past belief, for here is the verification." I surveyed that carcase and, having measured in a glance the distance to the mountains whence it had descended, I gazed into the blue sky in whose depths lurked the watching vulture. A plan of escape then came to me and I hastened to put it into operation. First I gathered as many diamonds as I could well dispose within my garments. Then, unfolding my turban, I approached the slaughtered beast, and, lying on my back, drew it over me and bound myself firmly to it.

I had not lain long in that position, with the heavy weight of the beast upon me, when a monstrous vulture came out of the sky, and, seizing upon the carcase with a loud scream, gripped it in its powerful talons and rose up and away with it and me. And it rose higher and higher, with a mighty flapping of its wings, until at last it alighted on a broad ledge near the summit of the mountain—a place which, judging by the bleached bones lying on every hand, was the favourite feeding-place of these birds. This was clearly known to the merchant who had cast the carcase down, for, no sooner had the vulture deposited his burden and started to tear at the flesh, than he sprang out with loud cries and scared it away.

Half smothered by the weight of the slaughtered beast I lost no time in freeing myself, and soon I struggled to my feet and stood there with my clothes stained and polluted with its blood. When the merchant saw me his fear was great; but his disappointment was even greater when, his fear mastered by the lust of gain, he turned the carcase over and found no diamonds sticking to the flesh. Pitying him in his sad case—for he was smiting hand on hand and calling

19

out against fate—I advanced and said, "Curse not fate, nor fear me, for I am of thy kind, and I bear with me an abundance of these stones the loss of which thou lamentest; and they are of the largest that a man can carry upborne by a vulture's wings. Of these will I give unto thee; therefore forget thy fear and bury thy disappointment."

On hearing this the merchant thanked me and prayed fervently for me and my family; and he ceased not to pray for the prolongation of my life until I had bestowed upon him the largest diamonds I could find within my garments. While he was thanking me for this there came his companions, each of whom had cast down a carcase; and, when they had heard the story of my escape, they congratulated me and bade me come with them, for they said, "By Allah! thou art greatly favoured by fate, since none but thee hath been in that valley and escaped to tell the tale."

After my perilous adventures, and my despairing sojourn in the valley of serpents, I was filled with the utmost joy at finding my fellow mortals around me; and, seeing this, they made me welcome among them, and I partook of their food and wine. We passed the night in a safe place, and, when morning came, we set forth over the mountain ranges overlooking the valley of the serpents and at length descended to a stretch of sea. This we crossed by means of the boats which they had moored by the shore, and came thus to a low-lying island where grew camphor trees in abundance, each of which might shield a hundred men from the sun. Here, too, upon the plains roamed the wild rhinoceros, of which wonderful tales are told by people who return from unknown lands. This beast impales an elephant upon its horn with ease, and wanders thus, with little hindrance to its

20

pasturing, until the fat of the elephant, melting in the heat of the sun, and flowing down into its eyes, renders it blind; whereupon it seeks the seashore and lies down until such time as the rukh may find it and carry both it and the elephant away as a morsel for its young. But I speak of what I know and, as I saw naught of this kind, I can but say that I know not.

I continued with my companions for some space, journeying from island to island and exchanging the diamonds we had acquired for rich merchandise. And, in passing through many countries unheard of in this city, I separated from them and went my way, coming at length to El-Basrah with a princely cargo of goods. Thence I journeyed to Baghdad, the Abode of Peace, and rejoined my family. Wealth I had in abundance, and I resorted to my former life of luxury, bestowing gifts and alms, wearing rich apparel, and eating and drinking with my companions. This is the story of my second voyage, and by the grace of God (whose name be exalted!) I will narrate to-morrow the still more remarkable adventures that befell me on my third voyage.

THE THIRD VOYAGE OF SINDBAD THE SAILOR

HAVING rested for a space in Baghdad, where I lived surrounded by every happiness and delight, I began again to experience that restless desire for travel and commerce which had drawn me forth on my former voyages. When the desire grew so great that I could no longer withstand it, I set out with a large stock of merchandise and arrived at the city of El-Basrah, where I took ship, together with a goodly company of merchants, and others of high standing and repute.

For many days we sailed outwards, buying and selling among the islands; until, one day, while we were in the midst of the ocean, a storm descended upon us and blew the ship out of its course. The wind continued from one quarter with great violence, and for a day and night we were hurled before it. When morning came it abated, and the master of the ship looked forth on every hand to ascertain where we were. Suddenly he uttered a loud cry and plucked his beard. "God preserve us!" he said. "The gale hath driven us to an evil fate. See! yonder is the Mountain of Apes! None hath ever come near it and escaped."

We looked and beheld a high mountain on an island, and, while we were gazing at it, and wondering where lay the danger at so great a distance, behold, the sea around us was swarming with apes which had swum out from the island. They were hideous black beasts, not of large size, but of malignant aspect; and so great was their number that we were powerless to stand against them. They climbed up the sides of the ship and seized upon the ropes, which they severed with their sharp teeth so that the sails were powerless and the vessel drifted with tide and wind to the shore. There we were seized by the apes and set on the land, after which they returned to the ship and bent fresh ropes and set the sails and departed over the sea we knew not whither. But we ceased to wonder at the manner of their going, for we were in a desperate plight, since all sailors feared the Mountain of Apes and no ship would ever approach the island to rescue us.

In our wanderings through the island, eating of its fruits and drinking of its streams, we came at length to an open space in which stood a house of gigantic size. The walls

22

and the folding doors of ebony were very lofty, and, when we walked into an immense apartment—for the doors were open—we found everything within it of a corresponding size. The cooking utensils were large enough to cook an ox whole, and, on the couch at the upper end, a hundred men might sit with comfort. But no occupant could we find, so we seated ourselves and rested for a while, and then we slept.

It was about sunset when we were awakened suddenly by a loud noise and a trembling of the earth; and lo, we beheld coming from the further end of the apartment a gigantic being in the shape of a man. His skin was black, and his eyes blazed like fire; two gleaming tusks protruded from his great mouth, his enormous ears drooped to his shoulders, and his nails were like the sharp claws of a beast of prey. We were stricken with great fear at the approach of this frightful being so that we could neither move nor cry out while he advanced to the couch and disposed his huge limbs thereon. Then, on turning his head, he caught sight of us and arose and came towards us. As I was nearest to his hand he seized me, and, taking me from the ground, turned me over and over in his palm, feeling my limbs to see if they were fat. But, by the grace of God (whose name be exalted!) I was lean and wasted with fatigue and affliction; so he set me down and seized another, whom he turned over and felt in the same manner. He, too, was lean, and he let him go; but he took one after another until he came to the master of ship—a big man and fat. With him he was satisfied. Then, seeing what he was about to do, we hid our eyes, and did not look again until the ogre, having cooked and eaten our master, threw his bones upon a heap of others on one side of the apartment. Afterwards he arose and laid himself down upon the couch and slept, and his snoring was like the roll of thunder.

We crept forth from that house in terror, feeling that it were happier to be killed by apes or drowned in the sea than to be roasted on live coals—a terrible death for a man! We then considered means of hiding, or escaping from the place. But there was no place to hide, and the ship, our only way of escape, was gone. While we were lamenting, a spell seemed to be cast over us, so that our very excess of fear drew us back to the ogre's house, wherein we sat as before, and slept.

Again we were awakened by the thunder of the ogre's approach, and again he came and selected one of our number. When, having eaten, he slept upon the couch, we conversed together, thinking to find some way of escape. One said, "By Allah! by Allah! let us kill him!" and he proposed a plan. "Listen, O my brothers!" I said on hearing this; "if we seek to kill him let us first prepare some rafts on which to escape, for we may fail of our purpose; and on these rafts we can at worst be drowned, which is better than being roasted." They answered me, "Thou art right!" So we set to work and gathered stout pieces of wood and carried them to the seashore, where we constructed rafts and stowed food upon them in readiness for a hasty departure. Then we returned to the giant's house to carry out our plan.

The sound of his snoring told us he still slept, so we took two sharp-pointed iron spits and heated the points red-hot in the fire. Then we approached him cautiously, and, at a given signal, thrust the red-hot points one into each of his eyes, and bore upon the spits with our combined weight. He arose with a mighty roar, and we fled right and left; for,

24

his sight being destroyed, we feared his blind rage. He searched for us, but, not finding us, he groped for the door, and went forth uttering loud cries which shook the earth.

In great haste, and lashed by mortal fear, we gained the seashore and launched the rafts; but, scarcely had we gained the water, when we saw the ogre approaching, led by a female more gigantic and more hideous than himself. We swam out, pushing the rafts before us; but they hurled great rocks after us, and many of our number were killed. Three alone, including myself, escaped, and, after much stress and peril, reached another island.

We had gained at length what seemed to us a place of safety, high and dry above the wave and far from the ogre's domain; and there, when night came on, we slept, but only to awaken to fresh terrors. Lo! in the act of coiling round us was a serpent of enormous size, its folds contracting and its head raised to strike. At sight of this, another and myself were more nimble than our companion, for we sprang clear of the serpent's embrace while he was seized in the huge jaws and slowly swallowed with a horrible crackling of bones. And we mourned our companion and went thenceforth in fear for ourselves. Dreading to sleep again on the ground we climbed a high tree, and, binding ourselves each in a safe position with our turbans, we slept fitfully. But alas! God hath given to all serpents the wisdom of the Evil One. That night the serpent mounted the tree, and, seizing my companion, proceeded to swallow him, while I looked on in helpless fear. Then, in descending the tree, it coiled its vast bulk round the trunk and I heard my companion's bones crack within its paunch.

When morning had come I descended from the tree feeling

D

that my safest course was to drown myself in the waves, for where else could I hide that the serpent could not find me? But life is sweet, and I pondered long upon a cunning plan to protect myself. Then, repairing to the seashore, I selected some pieces of wood from the raft, and took them to a dry place. Towards evening, when I had eaten of the fruits of the island and drunk of its streams, I bound a long piece of wood crosswise upon the soles of my feet and another crosswise upon my head; I secured a wide flat piece to my right side, another to my left side, and another to the front of my body; and there, having thrust my arms under the side pieces, I lay encased. And, as the evening wore on, the serpent saw me, and drew near; but it could not swallow me because of the pieces of wood. All through the night it tried to come at me, attempting in all ways to effect its purpose; but in every way it failed, while I lay like a dead man, gazing in speechless horror at the terrible creature. And it ceased not in its efforts to engulf me till morning broke, when it went its way consumed with rage and vexation. Then I freed myself from the pieces of wood and arose, trembling in every limb, but thanking God for my deliverance; for, look you, I was sorely tried by what I had endured from that serpent.

Not many hours later I had the good fortune to espy a ship far out upon the sea, and, as it was making as if to pass a headland of the island somewhat closely, I ran with all speed and established myself on the furthest point. There I waved my unfolded turban to attract the notice of those on the vessel. At last they saw me, and came and took me on board. They listened to my story with great astonishment, and congratulated me on my escape. Then they gave me clean raiment, and set food and drink before me, so that I was revived and comforted. And, as we proceeded on our way I was emboldened to look back on all I had suffered as nothing more than a terrible dream.

In the course of our journey we came to an island where the sandal wood grows, and here I landed with the other merchants. But they had goods to sell, while I, alas! had none. Then, strange to relate, the same kind Providence that had befriended me on my first voyage was at my service once more, and in the same guise. The master of the ship, seeing me without merchandise, came to me, and, taking compassion upon my poor condition, told me of some goods in the hold which belonged to a man whom they had lost during the voyage. He offered me these goods to sell upon the island so that, when an account had been rendered to the owner's family in Baghdad, there would be a recompense for my trouble and service. I thanked him gladly for this, and he ordered the goods to be brought up and landed on the island. And lo! when I saw the bales, I knew them, and showed how they were marked with the name of Sindbad the Sailor. Then, seeing that they were perplexed, I shouted in my excitement, "Do you not hear me? *I* am Sindbad the Sailor, and these are my goods!"

While some believed and others doubted I related my story from the time I had awakened upon the island to find myself alone; and, when I mentioned the valley of diamonds, a merchant came forward and confirmed my words, for it was he whose slaughtered beast had helped me to safety. "Hear me, ye doubters!" he said. "When I related this very thing to you, you believed me not; but see—this is the man I spoke of, and now you have it independently from his own mouth. Learn from this, O my brothers, never while living, doubt a true tale because it is marvellous." Then the master asked me what was the distinguishing mark of my goods, and I replied that it was such and such a mark, and I also called to his mind some conversation between him and me before the ship left El-Basrah. He was then convinced that I was Sindbad the Sailor, and he congratulated me and embraced me, saying that my story was most extraordinary.

The remainder of this, my third voyage, was occupied in buying and selling among the islands on the way to El-Basrah, whence, in good time, laden with wealth and rich merchandise, I proceeded to Baghdad to dwell in peace again, surrounded by my family and friends. Here, for a season, charmed with every delight, I forgot the perils and horrors I had endured. But the longing for travel and adventure found me out again, impelling me to undertake a fourth voyage ; and the events of this—more marvellous than those of the preceding voyages, O Sindbad, the Landsman—I will narrate to you to-morrow.

THE FOURTH VOYAGE OF SINDBAD THE SAILOR

LED by the desire to associate with other races, and to buy and sell for gain,—for the soul is prone to evil,— I departed from Baghdad with many precious bales, and set sail from El-Basrah in a large ship on which a company of other merchants embarked in like fashion.

For many days we had a pleasant journey among the islands, and all went well with us until, on reaching the wider sea beyond, a mighty wind came up against us. The sea rose in great waves as the tempest increased, and we were in dire peril. More and more violent grew the gale, lashing the sea into fury. The sails were rent, the masts were blown away, we sprang a leak, and slowly the vessel began to sink. We gave ourselves up for lost, and, indeed, when the waves passed over us and we sank, many perished. But, in the seething turmoil, it was my good fortune to be cast against a broad plank, which I seized and held. Others were struggling for life near by and I was able to draw some of them to me. Sore buffetted as we were by wind and wave we mounted that plank and sat astride of it. Thus, through a whole day and night, we drifted before the gale, now descending into despairing hollows of the sea, and now flung up on the mountain tops of billows. At dawn on the following day the sea cast us like dead men upon an island, where, for many hours, we lay exhausted. Albeit, strength began to return to us again, and we arose feebly, and staggered forth into the island. Fruit and herbs there were in abundance, and clear fresh water ; so we ate and drank and were revived.

That night we slept upon the shore, and in the morning we arose strengthened and invigorated. When we had broken our fast we set ourselves to explore the island, and had not gone far in this before we came to a great building. As we stood at the door of this, wondering who dwelt within, a party of naked men came out, and without a word, seized us and led us in to a spacious apartment, where we found ourselves standing before their King. He commanded us to be seated, and they brought us food of a strange kind, such as we had never seen. My companions ate largely of this but my stomach revolted at it and I ate but little—a thing which preserved me from a terrible fate. For, as my companions ate, they became mad with a ravenous hunger, and ate more and more. Presently they were given cocoanut oil to drink, and, when they had swallowed it, their eyes rolled in their heads, and they continued to eat in a frenzy horrible to behold.

I was consumed with fear at these things and said within myself, " This is a tribe of the Magi and their King is a ghoul ! " As I observed them attentively I remembered a story of these people : how they seize on travellers and set this loathsome food before them to eat, and give them the oil to drink, so that they swell out and eat more and more until they are fattened to an enormous degree and their minds are rendered like those of idiots ; whereupon, in due time, they kill and roast them and serve them up as food to their King. And all these things I saw in the days that my companions were fattening, for there were others who had been seized before us, and each day one of these was killed and roasted and set before the King.

While I was wasting away with fear and hunger—and it was on this account that they forgot me and left me to die in my own way—my companions had come to be like dull, heavy, stupid beasts of the field, so that they were placed in the care of a beastherd, who led them forth every day to the pasturage. As for myself, as soon as I observed that I was a failure in that I would not fatten, and that none took heed of me nor marked my coming or my going, I arose in the night and crept away among the trees surrounding the King's dwelling. Then, when morning came, I went forth with a heart of fear, knowing not what fresh terror I should encounter. In my wanderings back and forth I came about midday to a stretch of green pasture, where I beheld with

30

sorrow my late companions grazing on all fours, and fattening like beasts for the slaughter, while the beastherd sat upon a rock and piped on an oaten reed. I breathed a silent farewell to them as to those I should never see again, and turned sadly away.

My heart was cold within me, and my steps were faltering as I wandered on, pausing here and there to gather edible herbs and roots, which, for want of something better, served to sustain life in my body. Journeying in this way I came at length to a grove of pepper trees, and there were men at work in it, gathering the berries. Their aspect seemed to me to be peaceable, so I exposed myself, and they approached me and pressed upon me, asking my name and whence I had come, for my aspect excited their curiosity. Then I unfolded to them the tale of the adventures, the perils, and the horrors that had befallen me; and, when I had related the sad case of my companions, they wondered greatly at my escape. While they resumed their work, they made me welcome amongst them, and set nutritious food before me, the like of which I had not tasted for many days. I regaled myself on their bounty and rested, and was content.

When they had finished their work at the setting of the sun they took me with them to the seashore, and I accompanied them in their vessel to an island, not far distant, where they brought me to their King. And, there, before them and his court, at his command I narrated my adventures since leaving Baghdad, at which his interest was kindled, and he bade me sit with him and eat. And I did so gladly, for my body was thin and meagre, and my vigour was sorely wanting. After that, having shewn my gratitude to the King and offered praise to God for His saving grace, I rose, and, with the King's permission, went forth into his city. It was a well-conditioned, flourishing place, thronged with buyers and sellers; and there was an abundance of food and rich merchandise.

As day followed day and time drew on I had cause to rejoice at my arrival in that city, for I found favour with the King, and he magnified me over his people and his great men. Observing the ways of the people, I saw that the horses that they rode were without saddles; whereupon I went in to the King and spoke to him on the matter, describing a saddle and the ease and comfort of it. At this the King desired me to make him one, and placed at my disposal his cleverest carpenter with many tools and instruments. And I sat with the carpenter and instructed him how to proceed, so that the saddle, covered with polished leather and stuffed with teased wool, was soon complete. I attached stirrup-straps and girths, and showed the blacksmith how to fashion the stirrups. Then, with the aid of costly fringes and trappings, the work was complete. Full of satisfaction I sent for one of the King's finest horses, saddled and bridled him, and led him before His Majesty. He was greatly pleased at the sight of what I had done, and, when he had mounted the horse and sat in the saddle, he was overjoyed at the ease and pleasure of it, and bestowed upon me a large reward.

When the King's chief officials and the grandees of his Court saw the saddle which I had made, they each and all desired me to make others like it. Then, with the carpenter and the blacksmith, I employed many days in the construction of numerous saddles, and for these I received much gold, and rose to an assured position in the land.

The high rank and honour which the King had bestowed upon me had but half expressed his heart towards me. I was yet to learn that he had a further favour in store. One day, while I was sitting at his right hand discussing affairs of state, he said to me, "O my son, seeing thou hast now become as one of us and we cannot part with thee, I desire that thou give ear to a matter which I have planned and which will bind thee more closely to us." And I answered him, "For thy great kindness to me, O King, I am now and henceforth thy faithful servant. What dost thou desire me to do?" And he looked at me intently and said, "I would marry thee to a woman of high rank among us—one possessed of great beauty and wealth—so that thou mayest continue to dwell with us in pleasure and comfort and with a good heart. Thus shalt thou advantage greatly and receive every good thing at my hands; wherefore, refuse me not, nor oppose my wish."

I remained silent, for I was overwhelmed by his proposal and the stress of bashfulness it brought to my face. Seeing this, he rallied me and said, "Art thou dumb? Is not thy heart with us?" Then of a sudden I replied, "O King! Thy words took away my breath. As thou commandest, so I obey."

Pleased at my compliance the King immediately ordered his officials to bring the lady and the witnesses, and forthwith I was married to her with the King's blessing and the ac- clamation of all his Court. She was of surpassing loveliness, and she brought me a dowry of abundant wealth and possessions. And to this the King added a magnificent house with servants and slaves, and assigned me a handsome salary. And I lived in ease and comfort, our days being full of delights. Gone was all thought of the perils and hardships I had endured, and gone was the fear of adversities in store. But there is no strength nor power but in God, and He orders the fates of men as He will. On an evil day a great fear suddenly came to me by reason of a thing which I will make known to you.

A companion of mine suffered a bereavement in that his wife died; whereupon I went to him, and mourned with him, saying, "Take heart, O brother; God will fill her place to thee with one far better." But he continued to weep, saying, "Alas! How can I marry another when this very day I depart this life?" "Nay," said I, "that is not within reason, for thou art in good health and not like to die." He then raised his head and dried his tears, and said to me very slowly, "Hear me, O my brother! Knowest thou not that, to-day, they will bury my wife, and that they will bury me also in the same tomb with her? For such is our custom. When husband or wife is buried the other must be buried also, so that neither may continue to enjoy life alone."

"By Allah!" said I, smiting palm on palm, "this custom is wholly vile, and it toucheth me closely." Then, as we continued to discuss this matter, there came others who condoled with my companion, grieving not only for the loss of his wife, but also that they should never see him more. And, later in the day, came yet others bearing a bier; and on this they laid the woman and carried her forth prepared for burial with all her jewels and raiment and wealth. And the husband went with them.

Through sympathy with my companion, and to bid him a last farewell, I followed this funeral procession till it halted in a distant spot on the sea-shore. There a great stone was lifted and a vault exposed. Into this they threw the body of the woman, and then, by means of a stout cord, they lowered the husband gently till he rested by her side. A pitcher of water and seven cakes were then let down to him, and, when he had freed himself from the cord, they drew it up and closed the sepulchre and went their ways.

"By Allah!" said I within myself as I smote myself on my breast, "this manner of death is the worst of all!" And on my return I went in to the King with grief and fear gnawing at my heart. "O King!" I said, "Tell me why is this: that ye bury the living with the dead?" Said he, "O my son, it is the custom of our country and has descended to us from our ancestors: husband and wife are one, in death as in life." And I answered him with a question that concerned me nearly. "O my lord," I said, "and the stranger that sojourneth with thee: if his wife die, do ye treat him in like manner?" "Yea," he replied, "in like manner, even as thou hast seen." Then I departed from him in grief and mourning lest I should perchance be bereft of my wife. In vain did I say to myself, "Be comforted! Maybe thou wilt die before her—none knoweth." In vain did I give myself up to my manifold occupations. The fear was not to be dispelled.

And, within a short time, what I had feared came to pass. My wife was stricken with a fever, and, when I had reason to hope she would recover, she suddenly relapsed and died. My grief at this was overwhelming, but, as if to add to it, there came many to condole with me on her death and to mingle their tears with mine for that I should soon be departing this life. The King himself came and commiserated with me on my most unhappy fate. And he said, "There is no strength nor power in any but God. Farewell, O my son!"

And they prepared my wife for burial, arraying her in her richest garments and her finest jewels. But, when they carried her to the burial place and cast her down into the pit, and all my companions pressed upon me to bid me farewell, my gorge rose and I cried out upon them that their custom was vile. Loudly I spoke my bitter mind on the abominable nature of this thing; they would not listen, but took me by force and lowered me into the pit, together with the seven cakes and the pitcher of water. And when I had reached the floor of a vast cavern they called down to me: "Untie the ropes that we may draw them up!" I answered, "Draw me up with them!" "Nay, nay;" they replied, "we do but follow our custom." "To the ravens with you and your custom!" I retorted, for I had no stomach for this proceeding. Then, as I steadily refused to loose the ropes, they at last threw them down upon me, and, having closed the mouth of the pit, went their way.

Now was I in worse plight than I had ever been. On that cavern floor there were the bodies and bleached bones of those that had died a natural death cheek by jowl with those who had perished in the fulfilment of this abominable custom. And I said to myself, "Better to remain single and live, than to marry and be buried alive."

Nevertheless, knowing not night from day, I kept myself from death by eating sparingly of the cakes and drinking some of the water, for I was in no mood to die in so vile a manner after having come through great perils by mountain and sea. At length, when I had eaten all the cakes and drunk all the water, and hunger and thirst began to cry out within me, I arose and wandered to and fro in the cavern, stumbling and falling over dead bodies and biting the dust of bones that had

36

crumbled long since. By dint of much groping in the dark I at length found the wall of the cavern, and, selecting therein a cavity free from bones and corpses, I stretched myself and slept.

I was awakened later as if by hunger and thirst knocking at the door ; and, while I sat in gloom thinking of the plenty in Baghdad—fool that I was to leave it !—I heard a sudden noise. Looking forth from my cavity, I saw that the stone had been removed from the opening of the cavern and a dead body was being lowered. It was the body of a man, and after him was let down the living body of his wife. She was weeping and wailing for him and for herself. Then the mouth of the cavern was closed again and all was dark and silent save for the wailing of the woman echoing through the cavern. "Alas !" she cried, "that I should die this lingering death ! Had I the means to end my life, then would I do it. Would that there were one here to slay me !"

When I heard this I remembered that I had never been able to resist the pleadings of a woman. So I arose, and, taking a stout leg-bone in my hand, I slew her according to her desire. And I took her seven cakes and the pitcher of water, which she would no longer need, and, retiring to my cavity, I ate and drank. This thing occurred many times during my sojourn in that cavern, for a number of married men and women chanced to die. And, though they did not always cry out for me to slay them, I knew their prayer before-hand and answered it speedily. Thus the cakes and the water bequeathed to me stayed my spirit and I continued to live.

Time passed slowly, but yet it passed. I had no other means of measuring it except to call an hour a day and a day

a year. And I was weary to death of it all when an unwonted thing occurred. I was awakened suddenly from
sleep by a noise at the far end of the cavern. Then I heard
footsteps as of some beast. I arose, and, arming myself with
a stout bone, advanced upon the intruder; but it heard me
and fled from me, and I could not come at it. Yet, as I
followed its footsteps, I saw its form darken a pin-spot of
daylight at the end of a crevice of the cavern. This gave me
a glimmer of hope, for, where that beast had passed, I myself
might pass, and so gain the outer air. Over jagged points of
rock I clambered towards that opening, now losing sight of
it, and now gaining view of it again, until at last I reached
it and found that it was indeed a communication with the
outer country. With some difficulty I forced my way
through it and climbed down by a perilous pathway to the
seashore.

I had escaped from the sepulchre of the living and the
dead, and I praised God for the sight of the sky and the sea;
but, when I had looked into my position and found behind
me an impassable precipice, before me the wide stretching
sea, and above me the dome of heaven, I sat down on the
shore with my head on my knees and said within myself,
"There is no way out! I cannot scale the sheer cliff, neither
can I tread the fishes' pathways in the sea, nor walk in the
tracks made by birds in the air. There is no way out!"

Day followed day, and I strove to stay my hunger with
what shell-fish I could find; but the supply was meagre, and
again and again I was forced to return to the cavern to receive
reward of cakes and water in return for merciful death dealt
by my hand. Far be it from me to rob the dead, and none
can say I did so. It was in the spirit of a last gift generously

bestowed by those about to die that chains of pure gold were hung about my neck and rich jewels thrust upon me. These keepsakes of many I retained, assured that later I should carry them with me to a nameless grave in a desolate spot.

But God, in His infinite mercy, willed it otherwise, for one day, sitting sadly on the shore as was my wont, I espied a vessel on the sea. Hope surged high within my breast and I arose and stripped myself of a white garment and mounted it on a staff and ran wildly to and fro, waving it above me. And, when my signal was observed, the vessel stayed its course and sent a boat ashore.

"Who art thou, and what doest thou here?" cried one from the boat as it ran upon the beach. "Know ye not that this is a desolate coast, and none has ever been seen upon it?" And I greeted them with joy, and answered them, telling my strange experience in a few words. Then, their wonder strong within them, they took me across to the ship and led me before the master, who marvelled greatly at finding a man where none had ever seen a human being before. He asked me many questions, and when I answered him, giving him the whole history of my adventures as heretofore set down, he was a man bewildered. Raising his eyes to heaven he said, "By Allah! thy case is extraordinary!" And all around wondered that a man could experience such things and live.

In return for his kindness in rescuing me from my terrible plight, I tendered him some of the rarest jewels I had brought with me from the cavern. But he refused me courteously, saying, "Nay, O my brother; if we find one in like case with thee, we succour him and give him to eat and drink; and, if he be naked, we clothe him. Then, at the first city we reach, we set him on land with some valuable token of our goodwill;

for so it is with us of the sea that we are not unmindful of the sufferings of others." And, when I heard this, I prayed for him and his family, that he and they might live long in health and prosperity.

Our journey from that place, where I had suffered so much, took us from island unto island towards the city of El-Basrah. As we proceeded, the places where we cast anchor grew more and more familiar to me, and, as of old, I bought and sold as merchants do. At length we arrived at the city of El-Basrah, whence, having transacted business there for some days, bartering and selling the jewels I had acquired, I journeyed to Baghdad. There, in the bosom of my family, and surrounded by my companions, I returned to my former habit of life. These, then, were the experiences of my fourth voyage; and, O my brother, Sindbad the Landsman! if thou wilt honour me by thy presence to-morrow, I will relate to thee still stranger things that befel me in my fifth voyage.

THE FIFTH VOYAGE OF SINDBAD THE SAILOR

LOOKING back from the position of safety and comfort to which I had returned I came in time to make light of the perils I had encountered and the sufferings I had endured. The advantages that had come to me through these perils and sufferings now stood in the foreground of my thoughts and I said within myself, "It is the life for a man; for how otherwise can he come at the meaning of the great book of the world than by treading its pages?" And, moreover I had conceived the wish to become the owner of a ship, for thus the gain accruing from a voyage to other lands would be so much greater.

Having considered the matter deeply, I arose from my life of luxury and ease and departed with many bales of merchandise for the city of El-Basrah. There in the river I found at length a splendid vessel, which I purchased. I found a master and a crew, over whom I set my own trusty servants; and, having secured a goodly company of merchants as passengers, I embarked their bales and mine, and we set sail. We worked our way outwards, calling at island after island, and doing the usual business that merchants find in those places, until one day we came to a large uninhabited island.

Here, while I was engaged in matters concerning the vessel, the merchants landed and, as I afterwards learned, they found there the great egg of a rukh, such as I had met with on a former voyage. Mistaking it for a deserted structure, and, failing to find an entrance, they had amused themselves by casting stones at it, so that it broke; whereupon a young rukh came forth from the shell. And they set upon this monstrous chicken in its helpless condition, and slew it, and brought great slabs of its flesh back to the ship.

When I heard what they had done I was sore afraid and reproached them for their rash action. "For, look you," I said, "there is not a doubt the mother rukh will seek to revenge the loss of her young, and, seeing our ship, will attribute the deed to us, and attack us and destroy us." But they neither heeded my warning nor repented them of their rash action.

The vengeance of the rukh was sudden and dire. Scarce had I spoken when the sun was obscured from our sight, and, looking up, we beheld the gigantic bird descending upon the island. When it saw that its egg had been broken and its young one destroyed it flew above us, looking down at the ship and shrieking in a voice that filled the sky. On this it was joined by its mate, and the two circled round us, their hoarse cries of rage falling like thunder on the sea. In great fear I bade the master and the sailors hoist the sails and seek safety in flight.

Then, as soon as we began to draw off from the island, the rukhs left us and flew inland, so that we thought we had made good our escape. But soon they reappeared and came after us, each bearing in its talons a huge mass of rock. One of them flew above us and dropped the rock, so that we saw death descending upon us. But the great mass missed the ship by a narrow space, and, falling close astern, raised such a commotion of waves that the ship was flung up on a mountain of water and then hurled down against the bottom of the sea before little by little she came to rest on the level tide. Then the other rukh dropped the rock from its talons, and fate ordained that it struck the ship astern with a mighty crash. Amid cries of fear and despair we sank into the sea, and all seemed lost.

How I survived the shock and turmoil of that sudden shipwreck I cannot describe clearly, for I was like one stunned or wrenched from his mind apart. How I sought to save myself is gone from me by reason of the extreme peril. I can imagine only that I touched some wreckage and clung to it, for, when my mind returned to me, I found myself on the shore of an island sitting upon a plank, which, it seemed had borne me hither. That I had fought against wind and wave I knew, for I was well nigh exhausted. I could do nothing more than drag myself painfully to a sheltered spot, where I rested and slept.

42

When I arose later in the day, I was refreshed; and, having found both fruit and water, I ate and drank and my strength returned to me. I went forth upon the island, and to and fro in it, but I found no other's footprint on the shore, nor any sign of human habitation from coast to coast. But that there *was* a dweller there I was soon to learn, and to my cost.

It was on the following day towards evening, when I was walking among the trees, that I came upon an old man sitting on the bank of a stream. He was a comely old man, with flowing silver locks and an ample white beard. He was clothed, from the waist downward, with the leaves of trees threaded together. As I regarded him for some moments I felt that his whole aspect betokened a disposition of simplicity and mild benevolence. Advancing upon the bank I spoke to him, but he shook his head sadly and sighed; and I saw that his speech was gone. Then he made signs with his hands as if to say, "Mount me upon thy neck and carry me across the stream."

I felt kindly disposed towards this mild and gentle old man, and wished to do him a service; so I mounted him upon my neck and took him across the stream. "Now," I said, "Thou canst dismount when it pleaseth thee!" But, instead of dismounting, he wound his legs still more closely round my neck, and pressed his feet into my chest, so that I cried out with pain and rage and attempted to throw him from my shoulders. But my frantic efforts were in vain; he stuck like a leech, and I could not dislodge him. Indeed, he clung so tight that he nearly throttled me, and I fell to the ground exhausted. Then he belaboured me sorely with his feet until I arose with him again, and, in this way, he

43

compelled me to obey him. When he would go in among the trees he made a sign with his hand, and, if I obeyed not with alacrity, he beat me with his feet unmercifully. By reason of his behaviour I was at last compelled to cancel my first opinion of him and, though he cleaved to me night and day, we were by no means friends. I was his captive and he ceased not to remind me of it. If I dallied by the way, or stumbled, his hard feet would rain blows upon me; and, at night, when he slept with his legs wound tightly round my neck, he would often dream that I had disobeyed him and would beat me violently with his feet and hands.

For many many days I was ridden hither and hither at the will of this obstinate old fellow, who, though he could not torment me with speech, was truculent enough in his manner. And I reproached myself for having desired to do him a service, saying constantly in my mind, "By Allah! never again while living will I do a service to any!"

At length one day the old man guided and belaboured me into a space on the island where pumpkins grew in abundance. While he was eating some of these I took others that were ripe, and, having cleaned out the seeds and coarse matter through a small aperture, filled them with the juice of grapes; then I filled up the apertures and laid the pumpkins in the sun. Thus in a few days I procured pure wine, and, every day thereafter, while the old man on my neck ate of the pumpkins, I drank of the wine until I became intoxicated, and laughed and sang and danced about with him among the trees. And when, with fist and heel, he desired to know the cause of this, I showed him the wine that I had made. Seeing that its effect upon me was so agreeable he sought to achieve the same happy result by drinking largely

44

of it himself, so that he grew hilarious and broke a pumpkin over my head, rocking and rolling in his seat with laughter. Then, as he continued to drink, he gradually lost control of his limbs and lolled from side to side; whereupon I grasped his feet and unwound them from my neck and threw him on the ground. And so at last, to rid the earth of such a monster, I slew him, and left him there for the vultures.

After this, happiness returned to me and I went about the island like one relieved of a heavy burden, as indeed I had been. And day by day I sat by the sea watching for a vessel. But I lived upon the island many days before at last I saw a ship approach and cast anchor off the shore. When the passengers had landed I ran towards them and welcomed them, answering their many questions respecting my condition. They listened to my story with great amazement. Then someone said, "This old man of whom thou speakest is surely he whom they call the Old Man of the Sea. He hath ridden many to death, and none hath escaped but thee. Therefore, praise God for thy deliverance."

They took me to the ship and set food before me, and, after I had eaten, they brought me some clean clothes and I clad myself decently. As the ship set sail for El-Basrah my thoughts went before it to Baghdad, The Abode of Peace; but I was destined to mischance, for a strange thing befell me. We had journeyed but a few days when we came to an island whereon was a city with lofty spires and splendid houses. This was the City of Apes, of which I had heard that at night-time the people, fearing the apes, put out in boats upon the sea, so to sleep in safety.

I landed on this island with some companions, and, in our going about the city, I missed them. While I was

searching everywhere they must have returned to the ship,
thinking I had preceded them, for, when I reached the shore
later, the vessel had gone. I reproached myself for this
mishap, for I had already suffered once at the hands of the
apes. So I sat on the seashore bemoaning my fate.

While I was doing this, one of the people of the city
came to me and enquired as to my trouble, and I told him.
"Then come with us in our boat," he said, "for the night
is falling, and if thou remain in the city the apes will devour
thee." So I went with them, and we pushed off together
with a multitude of other boats until we rested about a mile
from the shore ; and there we remained and slept till the
morning, when everyone returned to the city and went about
his occupation. And in like manner as the inhabitants sleep
upon the sea by night, and dwell in the city by day, so the
apes infest the city by night and sleep in the forests by day.
Woe betide any remaining in that city after the sun goes
down, for he will of a certainty be torn limb from limb and
devoured.

I earned my bread in that island in a strange manner, and
was able to set by a small store of gold. It was in this way.
I observed many of the people gathering pebbles on the
shore and placing them in bags, and, when they had collected a sufficient quantity, they went forth into a valley
filled with lofty trees. Here slept the apes among the
branches, for the trees were so high that none but an ape
could climb them. It was the way of the people then to
pelt the apes with the pebbles, whereupon they awoke
screaming and chattering, and plucked the fruit from the
trees, and hurled it down at their tormentors. And I saw
that the fruit was the cocoanut. When a sufficient number

46

of these nuts had been secured the people gathered them up and returned to the city, where they sold them. Very soon, I, too, was gathering pebbles and pelting the apes in the trees, and in this way I amassed a great store of cocoanuts. These I sold, and bought merchandise and traded and prospered in the city.

In this way I continued for a long time, until at last I took to buying cocoanuts from the people and storing them against the arrival of a ship, when I hoped to sell them in bulk. At length a large vessel anchored off the island, and I bargained with the merchants thereon. They agreed with me upon a good price for my store. With the money thus obtained I bought more of the merchandise of the place, and embarked it on the ship; then, bidding farewell to my companions in the city, I took my departure.

The ship was bound for El-Basrah, but on the voyage we lingered to visit many islands that I had not seen before. Upon one we found an abundance of cinnamon and pepper, and here I noted a peculiar thing. On every bunch of pepper was a large leaf that hung down when the sun shone, but, when it rained, this leaf twisted and erected itself above the tendrils to shield them. And this is truth.

So we sailed onwards, past the islands of the aloes-wood, where the people are depraved and know not the call to prayer, until we came at length to the Island of Pearls. Here I gave some cocoanuts to the divers, saying, "Dive for me for luck!" And they dived in the sea and returned to the surface with pearls of great size, which they gave to me, assuring me that my fortune was of the best. So that when we reached El-Basrah I was rich with pearls and merchandise, some of which I sold there, and some here in Baghdad.

Once more in the lap of luxury, and reposing in the bosom of my family, I returned to my former life of revelry and ease, and soon forgot the hardships I had endured. And this is the whole story of my fifth voyage. Return to-morrow, O Sindbad the Landsman, and thou shalt hear from me the adventures of my sixth voyage, for they are even yet more wonderful.

THE SIXTH VOYAGE OF SINDBAD THE SAILOR

ON a day when I was living happily in Baghdad, having forgotten the perils and dangers of my former voyages, I was sitting at ease in my garden when a party of merchants came to me, and their tales of travel aroused within my bosom a great longing to engage again in the hazardous delights of those things. I pondered long upon the matter, and, though I had said within myself, "never will I set forth again," I found that my mind was made up in spite of me. Therefore I set about collecting merchandise, and, having packed a goodly number of bales, I departed for El-Basrah, where I took ship with a company of merchants and others of high repute.

The outward voyage was pleasant and fortunate, and we did as others do, buying and selling and amusing ourselves in different cities. But there came a day of disaster, when the master of the ship suddenly discovered that we had wandered from our course, and had lost our reckoning. He plucked his beard and smote his breast, and cried out in despair that we had sailed into an unknown sea, where dire perils awaited us. And so it proved, for not long afterwards, while we were sailing in a calm sea, a sudden wind burst

The Episode of the Snake.   Page 25

The Episode of the Old Man of the Sea.   Page 43

upon us and, before the sails could be loosed, the rudder was broken and the ship drifted and was driven at last upon the sides of a high mountain rising up to heaven. She was dashed to pieces by the violence of the waves, and, from that terrible wreck, few survived. There were some others besides myself who clung to the sides of the mountain, and, by tooth and nail, climbed to a place of safety.

Little by little, when the tide receded, we made our way down among the crags until we came to a strip of seashore, and from this point we could see that the island was of large size, its interior being sheltered from storms by the front of the mountain. But what took our wonder was this: on the seashore was amassed the wealth of a thousand wrecks. Scattered here, there, and everywhere, in foam and high dry, were flotsam and jetsam of richest merchandise, much of it spoiled by the sea, but much more cast high up and still of great value. All along the shore were planks and fragments of many vessels that had been wrecked on this inhospitable coast. And this was not all, for, when we proceeded through the island, we found a spring of pure ambergris overflowing into the sea; and by this the whales are attracted, but when they have swallowed it and dived to the depths of the sea it turns in their stomachs and they eject it, so that it rises to the surface in solid lumps such as are found by sailors. But the ambergris that is cast about the opening of the spring melts in the heat of the sun, and its perfume is blown about the island, wafted sweet upon the breeze like fragrant musk.

When we had explored the island and wondered at the many strange things it contained, we searched among the wreckage on the shore and found some few barrels of

G

preserved meats, and on these we stayed our hunger. With the provisions on the shore and the fruit we secured on the island we were in no danger of starvation, but a kind of fever seized upon our company and one after another sickened and died. This was a time of stress and despair. Day after day the living buried the dead until there was only one left, and that one was I. And I wept and waited, and, as if death would not come uninvited, I arose and dug myself a grave in readiness, for there was none left to bury me when I died. It was on the seashore that I made my grave, so that, when I should come to lie in it in my last moments, the wind should blow the sand upon me and bury me. And in this state of mind I blamed myself for setting out on this voyage in disregard of the lessons learned from former perils.

But God in His mercy led my footsteps forth and I roamed in the island, restless for the end. In my wanderings I came to a river gushing forth out of the side of a mountain, and, after flowing for a space between banks of verdure in a valley, entering again another mountain. Having followed it to this point, I sat down upon a bank against the mountain wall and pondered. And I said within myself, "This river flowing through caverns within the mountain must have an opening somewhere, perchance in a fertile country where people dwell." For a long time I turned the chances of this within my mind and at last decided to build a raft and commit myself upon it to the current; for at most it were better to die that way than in my present desolation.

By means of ropes and wreckage from the seashore my raft was soon constructed, and in its construction I omitted not to measure it according to the width of the river.

Then, full of a wild hope that I might at length reach an inhabited region, I stowed upon it rich goods from the shore, ambergris from the spring, and the rarest jewels I could find in the beds of the watercourses. As I set myself upon the raft and launched it, I said, "If I perish, I perish ; but if I come to the haunts of men, I come to them rich in precious things."

No sooner had I entered into the aperture of the mountain than I was suddenly encased in darkness, and, having no choice which way I went, flung myself flat on the raft lest my head should be shattered against the roof of the tunnel. Like this I floated on, sometimes feeling there was a wide space around me, and sometimes clinging to the raft lest some narrowing of the passage should sweep me to destruction. And all this time my terror was so acute that at last I swooned and lay face downward on the raft, the plaything of fate and the sport of the rushing current.

When I awoke I found myself in the open air. The sun was shining above and the birds were singing in the trees around me. I was still lying on the raft, which was tied to a stake on the shore of a beautiful lake. As soon as I had raised myself and looked about me a number of dark-skinned people gathered round and questioned me in an unknown tongue ; but I shook my head, understanding nothing of what they said. At last one advanced from among them, and, addressing me in Arabic, said, "Peace be with thee, brother ! " Then I seized him joyfully by the hand and greeted him, but I was weary and hungry and could give no account of myself because of my utter exhaustion. Seeing my state he called for food and wine, and they hastened to set them before me. When I had eaten and drunk and my strength had returned to me I told what I had come through, and the one who had addressed me in Arabic interpreted it to the others. They were filled with wonder at my story and insisted that I should accompany them to their King and acquaint him with the history of my strange adventure.

So they took me, with the raft and all the riches I had laid upon it, and led me before their King; and, from his state and magnificence, I knew that I beheld the King of Sarandib, whose name and power and learning are known through all the earth. He saluted me in the custom of my own people, addressing me in Arabic which fell easily from his tongue. This set me at my ease and I told him my story, to which he listened with great attention. When I had finished, he raised his hand and said, "By Allah! thou hast endured much, and thy case is extraordinary. Thou art greatly favoured by fate: wherefore I join my happiness with thine at thy deliverance and safety."

I was greatly moved at his words, and, begging his acceptance of a gift at my hands, I took the rarest jewels from the raft, together with a quantity of ambergris and aloes-wood, and laid them at his feet. He graciously accepted my present and immediately established me in a position of honour, bidding me dwell with him in his palace. I accepted his hospitality and remained in his land in great happiness and honour, associating with the grandees and the people of rank. And I said to myself, "I care not if the rest of my days are passed in this kingdom of splendour and magnificence."

It was indeed a land of wealth and abundance. And there the day is equally divided with the night the whole year round ; and, when the sun rises, light bursts suddenly upon the earth, and, when it sets, the darkness descends like a curtain that is loosed. There is a lofty mountain whose glittering streams contain the richest jewels, with rare minerals ; and everywhere, on hill and valley, are wafted the fragrant odours of spices. The delights of this realm held me enthralled for a long time, so that I forgot my own country, wherein is the Abode of Peace.

But, on a day when I ascended the high mountain and looked far out across the sea, I seemed to hear the voice of my own land calling to me. Then, with that far call still in my ears, I went in to the King and asked him to let me go. At first he demurred, and tried to induce me to remain with him and his people ; but, when I pressed for his permission, he relented and gave me a large sum of money for my journey, and also many gifts.

When I was about to depart the King called me to him and handed me a letter written on fine parchment. This he asked me to give into the hands of the Khalifah, Harun Er-Rashid. The substance of the letter was this :—" The King of Sarandib sends greeting. Peace be on thee, O Brother, from the King of Sarandib, who commands a thousand elephants, and in whose palace are ten thousand jewels. By the bearer of this we send thee a gift, for we have a deep affection for thee. The gift is all too trifling, but we beseech thee to accept it graciously and reply to us. Peace be upon thee ! " The present with which I was entrusted was a goblet of ruby, the inside of which was set with sparkling diamonds and priceless pearls—truly a kingly gift.

Having bade farewell to the King and such of his people that I had associated with I embarked in a large ship which was bound for El-Basrah. In good time we reached that port and I journeyed up the river to Baghdad.

My first thought was to deliver the letter and the gift into the hands of the Khalifeh. So I lost no time in approaching him and fulfilling my pledge to the King of Sarandib. He was greatly pleased with the letter, and, when he saw the sparkling goblet of ruby and precious stones, he was filled with delight.

"O Sindbad," he said, "this King must be exceedingly wealthy and powerful; what sayest thou?" And I told him of the wonder and magnificence of the land of Sarandib: how the King's seat of state is on a splendid throne placed upon a gigantic elephant with his courtiers and officials standing about him on a richly decorated platform; how there are around His Majesty a thousand other elephants on which sit the princes of the land; and, surrounding all, on every hand, ten thousand horsemen clad in silk and gold; and how a crier goes before the King exalting him to heaven, and another behind him proclaiming, "Great is he, but he will die! Again, again and again I say it: he will die!"

And as I continued to tell of these things the Khalifeh marvelled greatly at the wisdom and power of this King. "Report hath spoken truly," he said. "As thou hast witnessed to me, O Sindbad, the tales of his might and dominion have exaggerated nothing."

He then thanked me for my faithful service and bestowed rich gifts upon me, and bade me seek my own house in peace and content. There in the bosom of my family, I lived at ease, having put behind me the perils of travel and set fixedly before me the determination never to seek them again. Yet, O Sindbad the Landsman, my determination was overruled by the direct command of the Khalifeh ; and, if thou wilt honour me by thy presence again to morrow, I will relate to thee the events of my seventh and last voyage.

THE SEVENTH VOYAGE OF SINDBAD THE SAILOR

IN adhering to my vow never again to fare forth from my native land in search of strange wonders at the risk of deadly peril, I was contented and happy in my state. While I was sitting one day thinking on this and saying within myself, "I am here in the Abode of Peace, and Allah be praised ! I shall never quit it for the haunts of trouble ;" lo ! there came a messenger summoning me to the Khalifeh. I arose and followed him, and presently I was before his majesty, saluting him and kissing the ground. "Welcome, O Sindbad !" he said. "Know that I have a matter of importance for thee to execute." "Sire," I answered, "I am thy slave."

Then the Khalifeh unfolded to me his wish : which was that I should go to the King of Sarandib bearing a letter and a gift. "By Allah !" I cried when I heard this. "O my lord, be not displeased, but have I not already taken a vow that I will not go forth again upon the sea lest I suffer worse things than have already befallen me ? The bare mention of a voyage causes my knees to shake." And I repeated to him the terrible sufferings and perils I had encountered in my travels ; whereupon the Khalifeh raised his hands and said no man had endured worse things. "Nevertheless," he added, smiling upon me, "thou wilt go forth once more, for my sake, and thou wilt bear my letter and gift to the King of Sarandib."

It was not for me to disobey the command of the Prince of the Faithful, and I bowed my head in submission. I took from his hands the account of the items composing the gift, together with a letter and a sum of money for my expenses; and, bidding him farewell, went forth, saying to myself that fate was against me.

The Khalifeh's gift to the King of Sarandib was one of great magnificence. First there was a splendid white horse, the equal of which was not to be found in the length and breadth of Arabia. Its saddle and trappings were adorned with gold and set with brilliant jewels. Then, in addition to this, there were a priceless robe, fit for the king of all the earth; a great quantity of rich stuffs from Egypt and Greece, and a wonderful crystal goblet of such a kind that a man's whole lifetime would be required to make it. And the Khalifeh's letter ran as follows:—"Peace be on thee from the King Er-Rashid, highest in any land but thine—under God (whose name be exalted!) We rejoiced greatly at thy letter and we have sent thee some royal trifles, thy gracious acceptance of which will give us joy and happiness. Peace be with thee!"

With all these things I embarked upon a large vessel and set sail from El-Basrah with a company of merchants. We journeyed for long days and nights until at length we came to the island of Sarandib. There I went in to the King in his palace, and he gave me a joyous welcome.

"By Allah!" he said, "we have often thought of thee, O Sindbad; and now we rejoice to see thy face again." Then he bade me sit beside him, and asked with courtesy the reason of my visit. I informed him and told him of the Khalifeh's gift, handing him the letter. When he had read it he was overjoyed, and when at length he saw the gift and the richness of it, he marvelled greatly and conferred upon me all the honours befitting the ambassador of the Prince of the Faithful.

After some days of pleasure and happiness in his land, I made known to him my desire to depart speedily to my own country, but it was with difficulty that I obtained his permission. At last he allowed me to go, bearing friendly messages to the Khalifeh; and I set sail for my own land, glad that I was now free to return to the life to which I had vowed myself.

But, O Sindbad the Landsman! the chances of long voyages upon the sea are such as thou know'st not of. We had not been many days on our course when, as we were passing near an island, a fleet of boats put off from the shore and surrounded us. They were manned by a host of men clad in suits of mail. They looked more like demons than men and were armed with swords and daggers. They drew in on us and attacked us, slaying those who offered resistance, and taking the rest prisoners. They towed the ship to the island and took all the merchandise in the hold. Then they led us away to be sold as slaves.

It fell to my lot that I was purchased by a rich man of gentle mien. He took me to his house, gave me food and drink, clothed me well and treated me in a friendly fashion. Somewhat comforted I rested, giving my hands to light tasks about his house. After some days he called me to him and said, "Art thou skilled in any art or trade?" I answered him that I was a merchant, and was skilled only in the art of buying and selling. "Canst thou not use the bow?" he asked. Now, I was skilled in archery, and I offered to give him proof in the matter. He then placed a bow and arrow in my hands and I pierced a mark at fifty paces. "It is well," he said; "thou art skilled."

The next day he sat me behind him on an elephant, and, at nightfall, we journeyed to a place where there were some high trees. One of these he bade me climb and sit there with arrow on bowstring till the elephants came at dawn, when I was to shoot; and, if I was so fortunate as to kill one, I was to run to him in all haste and inform him of it. He then went away on his elephant, leaving me in the tree, full of terror.

When at last the sun rose, a great number of elephants came straying about among the trees, and when one came beneath mine I sent my arrows at him. Late in the morning a well-aimed shaft pierced the brain of a monstrous beast, and, with loud roarings, he fell and died. At evening time, when the other elephants had retired from the spot, I descended from the tree and ran with all haste to my master, who rejoiced at my news and sent his slaves to bring the beast in.

Day after day I continued at this sport, each day securing at least one elephant. But a day came when trouble gathered round that tree in which I sat. It appeared in the form of countless elephants of large size and ferocious aspect. One who seemed to be king among them led the others to my tree. After he had thundered round it many times until the whole world trembled, he made a dash at it, and, winding his trunk round it, tore it up by the roots and threw it down. When, half stunned, I found my way out from among the broken branches, the great elephant came upon me bellowing loudly, and, seizing me with his trunk, bore me aloft. In this manner he led the whole herd of elephants in a wild stampede that made the earth shake ; and they ceased not in their career until they came to a valley in which were a great number of elephants' bones and teeth and tusks. On a heap of these the king-elephant set me down very gently ; and, after that, he and the others turned and walked away, leaving me there.

I looked about in the valley and saw a wealth of gleaming white tusks on every hand, and I said within myself, "The elephants liked not the death of one of their number every day, and they have done this to show how I may come by an abundance of tusks without further slaughter."

Then I found my way back over a great distance to the abode of my master. He welcomed me as one returned from the dead, for, when he had found the tree torn up by the roots, he had concluded that the elephants had made an end of me. I told him what had befallen me and described the position of the valley where the tusks lay. When he heard this he was greatly excited and lost no time in mounting me behind him on an elephant and setting forth to find the spot where so much wealth was stored. We reached the valley without mishap and I showed my master the ivory, at sight of which his joy knew no bounds. We then laded the elephant with as much as he could carry and returned with it to the house.

This adventure of mine placed me in a most favourable light in my master's eyes ; and, because I had been the means of revealing to him a source of enormous wealth, he set me free and gave me permission to return to my own country. He was even better than his word, for, not many days later, he set me on board a vessel bound for El-Basrah and presented me with a large sum of money for my passage and expenses, together with many bales of merchandise. And my return journey was very fortunate. The traffic I did at the different cities on the way brought me great profit, and I bought many rare things suitable for gifts.

On my arrival at Baghdad I went in to the Khalifeh and told him all that had befallen me ; and he was so astonished thereat, and so delighted at my return, that he commanded his scribes to write my story in letters of gold. And he said to me, "O Sindbad, my son ; thou hast done well, and now thou shalt have the wish of thine heart and keep thy vow ; for, unless thou so desirest, thou shalt go forth no more upon the sea."

* * * * *

This, O Sindbad the Landsman, is the end of the story of my voyages ; and now, as I have conceived an affection for thee, thou shalt dwell with me and be my boon companion ; and we shall pass our lives together in a state of the utmost joy and happiness, strengthened by God (whose name be exalted !) the Great ! the Omnipotent Creator of sea and land !

ALADDIN AND THE WONDERFUL LAMP

KNOW, O King, that, once upon a time, in a far city of Cathay, there dwelt a poor tailor who had an only son named Aladdin. This boy was a born ne'er-do-well, and persistently resisted all his father's efforts to teach him a trade by means of which he would be able in future to earn a livelihood. Aladdin would sooner play at knuckle-bones in the gutter with others as careless as himself than he would set his mind to honest business; and, as to obeying his parents in the smallest matter, it was not in his nature. Such was this boy Aladdin, and yet—so remarkable is the favour of fate—he was strangely predestined for great things.

Stricken with grief because of the waywardness and idle conduct of his son the father fell ill and died, and the mother found great difficulty in supporting herself, to say nothing of the worthless Aladdin as well. While she wore the flesh off her bones in the endeavour to obtain a meagre subsistence Aladdin would amuse himself with his fellow urchins of the street, only returning home to his meals. In this way he continued until he was fourteen years of age, when his extraordinary destiny took him by the hand, and led him, step by step, through adventures so wonderful that words can scarce describe them.

One day he was playing in the gutter with his ragged companions, as was his wont, when a Moorish Dervish came by, and, catching sight of Aladdin's face, suddenly stopped and approached him. This Dervish was a sorcerer who had discovered many hidden secrets by his black art; in fact, he was on the track of one now; and, by the look on his face as he scrutinised Aladdin's features, it seemed that the boy was closely connected with his quest.

The Dervish beckoned to one of the urchins and asked him who Aladdin was, who his father was, and indeed all about him. Having thus learned the whole history of the boy and his family the Dervish gave his informer some coins and sent him away to spend them. Then he approached Aladdin and said to him, "Boy, I seem to recognise in thee a family likeness. Art thou not the tailor's son?" Aladdin answered him that he was, and added that his father was dead.

On hearing this the Dervish cried out with grief and embraced Aladdin, weeping bitterly. The boy was surprised at this and enquired the cause of such sorrow. "Alas!" replied the Dervish with tears running down his cheeks, "my fate is an unhappy one. Boy, I have come from a distant country to find my brother, to look upon his face again, and to cheer and comfort him; and now thou tellest me he is dead." He took Aladdin's face in his hands and gazed searchingly upon it as he continued: "Boy, I recognise my brother's features in thine; and, now that he is dead, I will find comfort in thee."

Aladdin looked up at him in wonder, for he had never been told that he had an uncle; indeed, he was inclined to doubt the truth of the matter; but, when the Dervish took ten pieces of gold from his purse and placed them in his hand, all doubt was out of the question, and he rejoiced at having found so rich an uncle. The Dervish then asked him

62

concerning his mother and begged him to show him the way to her house. And, when Aladdin had shewed him, he gave the boy more gold and said, "Give this to thy mother with my blessing, and say that her brother-in-law, who has been absent forty years, has returned and will visit her to-morrow to weep with her over the place where his brother is buried." With this he departed, and Aladdin ran to his mother to tell her the news.

"Mother! Mother!" he cried excitedly, bursting in upon her, "my uncle hath returned after forty years; he wept when I told him my father was dead; he salutes thee and—" "My son," she broke in, "what are these wild words? Thou hast no uncle, and the only one thou ever hadst died many years before thou wast born." "Nay, nay;" returned Aladdin, "this is my father's brother; he recognised my father's features in mine and wept, and gave me this to bring to thee, with a message that he would come to see thee to-morrow."

He handed her the gold, and, as the widow took it, her doubt was lessened considerably. "I wonder," she cried. "Can it be that my husband's brother did not die after all, or that he has risen from the grave? In either case he is rich and generous."

On the morrow the Dervish sought Aladdin in the street where he had seen him the day before, and found him there among his disreputable friends. Taking him aside he kissed him and embraced him; then, placing ten gold pieces in his hand, he said, "Hasten now to thy mother and give her these gold pieces and say that her brother-in-law would come to sup at her house this night."

So Aladdin left him and ran home to his mother with the

gold pieces and the message. Then the widow busied herself and prepared for the coming of this new-found relative. She bought rich food, and borrowed from the neighbours such dishes, utensils and napery as she required. When the supper was ready, and the widow was about to send Aladdin to hasten the guest, the Dervish entered, followed by a slave bearing fruit and wine, which he set down, and then went his way. The Dervish, weeping bitterly, saluted the widow and immediately fell to asking questions about the departed, finally desiring to know which was his empty seat. On being shown it he prostrated himself and cried, "Alas! that I should return to find his place vacant. Oh! woe; there is no power nor strength but in God!" And he ceased not to weep until he had convinced the widow that his grief was genuine.

Then, when he was comforted and they all sat at supper together, the Dervish told them how he had journeyed from a far land with one thought only: to see his brother once again; and how, with a great joy, he had chanced to find Aladdin, in whose face he had recognised his brother's likeness—a joy so suddenly turned to sadness and grief on his learning that his only brother was dead. At his words the widow fell to weeping, whereupon the Dervish, to change the subject of talk, turned to Aladdin and asked him if he knew any art or trade. At this Aladdin hung his head, and, as he was too ashamed to answer, his mother dried her tears and answered for him. "Alack!" she said, "he is nothing but an idler. He spends his time as thou didst find him, playing with ragamuffins in the street, and is never at home except at meal times. And I—I am an old woman and ugly through toil and hardship, and grief at his behaviour. O my

Aladdin finds the Magic Lamp.   Page 71

Aladdin and the Efrite.   Page 78

brother-in-law! It is he who should provide for me, not I for him."

"I am grieved to hear this of thee," said the Dervish, turning to Aladdin; "for thou art no longer a child, but a man of ability and kindness; and thou shouldst work to provide for thine aged mother so that she may live in comfort. Now, tell thine uncle what trade thou wouldst follow, and he will start thee in it so that in time thou mayst be able to support thy mother and thyself. Come, my son!" But Aladdin was still silent, and it was clear that he had no mind to work at any trade. Seeing this the Dervish made a better offer. "Wouldst thou like to be a merchant?" he asked. "If so I will give thee a shop with all kinds of merchandise, and thou shalt buy and sell and get gain, and rise to a position of importance."

Now Aladdin regarded a merchant as a well-dressed, well-fed being, who did no work to speak of, but, from the profits on his wares, lived in a state of perfect delight. So the suggestion pleased him, and he replied with a smile that, above all things, he would like to be a merchant. "It is well, O Son of my brother!" replied the Dervish. "Then, to-morrow, I will take thee to the market and purchase a fine dress for thee, so that thou wilt be well received amongst thy fellow merchants; and, on the following day, I will stock a shop and set thee up in it; for this is the least I can do to show the great affection I bear for the memory of my late lamented brother."

At this Aladdin clapped his hands with glee, and his mother was rejoiced. If at first she had been disposed to doubt the Dervish she now accepted him unreservedly as her brother-in-law, saying within herself, "Who but the boy's

uncle would behave with such great kindness towards him?"
And she chid her boy for his own good, and counselled him
straitly to obey his uncle in all things. The Dervish also
gave Aladdin much sound advice on the conduct of trade, so
that the boy's head was bursting with buying and selling, and
he could not sleep that night for dreams of rich stuffs, and
bales of merchandise. At last, when the Dervish arose and
took his departure, promising to return for Aladdin on the
morrow and take him to buy his merchant's dress, the wizard
felt that he had proved himself undoubtedly the best of
brothers-in-law, and the best of uncles.

True to his word the Dervish came on the morrow, and
Aladdin, holding him affectionately by the hand, went with
him forth to the market. There they entered a shop full of
the finest materials, and the Dervish asked to be shewn some
dresses such as a wealthy merchant might wear. The owner
of the shop laid a great variety before him and the Dervish
said, "Now, my son, choose what dress you like." This
delicate favour of choice pleased Aladdin greatly, for it seemed
that he had now at last reached the age of discretion. He
picked out one that he liked, and the Dervish paid the price
without any attempt at bargaining. Then they went together to the Hammam, and, when they had bathed and
rested, Aladdin clothed himself in his new dress and came
forth in great delight, kissing his uncle's hand and thanking
him again and again.

The Dervish then showed Aladdin the market and the
traffic in goods, saying that he must study all these things in
order to be apt in his profession. From the markets they
passed on to the mosques and other fine buildings in the city,
and thence to an eating-place where the finest food was served

on silver dishes, and the sherbet was of the rarest kind.
Here they regaled themselves sumptuously, and rested. And,
whenever Aladdin thanked his uncle for his kindness, the
Dervish replied, "Nay, boy; am I not thine uncle? Would
that I could do more by my brother's son."

When the afternoon came they strolled in the beautiful
gardens, and the Dervish delighted Aladdin by showing him
the pleasure grounds and the magnificent palaces. And so
they wandered on, hand in hand, until they came to a garden
full of every delight, where crystal streams flowed between
glorious banks of flowers, and fountains played and sparkled in
the sunlight. There they sat down by the side of the running
water and made merry, so that none observing them could
doubt that they were kind uncle and glad nephew.

After they had rested the Dervish suggested a walk, and
he led Aladdin through garden after garden until they came
to the confines of the city, beyond which stood a high hill.
"Shall we return, O my uncle?" said Aladdin, who was in
no mood for climbing the hill. "There are no more gardens
outside the city." "Nay," replied the Dervish, "on the
hillside is the loveliest garden of all. Bear up, my son, and
be a man; we shall soon be there." And, as they went, he
beguiled the boy with anecdotes, so that Aladdin forgot both
the length of the way and his weariness.

At last they came to a place on the hillside where the
Dervish paused and looked about him, saying to himself,
"This is the spot I have journeyed so far to find." But to
Aladdin he said, "Rest here awhile, O my son, and, when
thou art refreshed, gather some wood and we will make a
fire; then, if thou wish to see a most wonderful thing, I
will shew thee that which will take thy breath away."

At this Aladdin's curiosity was excited, and, with no thought of resting, he began at once to gather wood. When he had collected a sufficient quantity the Dervish lighted the fire, and, taking from his wallet a little box, drew some fine powder from it and scattered it over the fire, uttering an incantation. Immediately, amid rumblings of thunder, the earth reeled and opened. At this Aladdin fled in terror, but the Dervish, powerless to effect his purpose without the boy's aid, flew after him in a rage, and smote him over the head, so that he fell to the ground stunned.

When, presently, he regained his senses, he sat up and cried out, "What have I done, O my uncle, that thou shouldst strike me?" "Nay, my son," replied the Dervish, "I intended not to hurt thee. Come, now, be a man, and obey my wishes if thou wouldst see the wonderful things that I will shew thee." With such words as these he banished Aladdin's fears and smoothed him over. Then he directed him to the opening in the earth, where there was revealed a slab of marble with a brass ring let into it. The Dervish stooped and began to draw figures upon the ground, saying as he did so, "Obey me, Aladdin, in all that I say, for so thou shalt become richer than all the kings of the earth. Know, O my son, that beyond that slab of stone lies vast treasure which none but thee can acquire and live. Therefore, advance, my son, and take the brass ring in thy hand, and lift the slab from its place ; for it is predestined that thou art the only one on this earth that hath the power to do this thing." And Aladdin, stirred to great wonder by the words of the Dervish, would have done his bidding with alacrity, but, on looking at the marble slab, he saw that it was far too heavy for him.

68

"Never can I raise that alone, O my uncle," he said. "Wilt thou not help me?" "Nay," answered the Dervish, "it will yield to no hand but thine. Grasp the ring and repeat the names of as many of thine ancestors as thou canst remember, beginning with thy father and mother; for thine ancestors are my ancestors, O my son! By this the stone will come away quite easily in thy hand as if it were a feather. Am I not thine uncle, and have I not said it? And did I not cleave the hillside with my incantations? Wherefore, pluck up courage, and forget not that all the riches beyond that stone are for thee."

Thus encouraged Aladdin advanced to the stone, repeating the names of all the ancestors he could remember; and, taking hold of the ring, lifted the heavy slab from its place with perfect ease, and threw it aside. Then within the aperture lay revealed a stairway of twelve steps leading into a passage.

While Aladdin was gazing at this wonder the Dervish took a ring from his finger and placed it upon the middle finger of the boy's right hand, saying impressively as he did so, "Listen to me, O my son! fear nothing in what I am about to bid thee do, for this ring will be thy protection in all dangers and against all evils. If thou shouldst find thyself in evil case thou hast only to—, but of that I will tell thee presently. What is more important now is this. In order to come at the treasure, O my son, steady thyself and listen attentively, and see to it that thou fail not a word of these my instructions. Go down the steps and traverse the passage to the end, where thou wilt find a chamber divided into four parts, each containing four vessels of gold. Touch not these on thy life, for if so much as the fringe of thy robe cometh

69

in contact with any of them, thou wilt immediately be turned into stone. Linger not to gaze upon them, but pass right through to the end, where thou wilt find a door. Open this, repeating again the names of thine ancestors, when lo, thou wilt behold a beautiful garden before thee. Take the pathway that is ready for thy feet and proceed forty nine cubits until thou comest to an alcove, where is set a stairway of forty nine steps. Look not to ascend that stairway : it is not for thee nor me ; but direct thine attention to a lamp hanging above the alcove. Take it from its fastening, and pour out the oil therein ; then put it in thy breast securely, and retrace thy steps to me. Is it clear to thee, my son ? "

"O my uncle, it is quite clear," replied Aladdin, and he repeated the instructions he had received. "Pull thy wits together then, my son," said the Dervish, well pleased ; "and descend, for verily thou art a man of mettle, and not a child. Yea, thou, and thou only, art the rightful owner of all this great treasure. Come now !"

Filled with courage from the wizard's words, and enticed by the dazzle of untold riches, Aladdin descended the twelve steps and passed through the fourfold chamber with the utmost care lest he should touch any of the golden jars therein with so much as the fringe of his garment. When he came to the door at the far end he paused to repeat the names of his ancestors, and opened it ; then, lo, before him lay a beautiful garden where the trees were laden with many coloured fruit, while sweet voiced birds sang in the branches. He took the pathway that lay before his feet, and, as he followed it, he looked up and noticed that the trees bore, not fruit as he had supposed, but sparkling jewels flashing with many colours. On boughs where rosy apples might have

70

hung were blood-red rubies half hidden in the leaves, and, where the purple grape might have clustered, were branches of large sapphires. On some trees white blossoms grew, and every blossom was a pearl, while what seemed like drops of dew among the blossoms were purest diamonds. All the leaves of the trees were of mother-of-emerald, and on their under surface they held, like seeds, rows of the emerald itself. Virgin gold peeled like bark from the trunks and branches, and, when bird chased bird through the foliage, there fell such a rain of wealth on the dull earth's lap as would have enriched a king far above his fellow kings.

But Aladdin, though dazzled by the glitter, thought these sparkling things were but coloured glass; and it was for such that he plucked them with boyish delight until his pockets were full. "These are lovely things to play with," he said, and proceeded to fill his girdle also.

As he made his way along the garden path, plucking the bright jewels as he went, he caught sight of the alcove at the far end, and, remembering his uncle's instructions, hastened towards it. There was the stairway of forty-nine steps, and there, hanging from a crystal beam, was the Lamp. He paused, looking up at it. How should he reach it?" His uncle had said that the stairway was neither for Aladdin nor for himself, and yet he saw at a glance that the only way of reaching the Lamp was by mounting seven steps of the stairway. He hesitated, then, concluding that the Lamp was the whole object of his quest, and that he must reach it at all costs, he ventured. With some misgivings he mounted the seven steps and, reaching out, took the Lamp from its fastening and descended with it. Then, emptying out the oil, he placed it securely in his bosom, saying "Now, as my

71

uncle said to me, with this Lamp in my bosom all is mine!"

As Aladdin was returning along the pathway among the trees, laden with the precious jewels, fear assailed him lest his uncle would be angry at his delay, for it was borne in upon him that no great delight can come to a mortal without his having to suffer for it. Whereupon he hastened his footsteps, and, passing through the fourfold chamber without touching the golden jars—for the fear of that was still upon him,—he arrived quickly at the foot of the stairway of twelve steps. Heavily weighted as he was with the jewels and the Lamp he proceeded to mount the stairs at a run. But the jewels grew heavier, and the Lamp weighed upon his bosom, so that he was exhausted by the time he was half-way up. Kneeling on the seventh step he looked up and saw the Dervish urging him on with the greatest impatience.

"Bear with me, O my uncle," he said. "I am heavily weighted and am out of breath. I will soon come to thee." Then he climbed three steps and one step more, and sank exhausted before the last, which was far higher than the others. The jewels and the Lamp oppressed him with heaviness and he could not mount that last step. "O my uncle, give me thy hand and help me up," he cried. But the wizard dare not touch him, for so the spell of fate was worded and he must abide by it. "Nay," he called down, "thou art man enough! It is the Lamp that hampers thee. Reach up and place it on the ledge here; then thou canst mount easily thyself."

The Dervish held out his hand expectantly for the Lamp and his eyes glittered. Aladdin saw the evil light in them, and, having some mother wit, replied, "O my uncle, the Lamp is no weight at all; it is simply that I am exhausted

72

and this step is too high for me. Give me thy hand and help me up." "Give me the Lamp!" cried the Dervish holding his hand out for it, and beginning to rage. "Place it on the ledge before thee, and then I will help thee up." "Nay," returned Aladdin, growing obstinate, "if thou wilt not give me thy hand I will not give thee the Lamp, for it is in my thoughts that thou wantest the Lamp more than thou wantest me."

This enraged the Dervish to a point beyond control, and he said within himself, "If I get not the Lamp then may it perish with him!" And, taking a box from his wallet, he threw some powder on the embers of the fire, muttering curses and incantations as he did so. Immediately a flame shot up, and its many tongues went hither and thither, licking the air. The earth shuddered and groaned with a hollow thunder; then the marble slab closed of itself over the aperture, the hillside rushed together above it, and all was as before, save that Aladdin was sealed within that cavern without hope of escape.

Long and loud did Aladdin call to his supposed uncle to save him from a living death; but there was no answer to his cries, and, at last, when he was almost exhausted, he took counsel of himself and plainly saw the truth of the matter. The Dervish was no uncle of his, but a cunning wizard who had made a catspaw of him to secure treasure which, by the laws of magic and destiny, he was powerless to come at in any other way. The whole thing, from the very beginning, was a trick; and he saw it clearly now that it was too late. The way out was sealed, and the darkness pressed heavily upon him. Frantic with the desire to escape from this dungeon he thought of the garden and the stairway in the alcove ; but, when he had groped his way to the end of the passage, he found the door closed, and all his efforts failed to open it. The names of his ancestors were of no avail against the magic of the Dervish. At this he wept loudly, and continued to weep throughout the night, until his rage and despair were spent. At last he sank down exhausted on the lowest step of the stairway by which he had first descended, and, feeling himself utterly abandoned by man, he raised his hands to God, praying for deliverance from his calamity.

Now, while he was holding his hands in supplication, he felt the ring upon his middle finger—the ring which the Dervish had placed there saying, "In whatever difficulty thou mayst find thyself this ring will be thy protection ; thou hast only to—but of that I will tell thee later." The Dervish had perhaps given him the ring to gain his confidence, and had purposely omitted to reveal its secret. But now, in answer to Aladdin's prayer, the power of the ring was revealed as if by the merest chance ; for, when he felt the ring, he looked at it ; and, seeing a light from the jewel therein, he breathed upon it and rubbed it with his palm to increase its lustre. No sooner had he done this when, lo, the Slave of the Ring appeared, and gathered shape before him, first in a luminous haze, and then, gradually, in clearer and clearer contour.

"Ask what thou wilt, and it shall be done," said the apparition ; "for know that I am the Slave of the Ring and the slave of him on whose finger my master placed the ring."

Aladdin, seeing before him an Efrite after the order of those invoked by the Lord Suleiman, was terrified, and his

74

tongue clave to the roof of his mouth, so that he could not speak. But the Efrite reassured him with kindly speech. "Thou hast only to ask," he said, "and thy wish will be fulfilled; for, since my master's ring is on thy hand, I am thy servant."

At this Aladdin took heart, and, having considered his wish, resolved to put the matter to the test. "O Slave of the Ring!" he said, "my wish is that thou take me from this dungeon and place me in the light of day where the sun shines and the breezes blow—if indeed it *is* day, for here have I been for many, many hours."

Scarcely had he spoken the words when there was a clap of thunder. The cavern opened, and, by some mysterious power, he was conveyed through the opening. Then, when he sat up and looked around him, he was in the light of day upon the hillside, and everything was as it had been when he and the Dervish had first reached the spot.

Aladdin marvelled greatly at this, and said within himself, "I wonder if it was all a dream!" But, when he looked at the ring upon his finger and felt the Lamp and the jewel-fruit he had gathered from the trees in the garden, he knew it was not a dream. Besides, there was the spot where the fire had been; and it was now but a heap of grey ashes on the ground. Turning himself about, he saw the path by which they had ascended, and the gardens stretching below. Nothing had changed. The side of the hill which the Dervish by his magic had opened for his entrance, and the Slave of the Ring had now closed up behind him, was as it had been when he first saw it.

Seeing that he was safe and sound in the outer world, Aladdin fell on his knees and gave thanks to the most High

75

for his deliverance from a terrible death. Then straightway he arose and took the path that led down the hillside and through the gardens of the city in the direction of his home. At length, with wearied body, but elated mind, he reached the doorway of his dwelling, and, entering, found his mother weeping.

"Where hast thou been, my son?" she cried. "All night long I lay awake, anxious for thee; and now it is again near nightfall, and thou comest like one about to die. Where hast thou been, and where is thine uncle?"

But Aladdin could not answer her. What with utter weariness, and the joy of gaining his home once more, he fell in a swoon at her feet. Quickly she dashed water on his face and restored him. Then, when she had made him eat, she enquired gently what had befallen him.

"O my mother," said Aladdin, "how much thou art to blame! Thou gavest me over to a devil of a sorcerer who tried, by his evil arts, to compass my ruin. I have a stout reckoning against thee for this; for, look you; this vile and wicked one, whom thou toldst me was my uncle, was naught but a liar and an impostor. Think, mother, of the richness of his promises! What was he not going to do for me? His affection for me was overwhelming, and he ceased not to pretend in that lying hypocrisy until the cheat was exposed and I saw that his purpose was to use me for his own ends, and then to destroy me. Mother, the devils beneath the sea and the earth are not the equal of this vile sorcerer." And thus, having vented his anger at the false conduct of the Dervish, he proceeded to tell his mother, first about the lamp and the jewel-fruit, then about all that had happened on the hillside, from the opening of the earth

76

by a magic spell, to the closing of it again, and his sub-
sequent escape through the Slave of the Ring. "And
thus," he concluded, "thus did this devil's own shew me in
the end that he was accursed and that he cared no jot for
me, but only for the Lamp."

Then Aladdin took the Lamp and the precious stones
from his bosom and placed them before his mother, albeit
neither knew why the Lamp had been so coveted by the
Dervish, or that the stones were more valuable than any
possessed by kings. And Aladdin, now weeping for joy at
his deliverance, and now cursing with rage at the vile
hypocrisy of the sorcerer, found sympathy in both cases in
his mother, who wept and cursed with him, crying out that
the Omnipotent, who had graciously saved his life, would
most assuredly punish that wicked man for his abominable
actions.

Now, neither Aladdin nor his mother had rested for two
days and two nights, so that, exhausted at length with weeping and with heaping maledictions on the Dervish, they
slept; and, when they awoke, it was about noon of the
following day. Aladdin's first words on pulling his wits
together were to the effect that he was hungry. "Nay, O
my son," replied his mother, "there is nothing to eat in the
house, for thou didst eat yesterday all that there was. But
stay, I have some spinning that is ready for the market. I
will take and sell it and buy some food."

She was busying herself about this when Aladdin suddenly
called out to her, "Mother! bring me the Lamp, and I will
take and sell that; it will fetch more than the spinning."
Now, although Aladdin and his mother knew that the Dervish had greatly coveted the Lamp, they both imagined that

77

he had some strange reason of his own for this; and, as the Lamp was an article that would command a ready sale, the mother quickly agreed to Aladdin's proposal and brought the Lamp to him in answer to his call. On regarding it closely, however, she observed that it was very dirty. Well knowing that it would fetch a better price if it were clean and bright, she set to work to polish it with some fine sand; when lo, as soon as she started to rub the Lamp, the air before her danced and quivered and a chill gasp of wind smote her in the face. Then, looking up, she saw, towering above her, a being monstrous and terrible, with a fierce face in which gleamed fiery eyes beneath frowning brows. She gazed at this apparition in fear and astonishment, for she knew it was surely a powerful Efrite such as were under the power of the Lord Suleiman. Then the being spoke: "Thou hast invoked me; what is thy wish?" But she only gazed at him, dumb with terror. Again the awful being spoke: "Thou hast summoned me, for I am the Slave of the Lamp which is in thy hand. What is thy desire?" At this the poor woman could no longer endure her fear, and, with a cry, she fell in a swoon.

Aladdin had heard the Efrite's words and had hastened to his mother's side. He had already seen the power of the Slave of the Ring, and he guessed that now the Slave of the Lamp had appeared, and was ready to do the bidding of the one who held the Lamp. So he quickly took it from his mother's hand, and, standing before the Efrite, plucked up courage and said, "I desire food, O Slave of the Lamp! the finest food that ever was set before a king."

No sooner had he spoken than the Efrite vanished, but only to reappear immediately, bearing a rich tray of solid silver, on which were twelve golden dishes with fruits and meats of various kinds. There were also flagons of wine and silver goblets. As Aladdin stared in amazement at this magnificent repast the Efrite set the tray down before him and vanished in a flash. Then Aladdin turned to his mother and dashed cold water on her face, and held perfumes to her nostrils until she regained consciousness and sat up. And when she beheld the sumptuous repast set out upon the golden dishes she was greatly astonished, and imagined that the Sultan had sent it from his palace. But Aladdin, who was very hungry, fell to eating heartily; and, while persuading his mother to eat, he would tell her nothing.

It was not until they had satisfied their hunger, and placed the remainder aside for the morrow, that Aladdin informed her what had happened. Then she questioned him, saying, "O my son, was not this the same Efrite that appeared to thee when thou wast in the cavern?" "Nay," he answered. "That was the Slave of the Ring; this was the Slave of the Lamp." "At all events," said she, "it was a terrible monster that nearly caused my death through fear. Promise me, O my son, that thou wilt have naught further to do with the Ring and the Lamp. Cast them from thee, for the Holy Prophet hath told us to have no traffic with devils."

"Nay, nay, O my mother," protested Aladdin; "it were wiser to keep them, for did not the Slave of the Ring deliver me from death? and has not the Slave of the Lamp brought us delicious food when we were hungry?" "That may be so," replied his mother, "but hear my words, my son; no good thing can come of these dealings with accursèd spirits, and it were better for thee to have died in the cavern than to invoke their aid." And thus she pleaded with him to cast away the Ring and the Lamp, for she was sore afraid of the power of the Evil One. But Aladdin would not undertake to do this, although, in respect for her wishes, he agreed to conceal the objects so that she might never need to look upon them. He also agreed to invoke neither of the Efrites again, unless it were a case of dire necessity. And with this his mother had to rest content.

Mother and son continued to live on the food that remained, until, in a few days, it was all gone. Then Aladdin took up one of the dishes from the tray, and, not knowing that it was of pure gold, went out to sell it and buy food with the proceeds. In the market he came to the shop of a Jew—a man of exceeding vile methods of buying and selling; and he showed the dish to him. This Jew, as soon as he saw the dish, knew it for pure gold and glanced sharply at Aladdin to find whether he knew its value. But Aladdin's face told him nothing; so he enquired, "What price do you ask, O my master?" "Its value in the market," returned Aladdin; and at this the Jew pondered, saying within himself, "If he knoweth the value, and I offer him too little, he will give me a bad name in the market; yet, if he knoweth not, I should be ruining myself by offering him too large a price. Perchance he knoweth not." Then, preferring that others might call him a rogue rather than that the event might prove him a fool in his own eyes, he took a single gold piece from his pocket and handed it to Aladdin. On this and its issue, seeing quickly that Aladdin knew not the value of the thing—for he took the gold piece and walked away—the Jew repented him bitterly of his rash act, for he could have bought the dish for much less.

As for Aladdin, he hastened home and gave the gold piece to his mother, begging her to buy food with it. She did so, and they ate, and were comforted. And so, from day to day, they lived on the proceeds of one dish after another, which the unregenerate Hebrew bought at cheaper and cheaper prices, saying always that the metal was inferior and that the demand for such goods was not what it used to be. And, when at last the dishes were all sold, Aladdin summoned the Jew to the house to inspect the goblets and also the tray, which was too heavy for him to carry to the market. When the Jew saw how much silver there was in the tray and the goblets he forgot himself and offered ten gold pieces for them—at least a thirtieth part of their value. Aladdin took the gold pieces, and the Jew departed with the tray. So food was forthcoming for many more days ; but at last the money was exhausted and there was now nothing left to sell. At this Aladdin, who, in deference to his mother's wishes, had concealed the Lamp and the Ring against a necessitous occasion, brought forth the former and rubbed it, for so, he concluded, was the Slave invoked. His conclusion was right, for no sooner had he rubbed the Lamp than the Efrite suddenly appeared before him, immense and of terrible aspect.

"What is thy wish, O my master?" said the Efrite; "for I am the Slave of the Lamp and of him who holds it." "My wish," answered Aladdin, "is that you bring me another tray of food similar to the one you brought before." Immediately the Efrite vanished, and, in a moment, appeared again, bearing a tray of food exactly similar to the one he had brought before. He set this down before Aladdin and then disappeared.

"Mother! Mother!" cried Aladdin in delight. "Come here and see what we have for supper." When she hastened to him and saw the delicate food, and smelt the rich savours, she was pleased, although she knew that Aladdin had summoned the Efrite and commanded him to bring the tray. "Look at it, Mother!" cried Aladdin; "and thou wouldst have me cast away the Lamp by means of which we have gotten this repast!" "O my son," answered she, "if the Slave of the Lamp be a devil then he is a good devil; but, for all that, I know I should swoon again at sight of him."

And they ate and drank and were merry, the food lasting them some days. Then, just as a tidy housewife clears away the platter after a meal, so, when the food was all gone, Aladdin proceeded to dispose of the dishes as before. Taking one of them he went forth to find the Jew, but it chanced that on his way he passed the shop of a fair-dealing man— that is to say, not a Jew—who had no vile methods of buying and selling, but was just, and feared God. When this man saw Aladdin passing he called to him, and told him that he had frequently seen him selling things to the Jew, and warned him about it. "Thou knowest not how the Jew will trick thee," he said, "for the goods of the faithful are fair spoil to the Jews; and it was ever so, and ever will be. If, therefore, thou hast aught to sell, I will give thee its full value, in the name of the Prophet."

Then Aladdin shewed him the dish of gold and he took it, and weighed it on the scales. "Did you sell any of this kind to the Jew?" he asked. "Yes," answered Aladdin, "many—all of them exactly the same." "And what price did he pay you?" "A gold piece for the first, and afterwards less." The merchant looked grieved and spat on the ground. "My son," he said; "it is not meet that a servant of God should fall into the hands the Jew. Woe unto him, accursèd! He hath cheated thee sore, for my balance tells me truly the weight of this dish, which is of pure gold; and its value is seventy pieces of gold. Here is the price if thou wouldst sell."

He counted out seventy gold pieces and handed them to Aladdin, who took them and thanked the merchant heartily for his honest exposure of the Jew's wickedness. And thereafter he brought the remaining dishes, and at last the tray, to that merchant, and received from him their full value; so that Aladdin and his mother were placed above want and in a comfortable position for people of their station in life.

During this time Aladdin had changed his ways greatly. He no longer consorted with the ragamuffins of the street but selected for his friends men of standing and integrity. His daily practice was to go to the market and converse with the merchants in a serious and business-like manner in the endeavour to learn their methods and the value of stuffs. And often he would watch the jewellers at their work, and the goods they handled; and, through knowledge thus acquired, he began to suspect that the jewel-fruit he had gathered in the garden of the cavern was not glass, as he had imagined, but real gems. By this and that, and by comparing and asking questions, he came at length to the certainty that he actually possessed the richest jewels in all the earth. The smallest among them was bigger and more sparkling by far than the largest and finest he could see in any jeweller's shop.

One day, while his mind was engaged with this amazing thing, and while he was as usual studying the ways of the merchants in the bazaar and the varying quality of their goods, a thing happened which was predestined to have far-reaching results on his life. He was in the jewellers' market, taking note of things, when a herald came by, crying to all people : "Take heed ! By command of the Sultan, King of the Age and Lord of the Earth, let all doors be closed, and let none come forth from shop or dwelling on pain of instant death, for the Sultan's daughter, Bedr-el-Budur cometh to the bath ! Take heed ! "

Now, on hearing this, a great longing arose in Aladdin's breast to look upon the face of Bedr-el-Budur, the Sultan's daughter. "All people extol her loveliness," he said to himself ; "and I—even if I die for it—I will look upon her face ; for something—I know not what—impels me to gaze on Bedr-el-Budur the beautiful."

So, with this will, he speedily found the way. Hastening to the Hammam he secreted himself behind the door so that, unobserved himself, he might see her when she came in. And he had not long to wait, for, presently, the Sultan's daughter arrived ; and, as she entered, she lifted the veil from her face, so that Aladdin saw her features clearly.

What a wondrous beauty was there ! The witchery of her eyes ! The ivory of her skin ! The jet of her glossy tresses ! These, and the swaying of her graceful body as she walked, caused Aladdin's heart to turn to water and then to spring wildly into flame. "What a creature is this Princess !" he said within himself. "I knew not that God had ever created such a soul of loveliness." Then, suddenly, an overwhelming love for her took him by the heart, and gat hold of him utterly, so that he knew naught else for the very stress of it.

Like one walking in a dream Aladdin went home and sat him down in dejection of spirit. For a long time he answered

84

not his mother's questions as to what ailed him, but continued
like one who had beheld a vision so lovely that it had de-
prived him of his senses. At last, however, he looked up,
and said, "O my mother, know that until to-day I had believed
that all women were of thy fashion of face, but now I find
they are not; for to-day I saw the Sultan's daughter, and she
is more beautiful than all others on earth." And Aladdin
told her how he had hidden behind the door of the Hammam,
so that, when Bedr-el-Budur had entered and lifted her veil,
he had seen her clearly; and how, on that, a great love had
leapt up in his heart and filled him to the exclusion of all else.
"And there is no rest for me," he concluded, "until I win the
Lady Bedr-el-Budur, and make her my wife."

At these daring words Aladdin's mother regarded him
sharply, with fear on her face. "Art thou mad, my son?"
she cried. "For, if such an insane act is thine intention, then
God save thee!" "Nay, O my mother," he answered, "I
am not mad. But, as I risked my life to see her, so will I
risk it again to win her; for, without her, life is of no account
to me. I will go to the Sultan and ask him to give me the
lovely Bedr-el-Budur for my lawful wife."

Seeing his determination his mother was sore afraid, and
knew not what to do. For a long time she reasoned with
him anxiously, pointing out what a scandal it would be for
the son of a poor tailor to aspire to the Sultan's daughter—
the highest in the land, and one whom the Sultan would
scarce bestow upon a King who was his equal. Aladdin
listened very quietly, and then replied that his resolve was
unshaken; and, though he admitted the truth of all she had
said, he would nevertheless carry out his purpose, for the
Lady Bedr-el-Budur was the only thing in the world to him,

and if he did not win her he would die. In vain she suggested that there were many of his own class he might marry; besides, to approach the Sultan on such a matter meant certain death; unless, indeed, the Sultan thought to bind him on an ass, with his face to the tail, and parade him through the city with the heralds shouting, "Behold the reward of presumption and the payment of impertinence!"

These arguments, and more, his mother put before him; but Aladdin shook his head at all of them, and remained firm in his determination. "And further, O my mother," he said, "I wish now that thou go thyself to the Sultan and put my request to him, for am I not thy child? And is it not thy duty to perform this office for me?"

"O my son," she cried in despair, "wilt thou bring me into thy madness? I, a poor woman of humble birth, to go in to the Sultan and demand the princess for my son! Why, if I were to go even to one of our equals and demand his daughter, I should immediately be asked what money and goods we possessed; and, if I could not give a ready reply on that matter to an equal, what reply, do you imagine, could I give the Sultan? Besides all this, O my son, how shall I even gain access to the Sultan's presence for this purpose without bearing a rich gift to offer him? Out on thee, my son, for thy presumption! What hast thou done for thy country, or what are thy vast possessions that the Sultan should reward thee with his daughter?"

"Mother," answered Aladdin," thy words have served me well, for they have called to my recollection a thing which, through excess of love for the Lady Bedr-el-Budur, I had forgotten. Thou sayest that thou canst not approach the Sultan without a rich gift. Then, O my mother, if I place in thy hands an offering richer than any King in the world can make to any other, wilt thou carry out my desire?"

Thinking his words were wild as the wind, and that he could produce no such offering, his mother agreed; but, remembering the Slave of the Lamp, and what had already been done in that way, she stipulated with Aladdin that she would carry out his wish only on condition that it required no further invoking of the Efrite. Aladdin assured her on this and asked her to fetch him a china bowl. Wondering greatly she arose, and brought the bowl to him. Then Aladdin emptied into it all the sparkling jewels which he carried within his garments, and, when they were heaped together in the bowl they shone with a dazzling splendour. Liking well her amazement he explained to his mother how he had learned in the market place that what he had at first thought were mere glass were really the rarest of precious stones, the equal of the least of which could not be found in the treasuries of Kings. On hearing this, and at sight of the brilliant, flashing gems, his mother was dumbfounded, for she saw that this was indeed a treasure beyond all imagination, and worthy of the Sultan's acceptance. But, as she had naught to say, Aladdin spoke for her, and held her to her promise.

"Thou seest, O my mother," he said, "that this is an offering excelling all others. Now, therefore, according to thy promise, arise straightway and go to the Sultan, bearing these wondrous jewels. I am greatly mistaken if he accepteth not the gift." "But, O my son," answered she in dismay, "what can I say to him? The gift is fabulous indeed, but still more fabulous is the request thou desirest me to put to him. For, if I say I want his daughter for my son, he may be so angered at my impertinence that he will take the jewels and condemn me to death. And then he may search for thee, my son; and, when he hath found thee, and looked upon thy face, we shall assuredly die together."

Aladdin made a gesture of impatience at his mother's view of the matter. "On my head and eye," he said angrily, "though thou art my mother thou art verily lacking in sense. I put it to you: What man living, yea, even though he be the Sultan, would refuse to grant thy request when thou comest to him with the price of more than half his kingdom? Nay, my mother,—for such thou art,—thou art surely deficient in wisdom." And he took up the bowl of glittering jewels and weighed the chances of them in his hand.

But his mother, silenced as she was with his shrewd words, was terrified at the prospect of her visit to the Sultan, and still went on raising difficulties. "Haply, O my son, he will be pleased to see me, because of the gift; but what if he say to me, 'Who is this, thy son, who seeketh the hand of my daughter? What is his condition and state of life?'" "How can he ask thee that," answered Aladdin, "when the jewels in the bowl are crying out my state and my condition? Such a thing will never happen, except in thy mind. Do thou now arise and go to him, for I will no longer listen to these fanciful excuses." "Nay, nay, my son," she cried, seeing there was no withdrawing from her promise; "I will go, but give me till the morning to strengthen and prepare myself."

So Aladdin curbed his impatience and agreed to wait until the following day; but, since he realised that it was not impossible that the project might fail, and that he might have to seek to the Slave of the Lamp for advice and help in difficulty, he spoke to his mother on the matter. "O my mother," he said, "it was the condition of thy promise that I should not invoke the Slave of the Lamp in the furtherance of this my desire; yet it must be understood between us that if thou make a blunder—which thou needst not do—then, to extricate us from a dire calamity, I am free to rub the Lamp and see what its Slave can do for our salvation."

His mother assented to this, for she knew, if she failed with the Sultan, all was lost; and, in such case, even the aid of a demon would be acceptable. "Then," said Aladdin, "see thou to it that in thy gossip to our neighbours no word of the Lamp escape thy lips, for, if this wonderful possession of ours become known, it will speedily pass out of our hands and its virtues with it. Therefore keep thy counsel, O my mother, and babble not of our secret." "Fear nothing, my son," she replied, "the Lamp is our peculiar possession, and no word shall pass my lips concerning it." And they ceased not to talk of their project, and the saving powers of the Lamp, far into the night.

When morning dawned Aladdin's mother arose and prepared herself for the visit to the Palace, and, wrapping the bowl of jewels in a cloth, went forth early. When she arrived at the Palace she found herself among the first there assembled, and at once fell to watching the princes and nobles and high officials as they came in. When the audience was full the Sultan came in and seated himself on the royal divan. All bowed down before him, and then stood waiting with folded arms for his permission to be seated. And, when he gave permission, all sat down in their due order of precedence. Then he listened to their petitions in the same order, and gave his decisions, until the hour

M

grew late, and the audience was declared closed. The Sultan arose and went into the Palace, and the princes, with the nobles and the people, went their ways. Among them went Aladdin's mother, thinking to herself that this would be a matter of many days.

She hastened home to Aladdin, who, when he saw her with the bowl of jewels just as when she departed, cried, "What is this, O my mother? Hath he refused the jewels, and thy head still on thy shoulders?" "Nay, my son," she replied; "be patient! There were many before me and I had no opportunity." And she told him how she had gained a place in the audience, and how it was only a matter of waiting till her turn came to place her petition before the Sultan; perchance to-morrow or the next day.

Aladdin was overjoyed at this; and, though his exceeding love for the Princess probed him sore, yet he resolved to possess his soul in patience against the fulfilment of his desire. But what he momently expected was hourly delayed, and, from that time forth, the daily postponement of his request added fuel to the flame of love in his heart; for, on the following morning, his mother set forth again for the Palace and returned again in the evening but one day nearer to the putting of her petition. And every day thereafter she stood in the audience with the bowl of jewels under her arm and heard the petitions, but dared not for very timidity address the Sultan. And in this way she continued for a whole month, while Aladdin was nursing his impatient soul and waiting on the issue.

Now the Sultan, being observant, had noticed the woman present herself constantly at the levée; and, at length, one day, after the audience had dispersed and the Sultan had retired with his Grand Vizier, he said to him, "Hearken, O Vizier! for many days have I seen an old woman at the levée, and on each occasion she has carried a bundle under her arm. Knowest thou aught of her?" And the Vizier, who had little esteem for women, replied, "Doubtless a woman like other women, O our Lord! Maybe she cometh with a deadly grievance against her husband, whom she desires to be beheaded; and, when thou grantest her desire, she will plead for his life, supplicating thee with tears; for such was ever their way." But the Sultan was curious about the woman and her silent persistence, and was not satisfied to dismiss the matter so easily. So he commanded the Vizier to see to it that, should the woman present herself again, she be instantly brought before him.

And so it came about. Aladdin's mother, though weary with her many attendances, still persevered in her quest, feeling that, for the sake of her son, she would endure all delay so that the issue might come at last. And it came according to the Sultan's command to the Grand Vizier; for one day the Sultan saw her waiting in the audience chamber and ordered the Vizier to bring her forward that he might consider her affair.

Now, at last, she was face to face with the Sultan, making obeisance to him and kissing the ground at his feet. "I have seen thee here, O woman, for many days," said the Sultan; "and thou hast not approached me. If thou hast a wish that I can grant, lay it before me." At this she kissed the ground again, and prayed fervently for the prolongation of his life. Then she said, "O King of all the Ages, I have a request; but, peace be on thee, it is a strange one! Wherefore I claim thy clemency before I state it."

These words whetted the Sultan's curiosity, and, as he was a man of great gentleness, he spoke her softly in reply, and not only assured her of his clemency but ordered all others present to withdraw, saving only the Grand Vizier, so that he might hear her petition in secret.

"Now, woman," said the Sultan, turning to her, "make thy petition, and the peace and protection of God be on thee." "Thy forgiveness, also, O King," she said. "God forgive thee if there is aught to forgive," he replied. And at this Aladdin's mother unfolded the tale of her son's exceeding love for Bedr-el-Budur, the Sultan's daughter: how life had become intolerable to him because of this, and how his only thought was to win the Lady Bedr-el-Budur for his wife, or die—either of grief, or by the Sultan's anger. Wherefore, his life being in the balance in any case, she had come as a last resort to beg the Sultan to bestow his daughter on her son. And she concluded by beseeching the Sultan not to punish either her or her son for this unparalleled hardihood.

The Sultan looked at the Grand Vizier, whose face was of stone—for the Lady Bedr-el-Budur had already been promised to his son: a matter well understood between them. "What sayest thou?" said the Sultan, regarding him with merriment in his eyes. But the Grand Vizier only cast a contemptuous look at Aladdin's mother, and answered him: "O King of the Age! Thou knowest how to deal with this petition." At this the Sultan laughed outright, and, turning a kindly face to the humble suppliant, observed her minutely. "What is that bundle thou hast under thine arm?" he said at last, remembering that she had brought it with her on every occasion.

Aladdin's mother, greatly relieved to see the Sultan laughing, unfolded the wrappings of the bowl and handed it to him. As soon as he took it in his hand, and saw the size and splendid sparkle of the jewels, the Sultan laughed no longer, but gazed at them, speechless with wonder and admiration. Then at length, he handed the bowl to the Grand Vizier, saying, "Upon my oath, this is a marvellous thing! Tell me, O Vizier, have I in my treasury a single jewel that will compare with even the smallest of these?"

The Grand Vizier also was taken aback by their dazzling loveliness and beauty. He would have lied, saying they were glass or crystal, but the stones themselves flashed back the purposed lie in his teeth. All he could reply was, "Never, O my lord the King, have I beheld the like of these; nor is there one in thy treasury that could equal the beauty of the smallest of them." And, saying this, the Vizier turned very pale, for neither he nor his son could approach the Sultan with such a gift. And it was as he had feared, and as Aladdin had prophesied: the Sultan required to know nothing further than what was before him in the bowl, for it was evident that the giver of these rare jewels must take precedence of all others, since, if they were sold in the market, their price would buy a dozen Grand Viziers and their sons, to say nothing of princes and nobles with their palaces and all. Indeed, as the Vizier readily saw, the worth of the precious stones might equal the worth of the Sultan's kingdom, and this caused his knees to quake, for he quickly concluded within his mind that there was more behind this thing than what the eye beheld: perchance the old woman's story was but the curtain that concealed a richer treasury than Cathay had ever heard of.

"O Vizier," said the Sultan in dry and chilling tones, "it seemeth that in this land there are men greater than the greatest. What sayest thou? The man who sends me this kingly gift cannot conceal his greatness and worthiness behind the thin, loose yarn spun by his messenger here. That he is worthy of my daughter is clearly proved, O Vizier; and I, the Sultan, King of the Age, having power over all men, do withdraw my former promise to thee to bestow her on thy son. Bedr-el-Budur, the one beautiful jewel in the treasury of my heart, is my gift in return to the man who has sent me these priceless jewels."

The Grand Vizier bit his lips and pondered awhile. Then he spoke. "Peace be on thee, O King of all the Earth. But is not thy promise worth most of all? Thou didst pledge me thy daughter for my son, and with that pledge I went, thinking that the whole earth and all therein were not its value. Wherefore, O King, I pray that thou wilt allow this matter time. If thou wilt pledge this foster mother of a prince that thou wilt comply with her request in three months time, then it seems to me that, by so doing, thou wilt cement the good feeling and loosen the griefs of all parties concerned. And in the meantime—yea, I have good reason for saying it—there will come before thee, O King of the Age, a gift compared to which this thou hast seen is but dross."

The Sultan weighed the Grand Vizier's words in his mind, and concluded that it would be best for all concerned to accept the gift from Aladdin's mother and to grant her son's wish, but at the same time to felicitate the Grand Vizier by imposing a three months' stay of the nuptials. Accordingly, he said to the woman, "Tell thy son that he

94

hath my royal assent, and that I will give him my daughter in marriage; but, as every woman knows, these things cannot be hastened, for there are garments and necessaries to be prepared; wherefore thy son (on whom be peace) must abide in patience for, let us say, three months. At the end of that time he may approach me for the fulfilment of my promise."

Satisfied with this, Aladdin's mother thanked and blessed the Sultan, and, buoyed up with a burden of delight, almost flew back to her house. There Aladdin was awaiting for her, and, when he saw her hastening, and noticed that she had returned without the bowl of jewels, his heart rose high to meet her. "Hath the Sultan considered thy request?" he cried, as she came in panting. "Hath he accepted the jewels? Tell me that only, and I know the rest without a movement of thy tongue."

And his mother, whose haste and condition had already answered all his questions, answered them still further with "Yea, yea, yea!" Then she related to him the details of the interview, laying stress upon the fact that, although the Sultan had been moved at the sight of the jewels to make immediate arrangements for the marriage, a private word from the Grand Vizier had led him to delay the ceremony for three months. "Take heed, my son!" she concluded. "The Grand Vizier hath a motive for this counsel of delay. He is thine enemy. I saw it in his face. Beware of him!"

Aladdin was greatly relieved by her news. He felt like one jerked out of the grave; and, where the Sultan was favourable to his suit, he was in no mood to fear a Grand Vizier. "Nay, nay," he said, "the jewels have the eye of the Sultan more than the Grand Vizier hath his ear. Fear

95

nothing, O my mother! The Sultan's word is good, and I rest content to wait; though I know not how such a long time as three months can be got into the calendar."

Two of these long, weary months went by, and Aladdin nursed his soul in patience. Then a thing happened which gave him seriously to think. On a day in the first week of the third month his mother went forth into the market place about sunset to buy oil, and she saw that all the shops were closed, and the people were adorning their windows with bright garlands as if for some festivity. She wondered greatly at this, thinking the Sultan had either changed his birthday or that another child had been born to him. Yet she had gleaned nothing of any great event from the gossip of her neighbours. Having, after much difficulty, found an oil shop open, she bought her oil, and questioned the man. "Uncle," she said; "what is abroad in the city that the people close their shops and place candles and garlands in their windows?" "Thou art evidently a stranger," replied the man. "Nay, I am of this city," said she. "Then must thou cleanse thine ears," he retorted. "Hast thou not heard that the Grand Vizier's son is to take to himself this evening the beautiful Bedr-el-Budur? Surely, woman, thou hast been sleeping all day on thine ears, for the news went abroad early this morning. The Vizier's son is at the Hamman, and these soldiers and officials you see in the streets are waiting to escort him to the palace. And, look you, you are fortunate to get oil to-day, for all those who purvey oil to the Grand Vizier and his household have closed their shops as a mark of respect."

On hearing this, Aladdin's mother was so distressed that her knees shook, and she walked away without replying—

even forgetting to pay for the oil. But the man speedily called her back and reminded her that, though the Grand Vizier had never given him an order, she had, and the price of the oil was such and such. In confusion of face she paid him and then hurried away, the oilman looking after her and wondering what manner of woman was this. Had he known all, he might have wondered more, or ceased to wonder.

Meanwhile, Aladdin's mother went home in a state of great consternation. Though her feet hastened, her heart lagged behind her, for she knew not how to tell her son the terrible news. She was afraid that after his joy at the Sultan's promise, and his patient waiting, this blow would send him from his mind. Then she contrived it in her thoughts that it was best to provoke her son's anger against the Sultan, rather than his grief at the loss of Bedr-el-Budur. Accordingly, as soon as she entered the house and found him sitting thinking, as was his wont of late, she said, "O my son, who can put trust in a King? When I went to buy oil, I found that the Sultan had proclaimed a holiday, and all the shops were closed except one. Tush! There is no faith in Sultans!"

"How now, O my mother?" answered Aladdin. "Treason hath a loud voice. With the Sultan and the Grand Vizier, *hush!* What ails thee? Thy hand is a-tremble." And she answered him : "O my son, there is no faith nor trust but in God. Said I not to thee that the Grand Vizier was thine enemy? Out on him and the Sultan, for their word is but hot wind, and there is no faith in the promise of a King." "I see by thy face and by thy speech," said Aladdin, "that thou hast some bad news. What is it, O my mother?"

Then his mother told how that the Sultan had violated his covenant, and how the marriage of the Lady Bedr-el-Budur to the Grand Vizier's son was to take place that very evening. For this she heaped abuse upon the Grand Vizier, saying that it was only the worst of men that could so lead the Sultan to break his promise. When she had told all, and Aladdin understood how the matter lay, he arose, more in anger than in grief, and cried out against the Grand Vizier and cursed all the parties concerned in the affair. But presently he remembered that, when all seemed lost, he still had the Lamp, and that was something in time of trouble and difficulty. So he suddenly restrained his speech and fell to thinking what manner of death the Vizier's son should die. His mother, seeing him in better spirits, questioned him. "What now, O my son?" she said. "Is thy bitterness of feeling gone? What gift wilt thou send the wedded pair? Peradventure another bowl of jewels?" She spoke mockingly for she wanted him to spend his wrath and save his reason. "Nay, O my mother," replied Aladdin lightly; "they are not wedded yet; and, on my head and eye, verily it is not every knot that holds."

With this he arose and retired to his own chamber, where he brought out the Lamp. Then, having considered well the manner of his wish, he rubbed it. Immediately the Efrite stepped out of the unseen and stood before him, saying, "Thou hast invoked me: what is thy desire? I am the Slave of the Lamp in thy hand and am here to do thy bidding." And Aladdin answered: "Know, O Slave of the Lamp, that the Sultan promised me his daughter for my wife, but he has broken his word, and this night she is to be united with the Grand Vizier's son; wherefore I wish that, as soon as the pair retire, thou take them up, with the couch whereon they lie, and bring them hither to me." "I hear and obey," said the Slave of the Lamp, and immediately vanished.

Aladdin waited expectantly for some time, for he guessed that the moment would not be long delayed when the wedded pair would retire from the ceremonies. And his guess was right, for when he had waited a little longer, suddenly a cold blast of air swept through the chamber; the wall opened and there appeared the Efrite bearing in his arms the wedded pair upon the nuptial couch. They had been transported in the twinkling of an eye, and, when the Efrite had set the couch down at Aladdin's feet, they were both stupefied with astonishment at this proceeding.

"Take that scurvy thief," said Aladdin to the Efrite, pointing to the Vizier's son, "and bind him and lodge him in the wood-closet for the night." And the Efrite did so. He took up the Vizier's son in one hand, and, reaching with the other for cords, drew them from the invisible and bound the miscreant securely. Then he placed him in the wood-closet and blew an icy blast upon him to comfort him. Returning to Aladdin he said, "It is done, O Master of the Lamp! Is there aught else thou dost desire?" "Naught but this," replied Aladdin. "In the morning, when the Sultan is proceeding towards their chamber to wish them long life and happiness, convey them back thither in a state of sleep so that the Sultan's knock at their door may wake them." "I will obey," said the Efrite, and, in a moment, the air closed over him and he was gone.

And Aladdin smiled to himself to think that this thing had been done. Then he turned to the Lady Bedr-el-Budur,

99

who was sitting weeping on the couch. "O lovely one," said he, "weep not; for I would not hurt one hair of thy head, nor sully thine honour in any way. Know that I love thee too much to harm thee; but, since thy father the Sultan promised me thee, and has violated his word, I am determined that none other shall call thee his. Rest in peace, lovely lady; for neither am I thy husband nor the thief of thy husband's honour. Wherefore, weep not, but rest in peace."

So saying he took a sword that hung on the wall of his chamber, and, having placed it by her side in token of security, he stretched himself upon the couch so that they lay with the sword between them. Thus they passed the night. The Sultan's daughter wept the long night through, and Aladdin could not close his eyes for thinking of his unfortunate rival's condition in the wood-closet. Towards morning Bedr-el-Budur, utterly exhausted with weeping, fell asleep; and, as Aladdin gazed upon her, he saw that indeed her loveliness was rare; and, the more he gazed, the more he thought of the unhappy fate of the Vizier's son. Never was a man so badly treated as to be bound fast on his wedding night and laid in a wood-cellar in deadly fear of the dreadful apparition that had placed him there.

In the morning, while Bedr-el-Budur still slept, the Slave of the Lamp appeared according to Aladdin's command. "O my master," he said, "the Sultan hath left his couch and is about to knock at the door of the bridal chamber. I am here to perform thy bidding on the instant." "So be it," answered Aladdin. "Convey them together on the couch back to their place." And scarcely had he spoken when the Efrite vanished and reappeared with the Vizier's son, whom he quickly unbound and laid upon the couch beside the sleeping Bedr-el-Budur. Then, lifting the couch with the two upon it, he vanished, and Aladdin knew that, before the Sultan had knocked at the door of the bridal chamber, everything would be as it had been. Everything? No, not everything; for the Lady Bedr-el-Budur must awake as from a terrible nightmare; and, as for the Vizier's son, would he sing a song to the Sultan about spending the night in the wood-closet? Aladdin pondered over this and decided that nothing less than a repetition of the affair would wring the truth from either of them.

At this moment the Sultan knocked at the door of the bridal chamber in the Palace, and the Vizier's son, still cold from the wood-closet, arose and opened to him. The Sultan advanced to the couch, and kissed his daughter, and asked her if she was happy and content. By way of answer she glared at him in sullen silence, for she had not forgotten, in dreams or in waking, what had happened to her. The Sultan, not understanding what had befallen, and feeling annoyed, turned and left the chamber to lay the matter before the Queen, to whose ear their daughter's tongue might the more easily be loosed. So he came to the Queen and told her how Bedr-el-Budur had received him, concluding his recital with the remark, "Thus it is; there is trouble behind the door of that bridal chamber."

But the Queen smiled at his serious fears and answered him: "O my Lord the King, thou knowest little of the heart of a woman. When it is happiest, a trifle makes it sad; and, when it would send tears of laughter and joy to the eyes, it sometimes turns perverse against itself for very gladness, and sends tears of pain instead. Wherefore, be not angry with her, but let me go and see her. She will surely confide in me."

So saying, she arose and robed herself, and went to the bridal chamber. At first sight of her daughter's dejected attitude and pained expression she imagined that some lovers' quarrel over a mere trifle had occurred; but when she kissed her, wishing her good morning, and Bedr-el-Budur answered no word to her salutation, she began to think that some grave trouble rested on her daughter's mind. And it was not until she had coaxed her, and used every argument known to a mother, that she received an answer to her questions. "Be not angry with me, O my mother," said Bedr-el-Budur at last, raising her sad, beautiful eyes, "but know that a terrible thing has happened,—a thing which I hardly dare tell thee lest thou think I have lost my reason. Scarcely had we retired, O my mother, when there suddenly appeared a huge black shape,—terrible, horrific in aspect; and this—I know not what nor who—lifted the couch whereon we lay and conveyed us in a flash to some dark and vile abode of the common people." And then to her mother's astonished ears she unfolded the tale of all that had happened during the night till, suddenly, in the morning, she awoke to find the monstrous shape replacing them in the bridal chamber at the moment her father the Sultan had knocked at the door. "And that, O my mother," she concluded, "is why I could not answer my father, for I was so bewildered and stricken with unhappiness that I thought that I was mad; though, now I have thought about the affair from beginning to end, I know that I have my wits like any other."

"Truly, O my daughter," said the Queen with great concern, "if thou were to tell this story to thy father he would say thou wert mad. Wherefore, I counsel thee, child,

tell it to him not; neither to him nor to any other one."
"Nay, O my mother," answered Bedr-el-Budur, "dost thou
doubt me? I have told thee the plain truth, and, if thou
doubt it, ask my husband if my tale be true or not." But
the Queen replied, "Sweep these fancies from thy mind, O
my daughter; and arise and robe thyself to attend the
rejoicings which this day have been prepared in the City in
thine honour. For the whole people is in glad array, and
the drums will beat and music will delight the ears of all;
and the musicians will sing thy praises and all will wish thee
long life and happiness."

Leaving Bedr-el-Budur, then, with her tirewomen, the
Queen sought the Sultan, and begged him not to be angry
with their daughter, for she had been distressed with unhappy dreams. Then she sent for the Vizier's son to come
to her secretly, and, when he stood before her, she related
to him what Bedr-el-Budur had told her, and asked him if
it were true or if he knew aught of it. "Nay," he
answered, for he had thought the matter over and feared
that the truth might rob him of his bride; besides, his
acquaintance with the wood-closet seemed to him discredit-
able, and he felt little inclined to boast of it. "Nay, O my
lady the Queen," said he; "I know naught of these things
beyond what thou hast told me."

From this there was no doubt left in the Queen's mind
that her daughter had suffered from a nightmare so vivid
that she had been unable easily to cast it from her. Nevertheless, she felt assured that, as the day wore on, with its
gaieties and rejoicings, Bedr-el-Budur would be enabled to
rid herself of these troublous imaginings of the night, and
resume her former self.

103

All that day the City was thrown into a state of the utmost festivity which the Sultan and the Queen busied themselves to augment, for to restore their daughter's happiness was their chief concern. The Grand Vizier, who knew only that his daughter-in-law had been troubled by evil dreams, laid this not to his conscience in that he had persuaded the Sultan to break his pledge, but attempted rather to mend matters by adopting every means in his power to increase the universal gaiety. The drums beat, and music echoed through the City. Trumpeters went forth, fanfaring the beauty of Bedr-el-Budur; heralds proclaimed her graces in the streets and byways; singers extolled her charms; and the heavy burden of taxation was lifted from the people's backs for one month, so that they might stand up for a little and see what a great man was the Grand Vizier in the Sultan's eyes, and what a charming person his son must be to deserve the beautiful cause of these wonderful things. As for the Vizier's son, he ceased not to pursue all manner of gaieties, thinking thereby to convince himself that the wood-closet was naught but an odious dream. But all this festivity and rejoicing failed to dispel Bedr-el-Budur's gloom. Being of a sincere nature, she could not pretend like the Vizier's son, nor could she love him the better for stoutly denying what was plain truth to them both.

And, as the City went about its gladness without restraint, Aladdin strolled forth from his mother's house and viewed it all from the point of view of one who knows. When he surveyed the delighted rabble rejoicing over the happiness of bride and bridegroom he laughed within himself, saying, "Little they know!" But when he heard all men envying the great honour and distinction of the Grand Vizier's son, and praising him in that his excellent qualities had won the heart of the Lady Bedr-el-Budur, he feared that he might die for laughing. "Verily, ye glad people," he said within himself," ye would envy him to distraction if ye only knew that he would far sooner rest in a wood-closet than on the bridal couch. Ha! Ha! Ha! Ye doubt me? Then come and peep into the wood-closet to-night, ye rabble! and see for yourselves what a happy bridegroom he makes of himself, the gallows-bird that he is!"

At eventime, when the wild rejoicing of the City had fatigued itself against replenishment by wine, Aladdin retired to his chamber and rubbed the Lamp. Immediately the Slave appeared and desired to know his wish. "O Slave of the Lamp," said Aladdin, "do as thou didst last night. See to it that thou convey the bridal pair hither again as man and maid at the eleventh hour of their innocence." The Slave of the Lamp vanished in a moment, and Aladdin sat for a long time; yet he was content, for he knew that the wily Efrite was but waiting his opportunity. At length the monster reappeared before him, bearing in his arms the bridal couch with the pair upon it, weeping and wringing their hands in excess of grief and terror. And, at Aladdin's word the Slave took the Vizier's son as before and put him to bed in the wood-closet, where he remained, bound fast in an icy chill. Then having dismissed the Efrite with injunctions to convey the pair back in the morning as he had done the day before, Aladdin placed the sword between Bedr-el-Budur and himself and composed himself to rest, regardless of her weeping and restlessness; for, he said to himself, "I am sufficiently rewarded for all my trouble. The Vizier's son hath retired to the wood-closet. He careth not for this world's joys—

the gallows-bird! And he leaves me his bride to protect in the hour of need. Verily he is of a trusting nature." And Aladdin slept not nor stirred the whole night through; and it was as if Bedr-el-Budur's sobbing and tribulation were cut off from him by the sword that lay between them. And when it was morning, and the Sultan was about to knock at the door of the bridal chamber in the palace, the Slave of the Lamp appeared and conveyed the bride and the bridegroom swiftly back to their place.

On being set down in the bridal chamber, dazed and bewildered, they had not returned to their proper senses when the knock came at the door. The Sultan had come to wish his daughter good-morning, and to see also if she would behave towards him as on the former occasion. The bridegroom arose, shivering with cold,—for he had but a moment since left the wood-closet,—and opened the door. He made way for the Sultan, who entered, and, approaching the couch, saluted Bedr-el-Budur with a kiss. But, when he asked her if she was not the happiest of women, she made no reply, but met his gaze with an angry stare. It was easy to see that she was perfectly miserable. But the Sultan did not look at it in that light, he saw only what he took for sullen obstinacy, and, flying into a passion, drew his sword, saying, "By Allah! tell me what ails thee, or thy head will not remain upon thy body."

Then Bedr-el-Budur wept and supplicated him, and told him what had befallen on the second night as on the first, so that as she revealed it all his pity was aroused, and he sheathed his sword. "Thy words ring true, O my daughter!" he said. "But fear not, and be comforted; for at this moment I am minded to set a guard on this chamber so that no such thing may happen a third time. For the present, peace be on thee!"

The Sultan repaired immediately to the Grand Vizier and told him all; and asked him whether he had received the same version of this matter from his son. But the Grand Vizier shook his head in the manner of one who might be lying and might not. "Then," said the Sultan, "go at once and question him, for it may be that my daughter hath seen visions and dreamed dreams; albeit, I am unable to disbelieve the truth of her story."

So the Grand Vizier went and enquired of his son, and presently returned to the Sultan in great perplexity of face, for his son, whatever he had admitted before, had now confessed to everything, even to the wood-closet. And, moreover, he had begged and implored his father to obtain his release from this most unhappy marriage, since it was better to be without a bride and sleep in peace than to have one and perish with cold in a wood-closet. Thus it was with the Vizier's son.

"O King of the Age," said the Grand Vizier, who could not see his way to conceal the truth, "my son telleth the same tale as thy daughter, the Lady Bedr-el-Budur. Wherefore I beseech thee that thou set a guard this night, so that——" "Nay," broke in the Sultan angrily; "it is an unhappy marriage and bodes no good. Thou didst persuade me that my promise to that woman in respect of her son was not binding, but these unhappy events and ill-omened affairs make me think thou wast mistaken. Abide not another night, for worse may happen. Go forth, O Vizier, and proclaim the marriage annulled. Bid the people cease to rejoice, and command all to go their own ways and comport themselves as if the marriage had not been."

At this the Grand Vizier bowed his head and went forth exceeding wroth, and proclaimed the annulment of the marriage to all the people. Great was the wonder at this on every hand, for, among them all, none knew why, save one alone; and that one was Aladdin, the Master of the Lamp and of the Slave of the Lamp. He alone knew, and it was almost with regret that he decided the wood-closet need have no tenant that night.

Whether the Sultan had swiftly forgotten, or tardily remembered, his pledge, Aladdin troubled not to enquire. He waited patiently until the three months had expired, and then sent his mother to demand of the Sultan the fulfilment of his promise.

So it transpired that, on the day of the expiration of the term, the Sultan saw Aladdin's mother standing in the Hall of Audience. He was not astonished at this, for the matter of his broken or twisted pledge had somewhat disturbed his dreams. "Behold! there she stands!" he said to the Grand Vizier. "Bring her before me immediately." The Vizier arose, his face like autumn leaves withered in the wind, and did as he was bidden.

"What is thy suit?" asked the Sultan of Aladdin's mother as soon as she stood before him. Then, when she had kissed the ground and prayed for the prolongation of his life, she answered: "O King of all the Earth, the three months thou didst proscribe are at an end and I have come to ask thee to redeem thy pledge in respect of thy daughter and my son Aladdin."

The Sultan, who had not now the bowl of jewels before him to blind his vision, regarded her intently, and saw that she was of humble state; then, as he turned in perplexity to the Grand Vizier, he observed that the expression on his face was the expression of one who ponders the laying of a stratagem and the way it should be hatched. "What is thy thought on this, O Vizier?" he said. "My word is my word, and I regret that thou shouldst have explained it away; yet it seems to me that this woman is not of the kind that could mother-in-law my daughter. Hast thou a plan which is not a trick? If thou hast, whisper it in mine ear."

The Grand Vizier was pleased to hear the Sultan appealing to his ready wit in this way, for he was consumed with chagrin at what had befallen his son and desired only to non-suit this woman who had out-bid him with the jewels. So he unfolded his plan—his stratagem—his trick, privately to the Sultan's ear. "O King of the Age," he said, "thy pledge holds good, as ever it did; yea, as good as marriage vows. But verily, if this common woman's son desireth thy daughter for his wife, there should be a settlement befitting such a suit. Wherefore ask of him forty bowls of gold filled with jewels of the same blood and tincture as the woman brought at first, with forty female slaves to carry them, and a fitting retinue of forty. This thing, which is a Sultan's right to ask, it seemeth to me he cannot contrive to execute, and thus thou shalt be free of him."

"By Allah!" said the Sultan, "thou art of ready wit, O Vizier! Truly a marriage settlement is needed." Then, turning to Aladdin's mother, he said: "O woman! know that when one asketh the daughter of the Sultan one must have standing, for so it is in royal circles; and, to prove that standing, the suitor must show that he is able to provide for the Sultan's daughter and keep her in that state to which she has been accustomed. Wherefore he must bring to me forty golden bowls filled with jewels such as thou didst bring, with forty beautiful female slaves to carry them and forty black slaves as a retinue. Coming like this, thy son may claim my daughter, for the Sultan's word is the Sultan's word."

A sad woman then was Aladdin's mother. She returned to her son sick at heart, saying with herself, "Forty bowls of jewels, with forty maids and forty black slaves! How can my son do this? Better he had not entered on this affair!" Then, with bitterness, she added, "The Sultan asketh far too little: forty *five* bowls with forty *five* maids and forty *five* slaves and a palace to boot! Oh! what a thing it is to live up to such a demand as I have made." Thinking like this she found her son and spoke sorrowfully to him. "O my son," she exclaimed, weeping, "said I not to thee that the Grand Vizier was thine enemy? The Sultan remembered his pledge, but the Vizier—may his bones rot!—spake in his ear, and the outcome is this: forty golden bowls of jewels, forty female slaves to carry them, and forty slaves as an escort. With this dowry, O my son, thou mayest approach the Sultan and claim his daughter as thy bride."

Loudly Aladdin laughed to scorn. "O my mother," he said; "is this all the Sultan requireth? The Grand Vizier—may his bones rot as thou sayest!—hath proposed what he imagines an impossible thing; but it is not at all impossible. Now, mother, set some food before me, and, when I have eaten, I will tell thee."

And when his mother had brought him food, and he had eaten, he arose and went into his chamber. There he brought out the Lamp, and, sitting down, he rubbed it. Immediately the Slave appeared. "What is thy wish, O my master?" "Lo, O Slave of the Lamp, know that the Sultan hath promised me his daughter, but, repenting him of his promise, he hath required of me what he thinketh a dowry impossible for anyone to compass: forty golden bowls of rare and splendid jewels, carried by forty maids, with an escort of forty slaves. Therefore I desire all these things of thee." "I obey!" said the Efrite, and vanished.

In less than an hour he returned and led before Aladdin forty beautiful maidens, each carrying a golden bowl of jewels on her head, and each accompanied by a magnificent black slave. And when Aladdin's mother saw this array she knew that it was done by the Lamp, and she blessed it for her son's sake. Then said Aladdin, "O my mother, behold, the dowry is ready according to the Sultan's requirement. It is for thee to take it to him, to shew him what is in my power, and also that no time hath been lost in complying with his request."

Then the maids, with the golden bowls of precious stones, arrayed themselves in the street outside the house, and by each maid stood a slave. Thus, led by Aladdin's mother, they proceeded to the Sultan's Palace; and the people crowded in the streets to see this unwonted sight, for the maids were richly dressed, and all, with the sun shining on their raiment and flashing in the jewels they bore, made a magnificent spectacle. Never had the people seen such jewels, never such beauteous damsels, never such magnificent slaves. A cortège like this was a wonder beyond the reach of kings. But Aladdin's mother headed the procession unmindful of their shouts of acclamation, for she well knew

111

that she was going before the Sultan in a manner and with a gift that would take his breath away.

When they reached the Palace gates the wonder of the people spread to the soldiers and the guards, who, after a moment of speechless admiration, found tongue to say to one another, "Does this earth contain such splendid jewels? And are there such radiant maidens even in the Fragrant Paradise?" And amazement gat hold of them, and their hearts leapt in their breasts, so that not one amongst them could ever think to become an anchorite, or hope to call one grandson. And so it was with the commanding officers, the chamberlains, the officials of the Palace and the grandees and nobles there assembled; they were all cast into the depths of wonder, and the whole place effervesced and simmered with an excitement it had never known before.

Thus, in due course, came Aladdin's mother before the Sultan, leading the cortège into the Audience Hall. And so they stood before him, a magnificent array, before whose dazzle and splendour the richness of the place, the nobles and grandees with their costly robes, even the Sultan himself and the throne whereon he sat, all seemed poor and common by comparison. The maidens took the bowls of jewels from their heads and set them on the ground. Then they made obeisance, they and the slaves prostrating themselves before the Sultan; and, having done this, they all arose and stood before him in humble reverence. And, when the Sultan's gaze at last left the beauteous damsels and fell upon the bowls of jewels at their feet, he was beside himself with wonder and admiration; and he was the more amazed that surpassing wealth in this form could be brought before him in the short space of one hour. For some moments he was

The Lady Bedr-el-Budur at her bath. Page 84

The Lady Bedr-el-Budur.   Page 113

speechless; then, when he found words, he commanded that the whole cortège should present itself, with the jewels, to the Lady Bedr-el-Budur in her Palace. So, in due order and with perfect grace of movement, the damsels took up their precious burdens; and thus, escorted by the slaves, and led by Aladdin's mother, they went in to the Sultan's daughter. While they were laying this dowry before her, Aladdin's mother returned to the Sultan and spoke with him. "O King of the Age," she said, "'tis but a mere trifle, and scarcely worthy of the priceless rarity of thy fair daughter."

"What sayest thou?" said the Sultan, addressing the Grand Vizier. "He who can control such wealth is surely worthy of my daughter." But the wily Vizier, who had twice persuaded the Sultan, and had twice been beaten, was minded to chance a third attempt, for he could not bear to see the Lady Bedr-el-Budur pass to Aladdin without a struggle. "O my Lord," he said, green with envy, "rich though these things be, thinkest thou they are worth one single curl of thy daughter's head? Thou art the King of Earth, and the Lady Bedr-el-Budur is thy daughter: this gift is not worthy of her."

"Perchance that is why thy son feared to bring the like lest I should be displeased," returned the Sultan sharply, for he saw that the Grand Vizier was envious to excess. Then he added to Aladdin's mother: "Tell thy son he need fear not but that I shall keep my promise; but bid him come hither to me with all haste, so that I may look upon his face and accept him as my son-in-law; for the marriage shall be this very night."

Aladdin's mother flushed red with joy—redder than she had ever known as a girl. The Grand Vizier turned white with rage—whiter than his false heart had ever been, even when a boy. After a dagger-thrust of glances between them, Aladdin's mother made obeisance to the Sultan and thanked him. Then, with contempt for the Grand Vizier written plainly on her face, she withdrew, and returned home, walking on the air.

As soon as she was gone the Sultan dismissed the audience and repaired to his daughter's palace, where he found Bedr-el-Budur examining the jewels in a state of the utmost delight, and singing a song of their wondrous beauty. Then, when the Sultan told her that they came from her new bridegroom, she clapped her hands with joy and demanded to know what he was like, and where was his splendid kingdom. "I know not," said the Sultan in answer, "but he cometh to me shortly, and then he will reveal to me his state. Meanwhile, O my daughter, do thou regard him in the sparkling light of these wondrous jewels, and know that, while he regardeth them as not worth thy little finger, his love for thee must be great."

Now Aladdin, when he saw his mother returning swift-footed and on wings of joy, knew that good tidings came with her. But, before he could speak, his mother burst in upon him and embraced him, crying, "O my son! thy heart's wish is fulfilled. This very night thou art to wed the Sultan's daughter, and so it is proclaimed before all the world." Then did Aladdin rejoice that his expectations were fulfilled, and was continuing to rejoice when his mother addressed him suddenly. "Nay," she said, "I have not told thee all. The Sultan bids thee go to him immediately, for he desires to see his son-in-law. But how shalt thou approach the Sultan in thy merchant's garments? However,

114

I have done all I can for thee, and it is now thine own affair."

So saying, she withdrew to rest a little, and Aladdin, having blessed her, retired to his chamber and brought forth the Lamp. With a set purpose in his mind, he rubbed it, and at once the Slave appeared. "Thou knowest me: what is thy desire?" "I wish," answered Aladdin, "that thou take me to a bath which hath no equal in all the kingdoms, and provide me there with a change of raiment of resplendent glory, richer than any the Sultan has ever worn."

No sooner had he spoken than the Efrite bore him away in his arms, and deposited him in a bath the like of which no King could compass nor any man describe. Everything was there which delighted the eye, and not the least of the wonders of this splendid bath was a hall whose walls were encrusted with jewels. Seeing there was no one in attendance, Aladdin clapped his hands, and immediately came slaves to wait upon him. And one with marvellous strength and dexterity of hand washed him and manipulated his limbs until he was altogether refreshed. Then he sought the jewelled hall and found there, in place of his merchant's garb, a set of robes that exceeded all imagination. These he put on, and smiled to himself as if he looked down on kings; for, indeed, the robes were more than royal. And, when he had drunk the sherbets and the coffee which the slaves brought him, he submitted to the completion of his dress by delicate unguents and perfumes, and then went forth. At the door of the bath, he was met by the Efrite in waiting, who took up and bore him in a flash to his home.

"Hast thou still some further need?" asked the Slave of the Lamp, about to vanish. "Yea," replied Aladdin.

115

"Bring me here a Chief of Memluks with forty-eight in his train—twenty-four to precede me and twenty-four to follow after; and see that they have splendid horses and equipments, so that not even the greatest in the world can say, 'This is inferior to mine.' For myself I want a stallion such as cannot be equalled among the Arabs, and his housings must be for value such as one could purchase only in dreams. And to each memluk give a thousand gold pieces, and to the Chief Memluk ten thousand; for we go to the Sultan's palace and would scatter largesse on the way. Wait! Also twelve maidens of unequalled grace and loveliness in person to attire and accompany my mother to the Sultan's presence. And look you! whatever of grace and beauty is lacking in my person supply it to me on my natural plan of being. See to it, O Slave of the Lamp!"

"It is already done," said the Slave of the Lamp; and, vanishing on the instant, he reappeared at once at the doorway of the house, leading a noble white stallion gorgeously equipped, while behind came the twelve damsels and forty-nine memluks on magnificent chargers. The damsels were bearing rich stuffs in their arms; so Aladdin, guessing that these were the robes for his mother, led them in to her that she might be arrayed in a manner befitting the mother-in-law of a Princess. Then he sent the Chief Memluk post haste to the Palace to announce his speedy arrival. The memluk rode like the wind, and soon returned at full gallop, saying as he drew rein, "O my lord, the Sultan expecteth thee every moment."

Then Aladdin, having seen that the maidens had properly arrayed his mother, mounted his steed and set out for the Palace with memluks before and behind him, and his mother

116

following, supported by the maidens. It was a brave cavalcade that proceeded through the streets, and the people watched it in amazement. "Is not this the tailor's son?" said one to another. "Yea, we all thought so," was the reply; "but it seems we have never known the truth." For, when they saw Aladdin's courtly grace, enhanced as it was by the Slave of the Lamp, and beheld his memluks scattering gold, they said among themselves that he was the son of a potent king of far lands, and had been placed in the tailor's care; for see! his foster mother, magnificently robed, was following. Little did they think—for Aladdin's mother had not gossiped—that all this ravishing splendour was of the Lamp, which could work wonders for whosoever possessed it. And the cavalcade filed onwards amid the acclamations and blessings of the people, until the Palace was reached. And all the way they ceased not to distribute largesse to the people.

Now, when the Sultan had received word that Aladdin was coming, he informed his nobles and grandees of the meaning of this thing; so that, when Aladdin arrived, there was a vast concourse of people, and all the stateliest of the land were there awaiting his entry. And, as he rode in at the gates, he was received not only by the greatest personages of the Sultan's realm, but also by officials high and low, who did him homage and extolled him. There was no office too small to be performed for him—no word of welcome too great to greet him. As the sun rises in glory upon a waiting world, so came Aladdin to the Palace. At the door of the Hall of Audience he dismounted, while hands held his stirrup that had never performed such an office before.

The Sultan was seated on his throne, and, immediately he saw Aladdin, he arose and descended and took him to his breast, forbidding all ceremony on so great an occasion. Then he led him up affectionately, and placed him on his right hand. In all this Aladdin forgot not the respect due to kings. Forbidden to be too humble, he was not too lofty in his bearing. He spoke:

"O my Lord the Sultan! King of the Earth and Heaven's Dispenser of all Good! Truly thou hast treated me graciously in bestowing upon me thy daughter the Lady Bedr-el-Budur. Know, O King, that when I consider her grace and loveliness, which cometh from thee, I feel unworthy, like one of the meanest slaves. Yet, since thou hast so honoured me of thy Felicity, I cannot bring to thy feet a slave's humility, for, by the gift of this lovely lady, thy daughter, thou hast raised me above my fellows beneath thy sheltering wing. Wherefore, while my tongue knoweth no words to thank and extol thee for the magnitude of thy favour, it can still pray fervently for the prolongation of thy life. O King of the Age! be gracious and hear me yet further, for I have a request to make. Wilt thou grant me a site whereon to build a palace, unworthy as it may prove, for the comfort and happiness of thy daughter, the Lady Bedr-el-Budur?"

Now, while Aladdin was thus speaking with courtly grace and diction, the Sultan's attention was divided between his ears and eyes. While listening to Aladdin's words he was noting his more than princely raiment, his beauty and perfection of form, his magnificent retinue of memluks, and the royal richness of everything that appertained to him—all following his lordly wake without compulsion, as though it were natural from long custom so to do. And he was bewildered, and wondered greatly that this son of a thousand kings should have been heralded by a woman of the people, saying, forsooth, she was his mother. And, while he was wondering, Aladdin's mother approached, apparelled in robes more costly than any in his own Queen's wardrobe, and supported humbly and decorously by her twelve maidens of surpassing loveliness. At this, while the Grand Vizier came nigh to death with envy, the Sultan on a sudden turned to Aladdin and embraced and kissed him, saying, "My son! My son! How hast thou hid from me so long?"

Then the Sultan conversed with Aladdin and was greatly charmed with his courtliness and eloquence. Anon he ordered the musicians to play, and together they listened to the music in the utmost content. Finally he arose, and, taking Aladdin by the hand, led him forth into the Palace banqueting hall, where a splendid supper was awaiting them with the lords of the land standing ready in their proper order of degree. Yet above them all sat Aladdin, for he was at the Sultan's right hand. And, while they ate, the music played and a merry wit prevailed; and the Sultan drew nearer to Aladdin in their talk, and saw, from his grace, his manner of speech, and his complaisance, that indeed he must have been brought up and nurtured among kings. Then, while they conversed, the Sultan's heart went out with joy and satisfaction to Aladdin, and the whole assemblage saw that it was not as it had been with the Vizier's son.

The Grand Vizier himself would have retired early had it not been that his presence was required for the marriage ceremony. As soon as the banquet was over and the tables cleared away, the Sultan commanded the Vizier to summon the Kadis and the witnesses, and thus the contract between Aladdin and the Lady Bedr-el-Budur was duly executed. Then, without a warning word, Aladdin arose to depart.

119

"Wherefore, O my son?" said the Sultan. "Thy wedding is duly contracted and the festivities are about to begin."

"Yea, O my lord the King," replied Aladdin; "and none rejoiceth at that more than I; but, if it please thee, it is my thought to build a palace for the Lady Bedr-el-Budur; and if my love and longing for her be anything, thou mayest rest assured that it will be completed so quickly as to amaze thee." At this the Grand Vizier tugged the Sultan's sleeve, but received no attention. "It is well," said the Sultan to Aladdin; "choose what site seemeth best to thee and follow thine own heart in the matter. See! this open space by my palace! What thinkest thou, my son?" "O King," replied Aladdin, "I cannot thank thee enough, for it is the summit of my felicity to be near thee."

Then Aladdin left the Palace in the same royal manner as he had approached it, with his memluks preceding and following; and again the people praised and blessed him as he passed. When he reached his house he left all other affairs in the hands of his Chief Memluk with certain instructions, and went into his chamber. There he took the Lamp and rubbed it. The Slave appeared on the instant and desired to know his pleasure. "O Slave," answered Aladdin, "I have a great task for thee. I desire thee to build for me in all haste a palace on the open space near the Sultan's Serai,—a palace of magnificent design and construction, and filled with rare and costly things. And let it be incomplete in one small respect, so that, when the Sultan offers to complete it to match the whole, all the wealth and artifice at his command will not suffice for the task." "O my master," replied the Efrite, "it shall be done with all speed. I will return when the work is finished." With this he vanished.

It was an hour before dawn when the Slave of the Lamp returned to Aladdin, and, awakening him from sleep, stood before him. "O Master of the Lamp," he said, "the palace is built as thou didst command." "It is well, O Slave of the Lamp," answered Aladdin; "and I would inspect thy work." No sooner had he spoken than he found himself being borne swiftly through the air in the arms of the Efrite, who set him down almost immediately within the palace.

Most excellently had the Slave done his work. Porphyry, jasper, alabaster and other rare stones had been used in the construction of the building. The floors were of mosaics the which to match would cost much wealth and time in the fashioning, while the walls and ceilings, the doors and the smallest pieces of detail were all such that even the imagination of them could come only to one dissatisfied with the palaces of Kings. When Aladdin had wondered at all this, the Slave led him into the Treasury, and showed him countless bars of gold and silver and gems of dazzling brilliance. Thence to the banqueting hall, where the tables were arrayed in a manner to take one's breath away; for every dish and every flagon were of gold or silver, and all the goblets were crusted with jewels. Thence, again, to the wardrobes, where the richest stuffs of the East were piled in great gold-bound chests to an extent that baffled the reason. And so from room to room, where everything that met the eye dazzled and captivated it. And all this had been done in a single night.

Having surveyed it all, Aladdin knew not what to say, scarcely even what to think. It seemed to him that the most sovereign monarch of all the world could command nothing like this. But, when the Slave led him further and shewed him a pavilion with twenty-four niches thickly set with diamonds and emeralds and rubies, he fairly lost his wits. And the Slave took him to one niche and shewed him how his command had been carried out in that this was the one small part of the palace that was left incomplete in order to tempt and tax the Sultan to finish it.

When Aladdin had viewed the whole palace, and seen the numerous slaves and beautiful maidens therein, he asked yet one thing more of the Efrite. "O Slave of the Lamp," he said, "the work is wonderful, yet it still lacketh an approach from the Sultan's palace. I desire, therefore, a rich carpet laid upon the intervening space, so that the Lady Bedr-el-Budur may come and go upon a splendid pathway of brocade worked with gold and inwrought with precious stones." "I hear and obey," said the Slave, and vanished. Presently he returned and led Aladdin to the steps of the palace. "O my lord," he said, "what thou didst command is done." And he pointed to a magnificent carpet extending from palace to palace. The gold and the precious stones in the brocade gleamed and sparkled in the stars' last rays before the rise of dawn. When Aladdin had gazed upon it and wondered at it, the Efrite carried him in the twinkling of an eye back to his own home.

Shortly afterwards, when the dawn had arisen, the Sultan opened his eyes, and, looking forth from his window, beheld a magnificent structure where the day before had been an open space. Doubting the evidence of his senses, he turned himself about and rubbed his eyes and looked again. There, undoubtedly, was a palace more splendid and glorious than any he had ever seen; and there, leading to it, was a carpet the like of which he had never trod. And all those who awoke betimes in the Sultan's palace observed these wonderful things, and neither they nor the Sultan could keep their amazement to themselves. The news of it spread through the palace like wildfire. The Grand Vizier came rushing to the Sultan, and, finding him at the window, had no need to tell him the cause of his excitement. "What sayest thou, O Vizier?" said the Sultan. "Yonder stands a palace surpassing all others. Truly Aladdin is worthy of my daughter, since at his bidding such a royal edifice arises in a single night."

Then the Vizier's envy found vent. "O King," he said, "thinkest thou that such a thing as this could be done save by the vilest of sorcery? Riches and jewels and costly attire are in the hands of mortals, but this—this is impossible!" "Impossible?" said the Sultan. "Behold!"—and he pointed towards the palace—"there it stands in the light of day, and thou sayest it is impossible. Verily, O Vizier, it seems thy wits are turned with envy at the wealth of Aladdin. Prate not to me of sorcery. There are few things beyond the power of a man in whose treasury are such jewels as those sent me by Aladdin." At this the Grand Vizier was silent; indeed, his excess of envy well nigh choked him, for he saw that the Sultan loved Aladdin greatly.

Now when Aladdin awoke in the morning and knew that he must set forth for the palace where the nobles and grandees were already assembling for the wedding celebration, he took the Lamp and rubbed it. The slave appeared on the instant and desired to know his wish. "O Slave of the Lamp," said Aladdin, "this is my wedding day and I go to the Sultan's palace. Wherefore I shall need ten thousand gold pieces." "I hear and obey," said the Efrite, and, vanishing, returned on the instant with the gold packed in bags. These he placed before Aladdin, and then, receiving no further command, disappeared.

Aladdin called his Chief Memluk and ordered him to take the gold and see that it was scattered among the people on the way to the palace. When all was ready Aladdin mounted his steed and rode through the City while the memluks before and behind distributed largesse all the way. And the people were loud in their praises of his dignity and grace and loved him greatly for his generosity. Anon the palace was reached and there the high officials, who were looking for Aladdin and his train, hastened to inform the Sultan of his approach. On this the Sultan arose, and, going out to the gates of the palace to meet him, embraced and kissed him. Then, taking him by the hand, he led him in and seated him at his right hand. Meanwhile the whole City was in festivity. Pomp and ceremony went hand in hand with gaiety and mirth. Soldiers and guards kept holiday order in the streets where youths and bright-garlanded maidens made merry riot. Within the palace resounded music and singing and the murmur of happy voices, for this was the nation's day of joy.

Anon the Sultan commanded the wedding banquet to be served, and the eunuchs set the tables out with royal dishes of gold and silver filled with sumptuous viands and fruits that might have been culled in Paradise. And, when it was all ready, Aladdin sat on the right hand of the Sultan; and they, with all the nobles and foremost in the land, ate and drank. On every hand were honour and good will for Aladdin. Everyone was filled with joy at the event, saying that this wedding was as happy as that of the Grand Vizier's son was unfortunate. Aladdin's palace and the space around it were thronged with people of every degree who ceased not to wonder at its resplendent beauty and the fact that it had been built in a single night. "May his head survive us all!" said some; and others, "God give him every pleasure, for verily he deserveth it."

When the banquet was over Aladdin repaired with his memluks to his palace to make ready for the reception of his bride, Bedr-el-Budur. And, as he went, all the people thronged him shouting, "God give thee happiness! God bless thy days!" And he scattered gold amongst them.

Coming to his palace he dismounted, and went in, and seated himself whilst his attendants bowed before him. And, thinking of naught else but his bride, the Lady Bedr-el-Budur, he commanded them to prepare for her reception. And they did so. Meanwhile Aladdin looked forth from a window of the palace and saw the Sultan with his horsemen descending into the riding ground. At this he bethought him of his stallion and commanded his Chief Memluk accordingly. Then, mounted on his steed and accompanied by his retinue, he galloped down into the riding ground. There, javelin in hand, he displayed his prowess, and none could stand against him. Bedr-el-Budur, watching him from a window in her father's palace, felt her heart turn over and over in her bosom, and then, saying within herself, "He is my husband and none other," she renounced herself to the exquisite joy of sudden love.

At eventime, when the sport and play were over, the princes of the land surrounded Aladdin—for he had become the centre of all interest—and accompanied him to the

125

Hammam. There he was bathed and perfumed, and, when he came forth and mounted his matchless steed, he was escorted through the City by guards and emirs with drawn swords, while all the people thronged in procession before and behind and on every side, beating drums and playing musical instruments and singing for very excess of joy and revel. And when he reached his palace he dismounted and entered, and seated himself. And the nobles and grandees, submitting to the ruling of his Chief Memluk, were seated also, each according to his degree. Then refreshments were served without stint, even to the multitude without the gates. And Aladdin arose in the midst of this and beckoned to his Chief Memluk. "Is there any gold?" he asked. "Yea," answered the Memluk, "some thousands of pieces." "Then," said Aladdin, "scatter it among the people who throng the gates." And thus it was at Aladdin's palace.

Meanwhile the Sultan, on returning from the riding ground, commanded an escort to conduct the Lady Bedr-el-Budur to her husband's abode. On this the Captains of guards, the officers of state and nobles, well equipped, were mounted in readiness and waiting at the door of Bedr-el-Budur's apartments. Presently, preceded by female slaves and eunuchs bearing lighted tapers set in jewelled candlesticks, came forth a vision of liveliness. Bedr-el-Budur, aflame with love for Aladdin, appeared on the threshold like a pure white bird about to fly into space. All too slow was the procession that escorted her to Aladdin's palace. The stately pomp and splendour accorded not with the beating of her heart. She saw not Aladdin's mother nor the beauteous damsels, nor the mounted guards, nor the emirs, nor the nobles—her only thought was Aladdin, for her heart was consumed with love.

Thus from the Seraglio to Aladdin's palace, where Bedr-el-Budur, as one floating in a dream, was taken to her apartments and arrayed for presentation to the Court assembled. And of all that Court and multitude of people the only one who had no voice was Aladdin, for, when he looked upon his bride in her surpassing loveliness, he was reft of speech or thought, and stood silent before a joy too great for tongue to tell.

At last, when the presentation was over, Aladdin sought the bridal chamber where he found his mother with Bedr-el-Budur. And there, in the apartment all sparkling with gold and precious stones, his mother unveiled her and Aladdin gazed into her eyes and took no thought for the lustre of jewels. And while his mother went into raptures over the splendour of the place, Aladdin and Bedr-el-Budur exchanged one look of love—a thing which none could purchase with all the treasures of the earth. And so it was with Aladdin and his bride.

In the morning Aladdin arose and donned a costly robe of royal magnificence; then, when he had quaffed some delicious coffee flavoured with ambergris, he ordered his steed, and, with his memluks preceding and following, rode to the Sultan's palace. As soon as the Sultan was informed of his arrival he came to meet him, and, having embraced and kissed him with great affection, led him in and seated him on his right hand. And the nobles and grandees and high officials of the realm craved the privilege to approach him with congratulations and blessings. When this was over—Aladdin having shown an exceeding graciousness to all—the Sultan ordered breakfast to be brought. The tables were immediately laid, and all assembled ate and drank and conversed in a state of the utmost joy and happiness.

"O my Lord," said Aladdin to the Sultan when they had finished the repast, "I crave that thou wilt favour and honour me with thy presence, and that of thy Court, to dine with thy well-beloved daughter Bedr-el-Budur at her palace to-day. I entreat thy Felicity to refuse not my request." And the Sultan answered with a charming smile, "O my son, thou art too generous; but who could refuse thee anything?" Accordingly, in due course, the Sultan commanded his suite, and all rode forth with him and Aladdin to Bedr-el-Budur's palace.

Great was the Sultan's wonder and admiration when he saw the architecture and masonry of the structure, for, even without, it was all of the rarest and most costly stone in-wrought with gold and silver and fashioned with consummate skill; but when he entered and viewed the entrance hall his breath was snatched away from him, for he had never seen anything so magnificent in his life. At length, finding speech, he turned to the Grand Vizier and said, "Verily, this is the greatest wonder of all. Hast thou ever, from first to last, beheld a palace like this?" "O King of the Age," replied the Vizier gravely, "there hath never been the like of this among the sons of men. It would take ten thousand workmen ten thousand days to construct it; wherefore, as I told thy Felicity, its completion in a single night is the work of sorcery." At this the Sultan was not pleased. "Verily, O Vizier," he replied, "thou hast an envious heart, and thou speakest foolishly with thy mouth."

At this moment Aladdin approached the Sultan to conduct him through the rooms of the palace. And, as they went from one to another, the Sultan was simply astounded at the wealth of metal and precious stones on every hand, and at the workmanship thereof. As for the Vizier, he had said

128

The Sultan and his Vizier looking for Aladdin's magic Palace

Page 122

The Nuptial Dance of Aladdin and the Lady Bedr-el-Budur

Page 130

all he had to say, and followed sullenly, nursing an evil heart. At length they came to the kiosk, which was a crowning work of jewel-clusters so rich and splendid that the treasuries of the earth must have been emptied to fill them. The Sultan nearly went from his wits in the effort to calculate the fabulous wealth of this apartment alone. His thought sped onward through thousands, millions, of gold pieces; and, losing itself in the thousands of millions, fell back staggering and distraught. For relief he turned this way and that, gazing upon the niches, which were the most precious and wonderful of all. And in this way he came at length to the niche that had been left incomplete. This gave him speech. "Alas!" he said, relieved to find a flaw, "this niche, at least, is imperfect." Then, turning to Aladdin, he enquired the reason of it. "Yea, O my Lord," answered Aladdin, "woe unto it; it is indeed unfinished, for the workmen clamoured to be allowed to prepare themselves for the wedding festivities and I had not the heart to say them nay. So they left it as thou seest it." Then, while Aladdin stood by observing intently the effect of his words, the Sultan stroked his beard in contemplation. "O my son," he said presently, "the thought has come to me to complete it myself." "On the head and eye, O King!" cried Aladdin. "And may thy life be prolonged! If thou wilt honour me thus it will be a fitting perpetuation of thy memory in the palace of thy daughter." At this, the Sultan, vastly pleased, summoned his jewellers and artificers, and, empowering them to draw on the Royal Treasury for all they might require, he commanded them to complete the niche.

Scarcely had the Sultan finished his directions in this matter when Bedr-el-Budur came to greet him. And his

heart leapt with joy at her radiant face when he looked upon
her. Then, when she had confided to him how happy she
was, Aladdin led them into the banqueting hall, where all
was ready. One table was set apart for the Sultan and
Bedr-el-Budur and Aladdin, and another for the Sultan's suite.
Then the Sultan seated himself between Aladdin and his
daughter, and the meal proceeded. The viands were like
ambrosia, and the wine like nectar; and the serving was
done by eighty damsels, to each one of whom the moon
might have curtseyed, saying, "Thy pardon, but I have
stolen thy seat." And some of these damsels took musical
instruments and played and sang in a manner divine. The
Sultan's heart expanded, and he said, "Verily, this is a feast
to which a king might aspire."

When they had eaten and emptied their cups the Chief
Memluk opened the way to another room, where the most
delicious fruits and sweetmeats were set out against a wealth
of delicate flowers and greenery. Here the whole assembly
lingered long in perfect delight while, upon the soft carpets,
the beauteous damsels danced to the sound of sweetest
music. Never had any of them, including the Sultan himself,
been so near to Paradise before. Even the Grand Vizier shed
his envy for the moment and forgot himself to joy.

When the Sultan's soul was well nigh weary with
excess of enjoyment he rose, and, bethinking himself of the
unfinished niche, repaired to the kiosk to see how his workmen had progressed with their task. And when he came
to them and inspected their work he saw that they had
completed only a small portion and that neither the execution
nor the material, which was already exhausted, could compare
with that of the other niches. Seeing this he bethought him

of his reserve Treasury and the jewels Aladdin had given him.
Wherefore he commanded the workmen to draw upon these
and continue their work. This they did, and, in due course,
the Sultan returned to find that the work was still incomplete. Determined to carry out his design at whatever cost
the Sultan commanded his officials to seize all the jewels
they could lay their hands on in the kingdom. Even this
was done, and lo, still the niche was unfinished.

It was not until late on a day thereafter that Aladdin
found the jewellers and goldsmiths adding to the work the
last stones at their command. "Hast thou jewels enough?"
he asked of the chief artificer. "Nay, O my master," he
replied sadly. "We have used all the jewels in the Treasuries;
yea, even in all the kingdom, and yet the work is only half
finished."

"Take it all away!" said Aladdin. "Restore the jewels
to their rightful owners." So they undid their work and
returned the jewels to the Treasuries and to the people from
whom they had been taken. And they went in to the Sultan
and told him. Unable to learn from them the exact reason
for this, the Sultan immediately called for his attendants and
his horses and repaired to Aladdin's palace.

Meanwhile, Aladdin himself, as soon as the workmen
had left, retired to a private chamber; and, taking out the
Lamp, rubbed it. "Ask what thou wilt," said the Slave,
appearing on the instant. "I desire thee to complete the
niche which was left incomplete," answered Aladdin.
"I hear and obey," said the Slave, and vanished. In a
very short space of time he returned, saying, "O my
master, the work is complete." Then Aladdin arose and
went to the kiosk, and found that the Slave had spoken

truly; the niche was finished. As he was examining it, a memluk came to him and informed him that the Sultan was at the gates. At this Aladdin hastened to meet him. "O my son," cried the Sultan as Aladdin greeted him, "why didst thou not let my jewellers complete the niche in the kiosk? Wilt thou not have the palace whole?" And Aladdin answered him, "O my lord, I left it unfinished in order to raise a doubt in thy mind and then dispel it; for, if thy Felicity doubted my ability to finish it, a glance at the kiosk as it now stands will make the matter plain." And he led the Sultan to the kiosk and showed him the completed niche.

The Sultan's astonishment was now greater than ever, that Aladdin had accomplished in so short a space that which he himself could command neither workmen nor jewels sufficient to accomplish in many months. It filled him with wonder. He embraced Aladdin and kissed him, saying there was none like him in all the world. Then, when he had rested awhile with his daughter Bedr-el-Budur, who was full of joy and happiness, the Sultan returned to his own palace.

As the days passed by Aladdin's fame went forth through all the land. It was his daily pleasure to ride through the City with his memluks, scattering gold among the people, and there was no kind of generosity or kindness that he did not practise. His hospitality drew the nobles and grandees to his table, and his name was exalted far and wide. In the chase and on the riding ground there was none could vie with Aladdin, and frequently Bedr-el-Budur, watching from a window in the palace, would glow with love and pride at the sight of his graceful and daring horsemanship in the javelin joust. Then she would say within herself, "A lucky one am I to have escaped the Vizier's son."

Now it chanced that the Sultan's enemies from distant parts invaded his territory and rode down against him. The Sultan assembled his armies for war and gave the chief command to Aladdin, whose skill and prowess had found great favour in his eyes. And Bedr-el-Budur wept when Aladdin went forth to the wars, but great was her delight when he returned victorious, having routed the enemy in a great battle with terrible slaughter. Many were the tales the soldiers told of Aladdin's courage and strength, his daring when, at the head of his troops, he thundered down upon the enemy, sword in hand, and broke and dispersed them. A great triumph was held in the City, for Aladdin returned not only with victory, but with much plunder and many flocks and herds of which he had despoiled the enemy. And the Sultan rejoiced over Aladdin in that he had saved the realm and smitten his enemies; and Bedr-el-Budur wept upon his breast with delight that he had returned to her safe and sound and covered with glory. The City was illuminated, and everyone feasted and drank by order of the Sultan, and praised Aladdin by the dictate of their own hearts. So greatly was he magnified by the people of high and low degree that, if any swore, it was by Allah in Heaven and by Aladdin on earth. Such was his exalted position in the land.

Now the fame of Aladdin penetrated even to distant parts, so that his name was heard even in the land of the Moors, where the accursed Dervish dwelt. This sorcerer had not yet made an end of lamenting the loss of the Lamp just as it seemed about to pass into his hands. And, while he lamented, he cursed Aladdin in his bitter rage, saying within himself, "'Tis well that ill-omened miscreant is dead and buried, for, if I have not the Lamp, it is at least safe, and one day I may come by it." But when he heard the name "Aladdin," and the fame attached to it, he muttered to himself, "Can this be he? And hath he risen to a high position through the Lamp and the Slave of the Lamp?" Then he rose and drew a table of magic signs in the sand in order to find if the Aladdin of Destiny were indeed alive upon the earth. And the figures gave him what he feared. Aladdin was alive and the Lamp was not in the cavern where by his magic he had first discovered it. At this a great fear struck him to the heart, and he wondered that he had lived to experience it, for he knew that at any moment Aladdin, by means of the Slave of the Lamp, might slay him for revenge. Wondering that this had not occurred to Aladdin's mind he hastened to draw another table; by which he saw that Aladdin had acquired great possessions and had married the Sultan's daughter. At this his rage mastered his fear and he cursed Aladdin with fury and envy. But, though his magic was great, it could not cope with that which slumbered in the Lamp, and his curses missed their mark, only to abide the time when they might circle back upon him. Meanwhile, in great haste, he arose and journeyed to the far land of Cathay, fearing every moment that Aladdin would bethink him of revenge by means of the Slave of the Lamp. Yet he arrived safely at the City of the Sultan and rested at an inn where he heard naught but praises of Aladdin's generosity, his bravery in battle, his beautiful bride Bedr-el-Budur and his magnificent palace. This gave a biting edge to his envious wrath, and, when he went forth into the ways of the City and still heard groups

134

of people talking of Aladdin and the splendour of his state, he approached a young man, and, saluting him with feigned graciousness, said, "O my master, pray tell me, who is this great one that all extol?" And the young man replied, "Verily thou art a stranger in the City and from exceeding distant parts if thou hast not heard of Aladdin—whose glory be increased! His wonderful palace is the talk of the world." "Yea," answered the Dervish, "I am a stranger from very distant lands and there is nothing more to my desire than to see the palace, if thou wilt direct me." "On the head and eye," replied the youth; and, leading him through the City, he brought him to Aladdin's Palace. Then, when the Dervish scrutinised the wonderful building, he knew it to be the work of the Slave of the Lamp. "By Allah!" he cried when the youth had left him, "I will be even with this accursed tailor's son who got all this through me."

He returned to the inn, and, taking his instruments of divination, soon learned that the Lamp was not on Aladdin's person, but in the Palace. At this he was overjoyed, for he had a plan to get possession of it. Then he went out into the market and bought a great number of new lamps, which he put in a basket and took back to the inn. When evening was drawing nigh, he took the basket and went forth in the City—for such was his plan—crying, "New lamps for old! Who will exchange old lamps for new?" And the people hearing this, laughed among themselves, saying he was mad; and none brought an old lamp to him in exchange for a new one, for they all thought there was nothing to be gained out of a madman. But when the Dervish reached Aladdin's palace he began to cry more lustily, "New lamps for old! Who will exchange old lamps for new?" And he took no

heed of the boys who mocked him and the people who
thronged him.

Now Fate so willed it that, as he came by, Bedr-el-
Budur was sitting at a window of the kiosk; and, when she
heard the tumult and saw the pedlar about whom it turned,
she bade her maid go and see what was the matter. The
girl went, and soon returned, saying, "O my lady, it is a
poor pedlar who is asking old lamps for new ones; and the
people are mocking him, for without a doubt he is mad."
"It seems proof enough," answered Lady Bedr-el-Budur,
laughing. "'Old wine for new' I could understand, but
'old lamps for new' is strange. Hast thou not an old lamp so
that we might test him and see whether his cry be true or
false?"

Now the damsel had seen an old lamp in Aladdin's
apartment, and hastened to acquaint her mistress with this.
"Go and bring it!" said the Lady Bedr-el-Budur, who had
no knowledge whatever of the Lamp and its wonderful
virtues. So the maid went and brought the Lamp, little
knowing what woe she was working Aladdin. Then the
Lady Bedr-el-Budur called one of the memluks and handed
him the Lamp, bidding him go down to the pedlar and
exchange it for a new one. Presently he returned, bearing
a new lamp, and, when the Princess took it and saw that it
was a far better one than the old one, she laughed and said,
"Verily this man is mad! A strange trade, and one that
can bring him small profit. But his cry is true, therefore
take him this gold to cover his losses." And she gave the
memluk ten gold pieces, and bad him hasten. But the
memluk returned anon with the ten pieces, saying that the
pedlar had disappeared, having left all his new lamps with

the people. The Lady Bedr-el-Budur wondered at this, but knew not, nor guessed the terrible consequences of her act.

As for the Dervish, as soon as he had got the Lamp, he recognised it. Placing it in his bosom, he left all else and ran, which to the people was only a further proof of his madness. On and on he ran, through the City and its out-skirts, until he came to the desert, where at last he was alone. Then, and not till then, he took the Lamp from his bosom and rubbed it. In a flash appeared the Slave of the Lamp. "What is thy wish? I am the Slave of the Lamp which is in thy hands." And the Dervish replied, "I desire thee to take the palace of Aladdin, with all it contains, and convey it to the land of the Moors in Africa, and set it down upon the open space within the gardens of my dwell-ing in that land. Take me also with it. I have spoken." "O my master," said the Slave, "in the twinkling of an eye it is done. If thou carest to close thine eyes for one moment, when thou openest them thou wilt find thyself within the palace, in thy garden in the land of the Moors." And ere the Dervish could say, "I have closed my eye and opened it again," he found that it was even so, as the Slave had said. The palace and all in it were in his own garden, in his own country, with the sun of Africa shining in upon him.

Now the Lady Bedr-el-Budur was within the palace, but Aladdin was not. He had not yet returned from the chase. This thing had taken place after nightfall, so that as yet none had perceived it. But at the hour of the rising of the full moon, the Sultan looked forth from a window to admire Aladdin's palace in its silver light; what was his surprise to find that there was no palace there! All was bare and open space just as it had been before this wonderful palace was built. "By Allah!" he cried in distress and alarm. "Can it be that the Vizier was right, and that this splendid thing was but the fabric of sorcery, built in a single night and dissolved in a moment like a dream on waking? And my daughter, where is she? Oh woe! oh woe!" And the Sultan wrung his hands in grief. Then presently he summoned the Grand Vizier, and bade him look forth at the palace of Aladdin. And when the Vizier looked forth and saw no splendid edifice giving back the rays of the moon, but all as bare as it had been before, he turned to the Sultan, his face pale and twitching with excitement. "O King of the Age," he said, "doth thy Felicity now believe that the palace and all Aladdin's wealth were the work of sorcery?" And the Sultan did not reply, but beat his breast and plucked his beard; for, apart from sorcery, it was enough for him to know that Aladdin's palace was gone and his daughter with it. "Where is Aladdin?" he demanded at last in wrath. "At the chase," replied the Vizier. "Then I command thee to have him brought before me at once, pinioned and shackled."

A glad man then was the Vizier. With all alacrity he issued the Sultan's commands to the captains, who went forth with their soldiers to find and seize Aladdin. It was a difficult task for them, for they all loved him greatly; and, when they came upon him, they asked his forgiveness, yet took him and led him bound and manacled before the Sultan, whose word must be obeyed on the head and the eye. But when the people saw him thus, they one and all armed themselves and followed the soldiers with Aladdin to the palace, saying among themselves, "It will be a bad day for the Sultan if he cuts off Aladdin's head." But the Sultan knew not of this rising of the people, and, being filled with rage at the loss of his daughter, no sooner set eyes on Aladdin among his captors than he ordered him to the executioner. Now when this came to the ears of the people, they surrounded the palace and barred its gates and doors, and raised a great clamour without, so that the Sultan sent his Grand Vizier to ascertain the cause. Presently he returned, saying, "O King of the Age, the people have risen in a great multitude, and they are shouting that they will pull down the palace over thy head if any harm come to Aladdin. Wherefore it were better to pardon Aladdin, and so avert this great calamity, for it is evident the people love Aladdin more than they love us."

Meanwhile on the scaffold the executioner had spread the mat of death and Aladdin was kneeling thereon blind-folded, ready for the blow. The executioner walked round him thrice and then turned towards the Sultan, who stood at a window and awaited his command to strike. At this moment the cries of the people grew louder and fiercer and the Sultan beheld them scaling the walls of the palace. Then fear gat hold of him for the issue, and he signalled to the executioner to stay his hand, and bade the Vizier proclaim to the people that Aladdin was pardoned.

As soon as Aladdin was freed from his chains he begged speech of the Sultan, and said to him, "O my Lord, I thank thee for thy clemency, though I know not yet wherein my offence lay." "O base one," replied the Sultan; "hitherto I found thee blameless, but now—" he turned to the Grand Vizier, adding, "Lead him to the windows overlooking his palace, and shew him how it sparkles in the light of the sun." So the Vizier took Aladdin to the window and bade him look forth. Utter amazement fell upon Aladdin when he saw that his palace had completely disappeared, leaving no vestige to mark the spot where it had stood. He was so dazed and bewildered that he turned in silence and walked back into the Sultan's presence like one in a dream. "Well," said the Sultan, "where is thy palace? And, what is more to me, where is my daughter?" And Aladdin shook his head sorrowfully and spread his hands in helpless despair; but made no other reply for he was dumbfounded. Again the Sultan spoke: "It was my thought to set thee free so that thou mayest search for my daughter and restore her to me. For this purpose I grant thee a delay of forty days, and, if in that time thou canst not find her, then, by Allah! I will cut off thy head." And Aladdin answered him, "O King of the Age, if I find her not within forty days then I no longer wish to have a head left upon my body."

And Aladdin went forth sad and dejected. The cries of joy with which the people greeted him fell like lead on his aching heart. He escaped from their goodwill and wandered in the City like one distraught, greeting none, nor raising his eyes to any greeting. For two days he neither ate nor drank for grief at what had happened. Finally he wandered beyond the confines of the City into the desert. There, on the bank of a dark pool, he resolved to drown himself and so end his misery. But, being devout and fearing God, he must first perform his ablutions. So he stooped and took water in his hands and rubbed them together, when lo! a strange thing happened; for as his hands came together, he

chanced to rub the ring which was on one of his fingers.
In a flash the Slave of the Ring appeared and standing before
him, said, "O my master, what is thy desire?" Aladdin then
was seized with great joy, and he cried, "O Slave, I desire
my palace and my wife." "Alas!" answered the Slave,
"that I cannot bring about, for this matter is protected by
the Slave of the Lamp who hath put a seal upon it." "Then,"
urged Aladdin, "since thou canst not bring the palace and
my wife to *me*, transport *me* to the palace wherever it may
be upon the earth." "On the head and the eye," replied
the Slave, and immediately Aladdin found himself borne
swiftly through the air and set down by his palace in the land
of the Moors. Although the night had fallen he could
recognise it without difficulty, and close at hand was the
window of his wife's chamber. Great joy at this exhausted
what little strength remained to him—for he had neither
eaten nor slept for many days—and, overcome with fatigue
and weakness, he threw himself down beneath a tree hard
by and slept.

Awakened at dawn by the singing of birds in the garden,
Aladdin arose, and, having bathed in a stream, recited the
morning prayer, after which he returned and sat beneath
the window of Bedr-el-Budur's apartment. Now the Lady
Bedr-el-Budur, filled with grief at her separation from her
husband and her father, could neither sleep nor eat by reason
of her keen distress. Each day when dawn leapt into the
sky she would arise and sit at her window and weep. And
on this morning she came as usual, but did not weep, for
she saw Aladdin sitting on the ground outside. And they
both cried out and flew to one another ; and their greeting
was full of joy. She opened a side door for him,

bidding him enter, for she knew it was not the time for the accursed Dervish to come to see her as was his daily wont. Then, when they had embraced and kissed and shed tears of joy, Aladdin said to her, " O my beloved, before all else answer me one question : in my apartment there was an old copper lamp which—," " Alas," broke in Bedr-el-Budur, " that lamp was the cause of it all, for the man who obtained it by a stratagem told me of its virtues and how he had achieved this thing by its aid." And immediately Aladdin heard this he knew that it was indeed the Dervish who had worked this woe upon him.

" Tell me, how doth this accursed man treat thee ? " he asked. " He cometh once a day," she replied, " and he would fain win my love and console me for thy loss, for he saith the Sultan, my father, hath struck off thy head, and at the best thou wert of poor family and stole thy wealth from him. But he gets no word from me, only tears and lamentations." And Aladdin embraced her again and comforted her for what she had suffered. " Tell me," he asked again presently, " where doth this accursed keep the Lamp ? " " Always in his bosom," she replied, " where he guards it with the greatest care and none knows of it but me." Aladdin was overjoyed when he heard this, for he thought he saw a way to obtain the Lamp. " Listen, my beloved," he said, " I will leave thee now and return shortly in disguise. Bid thy maid stand by the side door to let me in. Then I will tell thee my plan to slay this accursed one and take the Lamp."

Then Aladdin went forth upon the road that led to the city, and he had not journeyed far before he met a poor peasant proceeding to his daily toil. Stopping him he offered to exchange his own costly garments for those the peasant was wearing. But the man demurred, whereat Aladdin set upon him and effected the exchange by force. Then, leaving the peasant battered and bruised but dressed like a prince, he went on into the city, and, coming to the market, purchased some powder of benj, which is called "the son of an instant," for it stupefies in a moment. With this he returned to the palace, and, when he came to the side door where the maid was waiting, she recognised him and opened immediately. Very soon he was exposing his plan to Bedr-el-Budur.

"O my beloved," he said, "I wish thee to attire thyself gaily, and adorn thyself with jewels in the sparkle of which no grief can live; and, when the accursed cometh, greet him with a smile and a look from thy lovely eyes; for so he will know thou hast turned his wooing over in thy mind and heart, and hast forgotten thy father and thine Aladdin. Then invite him to sup with thee, and, when thou hast aroused a blinding passion in his bosom, he will forget the Lamp which lieth there. See," he drew forth the powder, "this is benj, the 'son of an instant.' It cannot be detected in red wine. Thou knowest the rest: pledge him in a cup and see to it that the benj is in his and not in thine. Thou knowest how to ply him till he is careless, how to resist him till he is blinded by thy loveliness, how at last to wish him joy and happiness for ever by thy side so that he will drain the cup. Then, O my beloved, ere he can set it down, he will fall at thy feet like one in death. Thou canst do this?"

"Yea," replied Bedr-el-Budur. "It is difficult, but I will dare all for thee; and well I know that this accursed wretch deserves not to live. Yet will I add something to thy plan from a woman's wit. Lest he should suspect a

143

trick he shall find me weeping when he cometh; then will I take up some speech of his and dry my tears; and then, in a space—having all things ready—will I appear before him in a manner to dazzle his senses, and then—then—Oh! my Aladdin; fear not, for all will be well." And on this assurance Aladdin withdrew to a private chamber and sat him down to wait. He realised his extreme danger, for he knew that if the Dervish so much as suspected his existence in the flesh a rub of the Lamp and a word to the Slave would bring him instant death; but he did not know that Bedr-el-Budur, having learnt the virtues of the Lamp, had exacted a pledge from the Dervish that he would make no further use of it until she had given him her final decision as to whether she would come to him of her own free will and accord, which she maintained was a better thing than subsequently to be compelled by the abominable power of sorcery. Bedr-el-Budur, who in this was merely temporising, had not thought, in the joy and stress of their conversation, to tell Aladdin of it; while, as for the wizard, he had kept his pledge, deeming that a woman's love freely given was a better thing to have than any that could be acquired by magic spells.

According to the plan set forth for the Dervish's undoing Bedr-el-Budur ordered her slave girls to prepare everything of jewels and bright attire, ready for a rapid toilet. Then, when the Dervish appeared, she sat weeping as usual, and it was not until, in his protestations of love, he said words that were suitable to her purpose that she paused and half dried her tears as if it needed little more to make her weigh his petition with care. Observing this he drew near and sat by her side, and now, though no longer weeping, she had not yet found words for him. He took her hand, but she snatched

144

Aladdin finds the Princess in Africa.   Page 141

The Lady Bedr-el-Budur and the Wicked Magician.   Page 148

it away crying, "No, it cannot be! Never can I forget Aladdin!" He pleaded with her, and his passion made him eloquent. He showed her the uselessness of longing for a dead man when a living one was by her side. He told her too—and with the Lamp in his bosom she could not doubt the truth of it—that he and she could command the earth and look down on kings. Why had he not already won this as well as her love by means of the Lamp? Because he had pledged himself to wait and win her as a man wins woman. At this she turned her face to him on a sudden. A faint smile seemed to live in the corners of her bewitching mouth, and a look in her eyes convinced him that he was a much better man than he had thought since he could keep his pledge on so great a matter. On this, he drew still nearer to the lovely Bedr-el-Budur, and this time she did not snatch her hand away, but left it in his, pondering dreamily the while. Presently, on a sudden, she pushed him away petulantly. "Nay, nay," she cried, "I cannot rein my heart to thee at will. Give me, I pray thee, a little space of time— two days; and when my eyes are dim with weeping for Aladdin—" "Two days? Alas!" broke in the Dervish, "two days is a lifetime." "*One* day—I may decide in one, if weeping do not kill me." The Dervish smote his breast, "*One* day! one *hour* is the limit of my life. Think, O Lovely One, how I have waited to win thee as man wins woman, when in a moment I could call thee mine by other means." And his hand moved to his bosom where lay the Lamp. "Stay!" she cried, rising and standing before him. "Thy pledge! My decision is not yet. Having waited so long, surely thou canst wait another—" "Day? say not that." "Well then, at least, another hour." And, flashing

T   145

a look upon him that might hold his wits in thrall for that space of time, she turned to leave the apartment. "I go to weep," she said, throwing him a backward glance, "and my tears perchance will be for Aladdin, perchance for thee if I cannot bend my heart from him. Abide thou in patience. I will come to thee in one hour."

So she went, leaving the Dervish in an ecstasy of doubt. Time, times passed over his head as he sat weighing the issue, and yet he smiled to himself, for he knew that the Lady Bedr-el-Budur would sooner compel herself than be compelled by the Slave of the Lamp. And he was right. At the expiration of the hour the door opened and she stood before him a vision of loveliness in resplendent attire bedecked with priceless jewels. A smile was on her face and her answer to him was in her eyes. Yet, as he darted forward, her manner of approach showed him that, although he had won her, she was a surrendering princess demanding in her condescension a fitting control—even homage—from him. Having convinced him of this, she seated herself by his side and said boldly, "Thou seest how it is with me. My tears for Aladdin—who is dead—flowed till the hour was half spent; then, I know not why, they changed to tears of joy for thee, who art alive. Then I arose and arrayed myself gladly and came to thee. Yet even now I am not wholly thine, for tears—now grief now joy, I know not which—contend in mine eyes for him or thee. Wherefore come not too near me lest what thou hast won be forfeited. Perchance if we sup together with a jar of the red wine of thine own country—in which it may be that my soul will taste thine— then, who knows—" "O my life's delight," broke in the Dervish. "A jar of red wine and thee! I have many jars

146

in my house, and, not forgetting that tears contend in thine eyes as thou saidst, I will go and return in all haste with the reddest wine." "Nay, go not thyself," said Bedr-el-Budur, bethinking her of the Lamp. "Do not leave me. One of my slave girls will go. My tears have dried in my heart, leaving it thirsty for love." And the Dervish was cajoled, and he remained while a slave girl went forth for the wine.

While she was gone Bedr-el-Budur pretended to busy herself issuing orders to the household about the preparation of supper. And under cover of this she sought and found Aladdin. "It is well," she said as he held her to his heart and pressed his lips to hers. "But, O my beloved," he replied, "art thou sure that the Lamp is in his bosom?" "I will go and see," she answered. And she returned to the Dervish and, approaching him shyly, began to doubt the truth of this great thing—his love for her. As she did this she placed her hands on his shoulders and looked into his eyes; whereat the Dervish drew her close to him and she felt the Lamp in his bosom. Immediately she wrenched herself free and left him with a glance in which disdain and love were kindly mixed. "It is so," she said on returning to Aladdin, "the Lamp is in his bosom, and, since he embraced me—I could not help it nor could I endure it, beloved—it is a wonder the Slave of the Lamp did not appear to see how I tore myself away, I was pressed so close."

Meanwhile the slave girl returned with the wine, and, supper being ready, Bedr-el-Budur invited the Dervish to sit by her at the table. And when they had eaten somewhat, she paused and questioned him with a glance. It was for him to call for wine, and he did so. Immediately a slave girl filled their goblets, and they drank; and another and another until the distance between them was melted, and they became, so to speak, the best of boon companions. And he drank to her and she to him, and her tongue was loosed and she bewitched him with her charming eloquence of speech. But with it all was the dignity of the Princess, which repelled while it attracted. In this subtle manner she fanned his passion to a flame until his heart rocked and his head swam, and all else but her was as nothing in his eyes.

At length, when the supper was drawing to an end, and the wits of the Dervish were well mastered by wine, Bedr-el-Budur leaned towards him in an unbending mood. "This wine of thine has set me on fire, beloved!" she said. "But one more cup and then, if I say thee nay, do not believe me, for thou hast kept thy pledge and hast won me as man wins woman. And this shall be a loving cup, for it is the fashion in my country for the lover to take the loved one's cup and drink it." "O lovely one of my eye," he replied, "I will honour thy custom, since thou hast so greatly honoured *me* "

At this Bedr-el-Budur took his cup and filled it for herself, while a slave girl, who knew what to do as well as she hated the Dervish, handed him the cup which, though it contained the benj, she had just filled as if for her mistress. She even had to be told twice that it was not for her mistress but for the guest. So the Dervish took it, and felt for one moment like the conqueror of worlds and the Lord of two Horns as he looked into the eyes of Bedr-el-Budur brimming with love. But only for a moment. They drank, and immediately the Dervish fell senseless at her feet, while the cup, flung from his nerveless hand, clattered across the floor.

In the space of moments Aladdin was on the spot. Bedr-el-Budur's arms were round his neck, and she was sobbing on his breast, while the Dervish lay stretched helpless before them. "Come, come," said Aladdin, smoothing her raven hair, "thou hast succeeded: wherefore weep? Thou art the cleverest of women. Go now with the maidens, and leave me here with this accursed." And when he had comforted her she went, and the slave girls with her. Then Aladdin locked the door, and, approaching the Dervish, drew the Lamp from his bosom. This done, he stood over him and swore a fearful oath, then, without further shrift, he drew his sword and hewed off his head, after which he drove the point of the sword through his heart, for only in this way can a wizard be warned off the realm of mortals. And when the sword pierced the heart the look of hate on the upturned face of the wizard died out, and he was gone—for ever.

Once in possession of the Lamp Aladdin lost no time. He rubbed it and immediately the Slave appeared. "I am here, O my master; what is thy wish?" "Thou knowest," replied Aladdin. "Bear this palace and all that is in it to the Land of Cathay and set it down on the spot from which thou didst take it at the command of that." He pointed to the dismembered wizard. "It is well," said the Slave, who served the living and not the dead; "I hear and obey, on the head and the eye." Then Aladdin returned to Bedr-el-Budur, and, in the space of one kiss of love, the palace with all therein was carried swiftly back to the original site from which it had been taken.

When Aladdin and Bedr-el-Budur looked forth and saw the lights in the windows of the Sultan's palace they were overcome with joy. They feasted and drank and made merry far into the night. They kissed and embraced, and kissed again. And when Aladdin had told her all the wretchedness of his losing her she wept, saying it was nothing to what she had endured. Then Aladdin made her narrate her way with the wizard, point by point, till he exclaimed, laughing, that a woman's way in such was more than a man could compass in a thousand years. And so, full of delight for to-day and anticipation of joy for to-morrow, they rose and went hand in hand to rest—those lovers reunited. Thus it was with Aladdin and Bedr-el-Budur.

Now the Sultan was in grievous mood ever since the loss of his daughter—the apple of his eye. All night long he would weep, and, arising at dawn, would look forth on the empty space where once had stood Aladdin's palace. Then his tears would flow as from a woman's eyes, for Bedr-el-Budur was very dear to him. But, when he looked forth one morning and saw the palace standing as it had stood, he was rapt with joy. Instantly he ordered his horse, and, mounting, rode to the gates. Aladdin came out to greet him, and, taking him by the hand with never a word, led him towards the apartments of Bedr-el-Budur. She too, radiant with joy, was running to meet him. Like a bird of the air she flew to his arms, and for some moments neither of them could say a word for very happiness. Then in a torrent of words, she told him all about the accursed Dervish ; how by his sorcery he had conveyed the palace to Africa, and how Aladdin had slain him, thus releasing the spell and restoring everything to its place. But not a word did she say about the Lamp and its virtues. And the Sultan turned to Aladdin as if he might add something to the tale.

But Aladdin had nothing to add save that he had outwitted the Dervish and reversed his sorcery by cutting off his damnable head and plunging his sword through his heart. Then they arose and went to the chamber which contained the trunk and severed head of the Dervish. And, by the Sultans orders, these remains of the Sorcerer were burnt to ashes and scattered to the four winds of heaven.

And so Aladdin was restored to the Sultan's favour, and he and the Lady Bedr-el-Budur dwelt together in the utmost joy and happiness. And Aladdin guarded the Lamp with the greatest care, but, at the wish of Bedr-el-Budur, he refrained from seeking to it. "Let well alone, my beloved," she said; "there is no happiness for us in commanding everything at will. Besides, we are grateful to the Lamp for what it has done for us; any more is of sorcery." And Aladdin smiled to himself as he recognised the wisdom of a woman. Never did he gainsay her words. Never again did he rub the Lamp.

Time, times, and the Sultan died. Then Aladdin sat on the throne, and ruled the land wisely and well. And the people, with one heart, loved him and his Queen Bedr-el-Budur; and the realm continued in peace and happiness until at last the Great Gleaner came in their old age and knocked at the palace doors and gathered them in to rest.

THE THREE CALENDERS

ONE night, in the City of Baghdad, the Khalifeh Harun-er-Rashid went forth with Ja'far, his Grand Vizier, and Mesrur, his Executioner, all three disguised as merchants, for it was the Khalifeh's whim to wander abroad in this way at times, in order to learn how his people fared among themselves.

Taking their way at random, they had not gone far before they noticed a brilliantly-lighted house whence came sounds of music and revelry. "O Vizier," the Khalifeh said to Ja'far, "it is in my mind to enter this house, and see what entertainment we might find. Wherefore, devise some excuse whereby we may gain admittance." So Ja'far knocked at the door, and it was opened presently by a beautiful lady, tall and graceful as a windflower.

"O my mistress," said Ja'far courteously, "we are merchants from Tiberias, and, knowing not this City well, we have lost our way. I perceive that thou art kind, as well as beautiful; and I am emboldened to ask thee for safe shelter in thy house."

The lady regarded the three lost merchants with an approving glance, for, though she knew not their high degree, the dignity of state cannot be well concealed from a woman's eyes. "Wait a little," she said; "I will consult my sisters." And with this she retired within the house. Presently she returned, and bade them enter; whereupon they followed her into a sumptuously furnished apartment, where they found two other ladies as beautiful as the first; and with them was a porter—an amusing fellow, as full of quips and cranks as he was of wine—who had been entertaining them with joke and song and dance. The ladies smiled upon the three merchants, and welcomed them graciously, setting food and wine before them, and bidding them join in their merriment.

For a while the porter, who, like the three merchants, had come unbidden, but had been made welcome because of his versatility and ready wit in entertaining, kept the company in constant laughter, so that the Khalifeh said to Ja'far, "Verily, O Vizier, we should like this fellow's head and all it contains. Nay, O Mesrur," he added, turning to his Executioner, "I want not his head without the rest of him. He shall be my wag." "O King of the Age," answered the Grand Vizier, "I hear, and obey." Meanwhile, the porter continued to amuse them, but at length he became so intoxicated that his efforts to amuse were unsuccessful, whereat the entertainment flagged. "It seems to me," said the Khalifeh, "that these three ladies are no ordinary persons; perchance they have a history. Ask them to entertain us with their various stories." Accordingly, the Vizier singled out the eldest and put the question to her. But she liked it not, and, with a clouded brow, led him to the door, on the lintel of which she pointed out an inscription: "Ask not what doth not concern thee, lest thou hear what may not please thee." Ja'far returned and informed the Khalifeh of this, which only served to increase his curiosity. While he was planning a way with the Vizier to induce them to tell their history, there came a knock at the door. One of the sisters went to open it, and presently returned, saying, "There, are three Dervishes without, each of them clean shaven, and each lacking an eye."

"Ask them if they were born blind of an eye," said one of the sisters, "and if they are brothers." So the lady went and asked them these questions, and returned presently with the answer: "They were not born blind, but each lost his eye through an adventure; neither are they brothers, having met for the first time in this City, where they have lost their way. They are wandering Mendicants or Calenders."

At this, her sister turned to Ja'far. "Thou didst desire to hear our stories, O my master, but it seemeth that these Dervishes may have stories more interesting to hear. Shall we admit them?" The Khalifeh added his approval to that of Ja'far on this point, and the three Calenders were admitted. And strange looking men they were. Differing widely in feature and expression, they were all alike in the manner of their dress and general appearance. Each had lost one eye; and each had long black moustaches, twisted like silk, and drooping over a clean-shaven chin. Being of the order of mendicants, they bowed humbly, and stood silent. "Tell us how it is," said the eldest of the sisters, "that you three, being no relation one to another, and each lacking one eye, should be together." "In that," said one of the Calenders, "there is no more cause for wonder than that you three women, all unrelated one to another before birth, and all equally beautiful, should find yourselves sisters of one household."

At this the Khalifeh whispered to Ja'far, "This man's speech and address are not those of a mendicant. If I mistake not he hath moved in Royal Courts."

155

"Yet, O my mistress," the First Calender continued, "it may be that it was decreed by Destiny that we three, coming from three widely separate kingdoms, should meet in this City, the Abode of Peace, for our conditions appear to be similar. Each of us having lost, not only an eye, but a throne—for know that we are kings, and the sons of kings—has been led hither by the same stars, to kneel at the feet of the Khalifeh Harun-er-Rashid and implore his aid in the restoration of our royal state."

On hearing this, the Khalifeh looked down his beard, saying within himself, "If they knew, they would kneel and implore here and now. But they know not." Then a stratagem within a stratagem got hold of him, and he arose and bowed low to the three ladies.

"O my mistresses," he said, "whose beauty is unequalled, save by that of each to each, I crave your permission. It seems there is an entertainment in this matter. Here we have Three Royal Calenders suppliant to the Khalifeh—on whom be peace! Now, it will be good for them to rehearse their parts for our amusement; for so, when at last they gain audience of the Khalifeh, they will be well versed. Grant me then the privilege, O fair ones, to play the part of the Khalifeh, for I am not unskilled in the art of such play. Indeed, I have appeared before the Khalifeh himself—("In a mirror," assented Ja'far, in thought),—and he was greatly pleased with my impersonation and my appearance."

"Verily," said one of the sisters, in approval, "thou art a kingly man, and thou wilt play the part well. What say you, O my sisters?" she added, turning to the other two. They agreed, laughing, and clapping their hands, for they liked the idea of real suppliants rehearsing to a stage Khalifeh.

"Good!" cried one, "and these Calenders will approach thee as if thou wert in sober truth the Khalifeh."

"And," rejoined Er-Rashid, "as if these two were indeed my Grand Vizier, Ja'far, and Mesrur, my Executioner."

Loudly the two laughed at the Khalifeh's happy conceit, and preened themselves for office, Ja'far assuming his old look of terrible solemnity, while Mesrur, drawing his great sword, with a grin, struck an attitude that many had beheld for the last time.

The Calenders unbent to the play; the ladies sprang into animation; even the porter was rolled from a couch to give place to the Khalifeh, who sat himself thereon in royal state.

"On pain of death, O Calenders," said the Khalifeh—and all except Ja'far and Mesrur marvelled at his royal dignity—"I command you to make known to me severally the stories of your lives, for I would fain learn how each of you came to lose a throne, and an eye."

On this, the Royal Calenders, taking up the jest in a proper spirit, advanced and kissed the ground.

"Rise!" said the Khalifeh, imitating himself to perfection, "and see to it that your stories please not only me, but Mesrur, my Executioner; for his sword hath a cutting edge, and I observe that you have your heads with you." Singling out one of the three, he commanded the other two to stand aside. Then the first Royal Calender spoke as follows:—

THE STORY OF THE FIRST CALENDER

KNOW, O Prince of the Faithful, that I am a King, the son of a King, and one robbed of his heritage. My father's brother was also a King, and his son, my cousin, was born on the same day as myself. We two Princes were

157

friends, and paid long visits to each other. On one occasion, when I was staying with him, he made much of me, honouring me with a rich banquet. When this was over, and we were alone, and the wine had made us genial, he drew near to me, and said: "O my cousin, I desire thine assistance in a matter that concerneth me greatly."

"I will serve thee without question, O son of my uncle," said I. But he made me swear by the holiest oath that I would assist him in his undertaking. Then, when he was satisfied, he left me for a little, and returned with a beautiful young woman, dressed in the manner of a queen. "Lead this woman before me," he said, "to the place of sepulture, which thou knowest. Enter that place, and await my coming."

Wondering greatly, but questioning nothing, I led the woman forth, and we waited for him among the tombs. Soon he came, bearing a bowl of water, some plaster, and a pointed bar of iron. Approaching a certain tomb, he dislodged the stones with the iron bar, and disclosed a vault with a stairway descending into it. Then, addressing the woman, he said: "Hast thou chosen?" And she replied, with a steady gaze, "Yea, I have chosen." And she descended the stairway into the vault. Then he said to me: "Cousin, farewell! for I too descend. Place the stones together above us, and cement them with the plaster moistened with the water, so that none can say, 'This vault is not as it should be.' Farewell! And may thy head long survive mine!" With this, he descended into the vault.

Bound by my oath, and like one compelled against his will, I did his bidding, ceasing not until I had closed up the tomb in such a way that none could tell it had been opened. But that night I was visited by terrible dreams, which

magnified the enormity of what I had done. Repentance
pricked me, and I arose, and went to the place of sepulture.
There I searched for the tomb, but alas! so cleverly had I
done my work that I could not trace it. All day long I
sought it, but in vain; and, when evening fell, I returned
to the Palace burdened with grief and remorse. Again my
sleep was disturbed with dreams of horror, so that at daybreak, repenting of my action still more keenly, I repaired a
second time to the burial place. But again my search was
unsuccessful. And so I continued for seven days, searching
and calling out among the tombs, but never could I find the
place of my quest, nor from any tomb came back an answer
to my cry. At last, nearly mad with grief and remorse, I
left my uncle's palace to return to my father. But there
fresh trouble awaited me, for, no sooner had I entered the
gates of the city, than a party of guards sprang upon me,
and bound me, and cast me into a dungeon.

O Prince of the Faithful, imagine my despair. I was
the son of the King, and his servants had treated me in this
manner. With anger I enquired the cause of this, but none
answered me. At last I saw one who had been my own
servant, and had received many benefits at my hands. I put
the question to him, and he replied: "O my master, thy
father is no more, for the Grand Vizier hath killed him, and
now sitteth in his place." At this I bowed my head in
grief for my father, and despair for my own life. And they
led me before the Grand Vizier who had slain my father.

Now this Vizier had never been my friend, especially
after an accident in which I was made instrumental by fate in
depriving him of one of his eyes. It happened in this way:
One day I was using the cross-bow when I saw a rare bird

alight on the parapet of one of the windows in the Vizier's palace. I shot at it, but the missile struck not the bird, which was protected by Providence. Passing it narrowly it sped in at the window, and, guided by destiny, struck out the eye of the Vizier. My father being King the Vizier could do nothing against me, but the malice and hatred with which he had always regarded me from two eyes lost naught through being concentrated into one. No wonder then that now, my father being dead, and I standing before this regicide, bound and helpless, he fiercely commanded the executioner to strike off my head.

"What is my offence?" I asked. "Offence!" he cried. "Is not this offence enough?" and he pointed to the socket where his eye had been. "That was done by accident," I said. "And this by design," he answered, advancing swiftly and thrusting out my left eye. He then commanded me to be bound, and placed in a chest, and when this was done, he said to the Executioner: "Take this carrion, and convey it beyond the confines of the city. There draw thy sword, and cut it in pieces, so that the wild beasts may the more readily devour it."

Accordingly, the Executioner carried me forth upon a mule into the desert, where he took me out of the chest, and was about to kill me, when I implored him to spare my life, reminding him of the many kind deeds my father and I had done to him and to others. He was moved by my supplications, but shook his head, saying: "O my master, if I slay not thee, the Vizier will slay me." "The Vizier is not here to see," I said. "There is none here but thee and me."

He was silent for a little. Then he said: "Depart with thy life, and return not to this country, lest both our lives be

The Porter and the Ladies.　Page 154

The Prince leads the Lady to the Tomb.   Page 158

forfeit." When he had said this, I thanked him, and kissed his hands; then, lest he might change his mind, I fled from him, and ceased not to journey night and day until I reached my uncle's palace. There I related to my uncle all that had taken place, and he wept with excess of grief. "Woe cometh on woe," he said, "for know that thy cousin, my son, hath gone from me, and hath not returned for many days. None knoweth where he is, nor what fate hath overtaken him. Nephew, thou hast lost a father, and one of thine eyes; and now, woe is me! I have lost a brother, and an only son."

On witnessing his terrible grief I could no longer remain silent regarding the disappearance of my cousin. I told him all. "By Allah!" he cried, joyfully. "Where is this tomb of which thou speakest?" "Alas! O my uncle," I replied; "I know not. I searched for it for many days, but could not find it." On this my uncle commanded a company of work-men to proceed to the burial place, and there, in our presence, they opened tomb after tomb.

In this manner, on the evening of the second day, when a great number of tombs had been opened and closed again, we came upon what we soon discovered to be the right one. When the stones had been dislodged, my uncle descended the stairway, and I followed. On reaching the bottom, we were met by a blinding smoke. Enduring this, we found our way into an apartment wherein was a table bearing food of many kinds. At the far end of this apartment we found a curtain. My uncle drew this aside, and we looked within upon a sight of horror. There, side by side upon a couch, were the forms of my cousin and the lady, charred by fire, as if they had been thrown into a furnace.

On seeing this terrible thing, my uncle uttered a loud cry, and spat upon his dead son's face. "Wretch!" he exclaimed. "Thou art come into thine own, and hast gone where worse awaits thee for this deed. May thou never find forgiveness!" And he spat again upon the charred face.

"Wherefore, O my uncle?" I said. "Is not his state already grievous enough that thou must invoke a worse fate upon him?"

"O son of my brother," he replied, "thou knowest not the sin of this accursed. From his youth he was inflamed with love for his foster sister, who now lies there upon the couch, and, in defiance of my will, he persisted in and encouraged this passion. While they were children I let it pass, saying, 'They are young: they will grow out of it.' But, alas! when they came of age I discovered that they were both deeply enamoured of each other. Then I took my son, and counselled him, and bade him beware lest any act of his should bring us to dishonour, and I told him that if such occurred, I would slay him with my own hand. I then took steps to separate them, but who can lock love out? For when he knew my will, he called the Devil to his purpose, and he entered and took possession of them both. And so it was that he made this secret place among the tombs wherein they met. But fire from Heaven consumed them, as thou hast seen, and now they are further punished in the fires of Iblis." Then he wept bitterly, and I covered my head, and wept with him. And when at last he could speak, he said: "But his place shall be filled by thee. Thou art now my son in his stead."

Long time we wept together there in the tomb by the side of the charred bodies of the dead, for we had no lack of trouble upon our heads. Then we arose, and ascended the stairway, and my uncle ordered the workmen to replace the stones upon the tomb. Sadly we turned away, and retraced our steps to my uncle's palace. There we were about to dispose ourselves to rest when we heard unwonted sounds without—the tramp of an advancing host; the clank of armour, and loud cries of dismay from the populace. Drums beat and trumpets sounded; shrieks came out of riot, and groans issued from the wake of galloping hoofs. Then came a eunuch running, his face distorted, and his garb dishevelled. "The City is lost!" he cried. "On a sudden, being taken unawares, it is surrendered to the enemy. O King, thy brother's Vizier hath slain him, and he hath now come hither with his army, and none can stand against him."

At this, my uncle arose, and hastened forth; but I, knowing full well what would happen to me if I fell into the Vizier's hands, remained, and took thought on how I might escape unobserved by any of my father's city. I could think of naught but to shave off my beard, and change my clothes, thus disguising myself. This I did in all haste, and so made my way through the turbulent crowds of people, and escaped.

Far, far to the North I knew was the City of Baghdad, the Abode of Peace; and I bent my steps hither, for I said within myself, "There abideth the Khalifeh, the Prince of the Faithful, and the King of the Age. I will go and kneel at his feet, and humbly entreat him to strike mine enemy, and restore to me my father's throne." And when I arrived in this City some few hours since, it was night. I stood at the cross roads, not knowing which way to turn, when one like myself, a mendicant, drew nigh, and I saluted him. "I am a stranger," I said. "Canst thou direct me to a khan for shelter?" And he replied, "I too am a stranger, and would put the same question to thee." But lo, as I looked at him, I saw that he was in like case with me, having lost his left eye. I was about to question him on this, when a third mendicant came out of the night, and accosted us. "By Allah!" cried the two of us in a breath, "and thou too hast lost an eye!" "Verily," said he, "we are all strangers one to another, but the stars have enmeshed us in their network, and so have drawn us together with one purpose." "And that is?" we asked. "To seek audience of the Khalifeh," he answered; "for the tables of the stars have told me that I, a King, and the son of a King, should meet in this City two others who, royal like myself, have planned to seek the Khalifeh of the Lord of all creatures, craving redress for wrongs."

And the three of us marvelled at this thing, and at the exact computation of time and space in the mind of Destiny. And thus, from strangers we speedily came to be friends, having a common object. Then, proceeding forth together, we came at length to this house, where, by the grace of these hospitable ladies, we relate our true stories as if to the——

"As if?" cried Mesrur, grasping his sword, and clanking it on the table before him.

"As if!" echoed Ja'far, springing from his seat with well-feigned indignation.

"Silence!" cried Er-Rashid, rising in stately wrath. "O Calender, thy story is good, but if thou wert about to say 'as if to the Khalifeh' thou wert out of order. When I play a part, I play a part. I *am* the Khalifeh! The Prince of the Faithful! The King of the Age!"

The ladies laughed, with beaming eyes. The three Royal Calenders yielded to the jest with winks and nods to one

164

another; then, as the porter grovelled the floor in mock obeisance to the Lord of the Earth, the others followed in like spirit, and prostrated themselves in all humility.

"Peace be on you!" said Er-Rashid. "Rise, and be seated! As for thee, O Calender, thy case is extraordinary, and I will see to it that thou art restored to thy throne. Now it is our royal will that ye proceed with this entertainment."

At this, the second Calender advanced, and, having kissed the ground, rose, and spoke as follows :—

THE STORY OF THE SECOND CALENDER

O KING of the Age, my story is such that none hearing it need lack a lesson or a warning. I, a King, the son of a King, devoted my youth and early manhood to the study of the arts and sciences, so that I became proficient, and excelled greatly in all branches of learning. My fame as a scribe spread far and wide, even to India, so that the King of that land sent a messenger with rich gifts to my father, requesting that I might be allowed to visit him. This pleased my father, and he fitted out a fleet of ships laden with rich gifts, and set them at my disposal.

With a goodly company I sailed eastward, and after many days reached land. Disembarking some splendid horses we had brought with us, we loaded them with gifts and set out for the King's capital, but we had not proceeded far when a cloud of dust arose in the distance and swept rapidly toward us, with a sound like thunder; and, not until it was near at hand did we observe, outstripping the cloud, a large body of horsemen. Wild-eyed and fierce, and with lances poised, these rode down upon us. We shouted to them that we were ambassadors to the King of India, but this was of no service to us, for it appeared that these men were robbers and recognised no king. This we learned from their cries and shouts as they swept upon us, slaying all within reach of their spears. Some of us fled. I was one of them, though I was wounded; and so closely were the robbers occupied with the treasure upon the horses, that they did not pursue.

Separated from the other survivors, and not knowing which way to search for them, I journeyed on and on, weak from loss of blood, and wretched from my change of state, until in the evening I discovered a cave at the foot of a mountain. Here I rested until the morning, when, after having journeyed on for some hours, I found I was approaching a great city. With joy I made my way towards its sunlit towers and spires, passing through gardens of ever-increasing luxuriance, until I came to the busy parts of the thoroughfares, where merchants thronged the market places, buying and selling.

Not knowing how to proceed in this city, I looked about for someone who might give ear to my tale, and advise me what to do. At last I espied a tailor sitting at work in his shop, and decided that I would speak with him. He received me kindly, and I told him my tale, acquainting him with all that had happened since I left my father's capital. When I had finished he shook his head gravely, and said : "My son, verily thou art in hard case, though it is fortunate thou camest to me with thy story, and not to another. Knowest thou not that the King of this city is thy father's greatest enemy, having a blood-debt against him ? Wherefore, tell not thy tale again to any, lest the King hear of it, and inflict an injury of vengence upon thee." The tailor then treated me with hospitality, setting food and wine before me, and bade me remain in his house awhile.

When he had harboured me for some days, the tailor desired to know if I had any trade by means of which I could earn my living. Whereat I informed him that I was learned in the arts and sciences, and a fine writer. "Alas!" he said, "there is no profit in such things. This is a city of commerce, where people devote themselves to getting money. Arise, therefore, O my son, and work for thy living."

He then fetched an axe and a coil of rope, and bade me go to the forest without the city and hew firewood, which, on my return in the evening, I might sell for a good price. So I followed his counsel, and, when I found that my day's work brought me half a gold piece, I continued to dwell with the tailor, and hewed wood for the space of a whole year, paying my way, and steadily setting by something of my earnings day by day. Then a strange thing happened to me.

One day, while I was clearing the earth from the roots of a tree in the forest, I came upon a ring of brass. This, I soon discovered, was attached to a trap door, which, with some difficulty, I removed. Then, seeing before me a staircase, I descended until I reached a door, by which, on opening it, I found admittance to a large underground palace, richly furnished. On wandering through the rooms of this place, I came at length to one more richly decorated than all the others; and here, reclining upon a couch, was a lady of surpassing loveliness. The rarity of her charms dazzled me and took my breath away, so that I stood speechless before her. "Art thou a man?" said the lady, regarding me intently, "or art thou an Efrite?" This loosened my tongue, and I replied, "I am a man, as thou art a woman." She answered, "Yea, I am a woman, and thou art the first man I have seen for a space of twenty-five years, every day and night of which I have spent in this place. How camest thou hither?"

Her voice was sweet as her face was fair, and my heart was melted at the thought of her long captivity. I resolved to tell her my story, for here at least was one who could not spread it abroad in the bazaars. Accordingly I seated myself on the couch at a little distance from her, and related my story from beginning to end; whereupon she wept at my hard lot, saying, "O my master, thy case is not unlike mine." And she proceeded to acquaint me with it.

"I am the daughter of the King of the Ebony Isles," she said. "My father married me to my cousin, but on the night of our wedding an Efrite—a true son of Iblis—appeared, and, snatching me from my husband, carried me through the air to this spot where he had built this palace and filled it with all things necessary to my comfort. And from that night, twenty-five years ago, to the present, I have never seen the outside world. On every tenth day he cometh to me, to leave me on the following morning, but if I desire his instant presence at any time, I have but to press this panel of the wall whereon are inscribed some magic characters, and immediately he appeareth before me. Four days have now passed since he was here, so that there remain six of the ten. Do thou therefore dwell here with me for five days, and depart one day before he cometh."

I agreed to this, and when I had bathed, and put on some garments which she gave me, I sat by her side, and we ate and drank, and conversed happily together. Presently she sang to me in a sweet low voice, and, being fatigued, as well as drowsy with wine, I slept.

When I awoke, she was bending over me, with joy on her face. "Allah hath been good to me in sending thee here," she said; "for I was nigh to death with loneliness." At this my heart swelled with love for her, and I could think of naught else but her wondrous charm and beauty. And when I told her this, she said nothing, but the light of her eyes told me all there was to tell. And I remained with her in the greatest joy and happiness. We feasted, and drank, and sang; and, while I played upon musical instruments, she danced with a grace and skill that I had never seen before. At length, on the third day, when I was drunk with love and wine, I said to her: "Let me take thee from this sumptuous dungeon, and free thee from this vile Efrite." But perchance she knew that this would be impossible, for she replied, laughing softy, "Hold thy peace, O man; thou hast nine days out of the ten." This inflamed me, and my passion made me valiant. "It is the tenth day I want," I cried, "and the other nine as well. Lo here! I am a slayer and a conqueror of Efrites. I will this instant break this panel with the magic signs, so that the Efrite may come and be slain." With a cry she sprang forward to stop me, but I escaped from her embrace, and, aiming a violent kick at the panel, broke it.

"Flee for thy life ere he cometh," she cried, pointing towards the door. I scarcely knew whether to flee or to remain and face the Efrite, but my feet settled the matter for me, and I gained the doorway in a bound. Then, turning my head, I saw the ground open, and there rose into the room an Efrite of terrible aspect, who looked threateningly at the woman, and demanded to know the cause of his being

summoned in such a manner. "Nay, it was naught," said
she, "save that I tripped and fell against the panel, breaking
it as thou seest." "Thou liest!" he cried, in a voice of rage,
and, as he said it, his eyes, rolling round in his head, fell
upon my sandals and my axe, which in my haste I had left.
"Ha!" he exclaimed, snatching them up, "some man hath
visited thee, and hath left his axe and his sandals. Confess,
vile woman!"

But she denied it, saying, "No man hath visited me, and
thou must have brought these things with thee, for I have
never set eyes on them until this instant." "Again thou
liest!" he roared, "and unless thou tell me his name, I
will beat thy body black and blue." With this he turned
to look for the wherewithal to beat her, and, at sight of his
fierce face and huge bulk, my heart turned to water within
me, and I fled up the stairway. Before I reached the top I
heard the sound of blows, followed by loud cries and shrieks
from the woman. Full of bitter repentance that she should
suffer thus on my account, and unable to endure the sounds
of torture, I hastened through the trap door and fastened it
behind me. Then, when I had covered it with earth, I fled
through the forest and paused not till I had gained the house
of the tailor.

I found him in a state of great anxiety on my account,
for I had been absent three days and three nights. "I feared
thou hadst fallen a prey to some wild beast," he cried, "but
praise be to God that thou art safe!" I thanked him, and,
saying that I was fatigued and would tell him all later, went to
my own apartment to weep over what had come to that poor
woman through my rash action. But I had not been there
many minutes when the tailor came to me, saying, "There

is one, a foreigner, in the shop, who desires to speak with thee. He hath an axe and a pair of sandals, which he thinks are thine, and the other woodcutters have directed him to thee; so come forth to receive them, and to thank him." With this, he returned to the shop, leaving me pale with fear, for well I knew the meaning of this thing. While I was planning what to do—whether to go into the shop, or escape by some other way—the floor was rent asunder, and there rose from it the Efrite. In a loud voice he told me that he had tortured the lady nigh to death, but without avail, for she would tell him nothing; whereat he had taken the axe and the sandals, and, by enquiries, had traced me to the tailor's abode. With this, he seized me and bore me aloft through the roof of the house, and thence rapidly through the air into the forest, where he descended through the earth and placed me within the chamber of the palace from which I had fled. There, on the floor, laid the lady, bleeding from the wounds inflicted by the Efrite's torture. "Shameless woman!" cried he, standing over her; "here is thy lover: deny it not." She glanced at me, and answered him: "I have never set eyes on this man before." He appeared to take thought for a moment, and then he said: "Thou wilt swear that thou lovest not this man?" She answered him: "I know him not; I love him not." The Efrite drew his sword. "If thou lovest him not," said he, "take this sword and strike off his head."

She took the sword from him, and, coming towards me, raised it to strike; but I made a sign with my eye, imploring her pity. She replied also with a sign, as if to say, "I have suffered all this through thee." But I still implored her with the speech of the eye, for, as the poet saith:

171

The language of the eye, like the kisses of the mouth
is sweet as honey, and only lovers understand it.
When the lips are closed, love openeth the windows of
the soul, and conveyeth its meaning by soft glances.

And when my meaning was thus conveyed to her, she flung
away the sword and faced the Efrite, crying, "I cannot slay
him, for he hath done me no injury." The Efrite answered
her not, but, taking up the sword, handed it to me. "Strike
off her head," he said, "and I will set thee free." I took
the sword, and arose to do the deed ; but, while my arm was
raised to strike, love spoke again from her eyes. My hand
trembled, my heart melted. I flung the sword from me.
"Wherefore should I slay this woman, who hath done me no
injury, and whom I have never seen before?" I said to the
Efrite. "Never before God can I commit this crime." The
Efrite took the sword, and saying, "It is clear there is love
between you," he cut off one of the lady's hands, then the
other, and then both her feet. And, in her pain, her eyes
were turned on me, and the words of love were in them.
The Efrite saw her look, and cried, "Is it not enough? Wilt
thou still commit the crime of unfaithfulness with thine eye?"
And, raising the sword again, he cut off her head.

"O man," he said, turning to me, "it is lawful for one,
having known his wife for twenty-five years, to kill her for
the crime of unfaithfulness. As for thee, I will not permit
thee to join her. I will not take thy life, but, as I am
minded to punish thee, I will give thee thy choice as to
whether thou wilt be changed into the form of a dog, or an
ass, or an ape." Since he had shewn me this clemency, I
thought by pleading to melt him further, so that perchance
he would pardon me altogether. Therefore, I recited many

172

instances of kindness and generosity shewn by Efrites to mortals, some of which I had gleaned from books, while others I invented then and there, with a ready wit. But, though the Efrite listened, his bearing changed not towards me one hair's breadth. "Thou hast been misinformed," he said at last. "The Efrite knows neither kindness nor generosity: he is only constrained by the justice of those who have sovereignty over him. Wherefore, hold thy peace, and neither fear that I shall slay thee, nor hope that I shall pardon thee. Thou shalt be punished by the power of enchantment, and thou knowest not how to prevent it."

Immediately on these words, he stamped the floor with his foot, and the sides of the Palace rocked on their foundations, and fell together; but seizing me, he clove a way through the falling structure, and bore me aloft to a great height. Presently he set me down upon the summit of a high mountain, where he took up a handful of dust, and, having chanted some strange words over it, cast it upon me, crying, "Change thy form, O Man! Retain thy form, O Ape!" And immediately I suffered a rending pang in my bones and flesh, and behold, I was a man ape, old and ugly, and clothed only with hair. When I looked up from examining my ungainly limbs, the Efrite had disappeared.

Long I remained, crouching on the summit of that mountain, realising my punishment, the keenness of which lay in the fact that it was only my form that was changed. My memory, my mental powers, and my likes and dislikes all remained to me, though I was bereft of the power of articulated speech. At last, rousing myself, I descended the mountain, subdued and resigned, to meet whatever further fate awaited me. I journeyed on through strange places,

173

meeting no human being nor any of my present kind in the forests and deserts through which I passed, and subsisting on berries which I gathered from the trees. Finally, I came to the seashore, and lo, there was a vessel making towards the land. Presently the ship cast anchor, and some sailors landed in a small boat with some barrels, by which I knew that they were seeking water. There were six of these barrels, and when they had filled three of them from a spring some little distance inland, and had gone again with the other three to fill them also, I jumped into the boat, and secreted myself behind the three barrels, saying within myself, "If I can get on to the ship unobserved, and hide, I may reach a better land than this."

Presently the sailors returned with the remaining barrels, and placed them in the boat. I remained undiscovered, and when we reached the vessel's side, I leapt on board, and hid myself. But alas! I was soon observed, and not being able to explain my position there, knew not what my end would be. Moreover, the merchants who found me clamoured that I should be cast into the sea to drown, for they said, "This ugly brute will be unlucky to us, and, if he remain on the ship, we shall meet with some grievous misfortune." While they were discussing among themselves whether to slay me with the sword, or cast me overboard to drown, the master of the ship chanced to spy me, and as soon as I saw him, and knew him for the master, I ran forward and threw myself at his feet, clutching and tugging his garment in the endeavour to excite his compassion. And in this I was successful, for he looked down at me with interest, saying: "In truth, this is an intelligent ape; see how he claims my protection! By Allah! he shall have it! Know, O ye merchants, that this is *my* ape, wherefore harm him not, nor hinder him in his coming and going." He then took me, and treated me henceforth with the greatest kindness; and, in return for this, I proved myself still more intelligent by serving him in every way I could. When he discovered that I could understand everything he said to me, although I could not speak myself, his astonishment was great. "By the Prophet!" he cried, with a great laugh, "methinks this ape hath already forgotten much that I have yet to learn."

Meanwhile, we sailed many days upon the sea, until at last we reached a great City built upon the side of a mountain. The houses of this City were numberless, and the inhabitants thereof beyond all reckoning. Scarcely had we cast anchor, and set foot on land, when there came to us some high officials of the King of that City, with many greetings and congratulations on our fortunate journey. "Our King hath seen thy vessel drawing near," said one of them to the master, "and he bade me say to thee: 'Thine is a large vessel, and no doubt there are many passengers on board. Is there, perchance, one amongst them who is a skilled caligraphist?' For thou must know, O my master, that since the death of one of the King's Viziers,—a marvellous writer,—he hath searched the City in vain to find his equal. Wherefore he hath sent thee this roll of parchment whereon he desireth that each of thy company write a line as candidate for the high office left vacant."

Immediately on hearing this, I sprang past the master, and seized the parchment, whereat there was great consternation lest I should tear it to pieces. But when I ran to a bale of goods near by, and, seating myself upon it, held the paper correctly with one hand, while making the motions of writing with the other, the master said, "Let him write. He is a most marvellous ape, and I have yet to discover the full extent of his intelligence." Out of curiosity, the officials, who were incredulous in the matter, agreed, and I was supplied with pen and ink. Then I wrote in a large formal hand :—

He who writes will perish, though his writing live after him ;
Let him write, therefore, only what will stand to the end of time.

Then in the epistolary hand I wrote :

O King, thy virtues are so many and so great,
Fame has not space to set them on her page.
Ten thousand writers, writing for an age,
One half thine excellence alone could indicate.

To these I added, in several smaller and different hands, other quatrains in praise of the King ; and, having finished, I gave the parchment to the official. When he saw my writing he could not contain his astonishment. He passed it round among the merchants, all of whom marvelled greatly, while some, thinking they could outwrite what I had written, took pen and ink, and wrote. Finally, the official and his party returned with the parchment to the King.

Now, it seems that when the King had read all that was inscribed upon the parchment, he liked none of it but mine ; and, having summoned his attendants, he said to them : "Take this parchment and find the author of this handwriting. Clothe him in a splendid robe, and mount him upon the best of my horses, and bring him hither." On this, the officials who stood by could not restrain their laughter, so that the King was incensed at their behaviour, and was about to mark his displeasure by swift punishment when their chief advanced and explained the matter. "O King, didst thou only know

The Prince meets a noble lady in the underground Palace
Page 169

The Princess burns the Efrite to death.   Page 183

why we laugh, thou wouldst laugh louder than any of us.
We crave thy Felicity to pardon us, but this writing was
done, not by any son of Adam, but by an ape, which belong-
eth to the master of the ship." "What?" said the King,
"this excellent work done by an ape?" "Yea, your Majesty,
it is even so, on the head and the eye. This ape, which is at
least a hundred years old, and proportionately ugly, wrote
those quatrains in our presence." The King laughed heartily
and said, "Make haste, and bring this ape before me in the
manner I commanded, for I have never heard of anything so
wonderful." And he gave them a written and sealed order
to the master of the vessel.

O Prince of the Faithful, I learnt all this that I have told
thee from their narration to the master on their arrival. On
seeing the King's order the master handed me over to them,
and they clothed me with the splendid robe, and placed me
upon the King's horse. Great was the wonder of the people
when the procession started for the palace. Seeing an ugly
ape, dressed in a royal robe and mounted upon the King's
most splendid steed, their laughter died a sudden death in
their throats, and they gaped and wondered. The rumour
of my progress went before, and the way was soon thronged
with people of high degree and low, while from the windows
of houses and palaces looked forth a multitude of citizens to
witness this strangest of all spectacles. Then, gradually, arose
a great cry of wonder and astonishment, which spread throughout the city: Had the King chosen an ape for his Grand
Vizier? What marvellous thing was this? But the King was
the King, and the people was the people, and none among
them could doubt his doings. And so I rode on in dignified
procession.　　　*　　*　　*　　*　　*

z　　　　　　　　177

[At this point in the story, the Khalifeh, set off by the three ladies, could not forbear laughing. "Verily," he said, slapping his hand on his knee, and rocking with mirth, "were I in reality the Prince of the Faithful, and not a poor impersonator, so would I laugh at the thought of this solemn ape, clad in a royal robe, and mounted on the King's horse, proceeding in stately dignity through the city." Then, mastering his laughter, he added, to Ja'far, "O Vizier, I play my part badly when I say 'were I in reality the Prince of the Faithful,' for thou knowest, and my Executioner knows, that I *am* the Khalifeh!" Loudly did Ja'far and Mesrur laugh at this, and the others joined them, and clapped their hands, saying it was an excellent piece of play acting. "Proceed, O Royal Brother!" said the Khalifeh with grave dignity; and the story was resumed.]

Arriving at the palace I soon found myself before the King seated on his throne in a vast chamber, where were assembled the great ones of the earth. I made my obeisance three times to the King, and then, when he motioned me to be seated, I sat down, in the fashion of an ape, upon my haunches. So far, my intelligent respect to royalty commanded the admiration at once of the King and his subjects, for my performance required only the gift of speech to render it perfect. The King then ordered his Court to withdraw, saving only his chief Memluk, a young slave, and myself. He then bade us follow him into his private apartment, where he ordered food to be served. When it was ready, he beckoned me to approach and eat. At this I advanced and kissed the ground before him seven times, after which I sat down at the table and ate. When the repast was over I took a broad leaf from the flower-pod of a palm near at hand, and

having signed to the slave to bring me pen and ink, wrote
upon it the following verse :

> Know, O blade that enclosed the flower of the palm !
> That what thou protectedst less beautiful seems,
> Being now thus revealed, than the favour of Kings
> Unbladed to me by the finger of fate.

Having written this, I placed it before the King and
arose, and seated myself at a little distance. But when he
had read it, his face was distressed with wonder. "This
surpasseth all," said he. "How can an ape possess such skill in
the writing and rounding of a verse?" And he was overcome
with astonishment. He motioned me to approach him, and
said, "Thou art a wonderful ape: drink to me in this my
favourite liquor!" And he handed me his cup. I took it and
drank, and as soon as I felt the warm impulse of the liquor I
was quickened in my inspiration, and wrote upon the cup :

> Stronger than the blood of heroes,
> Sweeter than a woman's kiss ;
> Rare and royal though its savour,
> Joy less fine than Kingly favour
> Lies in this.

The King took the cup, and read what I had written.
"By Allah !" he exclaimed. "Find me the man who hath
the skill of this ape !"

Still wondering greatly as to the extent of my learning
and intelligence, the King called for a chessboard ; and,
setting it before me, questioned me by signs as to whether I
understood the game. By way of assent, I kissed the ground,
and humbly seated myself before the board. Now my name,
as a chessplayer, had gone forth through all lands, but it still
remained for me, as an ape, to justify that name. Solemn and
silent we sat at the board—the King of a vast territory matching

his skill (of which I had heard, as he had heard of mine, from afar) against that of an ape. Knowing all the science of the game, much of which I had myself discovered, I tested his skill by various openings, saying within myself, "This game I will not win, provided that I learn his measure." It so fell out that I lost, and the King, noting the character of my play, was pleased at his success. "Another game," said he, resetting the pieces.

This time, knowing his play, I held back in my moves, and awaited his openings. At length he made one which I knew, for I myself had invented it. "That," said he, "is the opening of Prince Eymar, whose treatise I have studied. I will allow thee a space to study it, and reply." What was his surprise when I replied immediately with the counter move! At that, from excess of wonder, he was unstrung, and, knowing not the following moves as well as I, he lost. Again we played, a third time, and I, seeing from his eagerness that he had still something to spring upon me, fell in with his moves until we reached the position which was the crowning point of my treatise. At length it came to a pass which I well knew. There was only one way out—a pawn in a distant corner of the board. I moved it readily. "By Allah!" he cried, upsetting the board with all that was on it, "thou art the most intelligent—as well as the ugliest—ape I ever saw." Then, to appease him, I bethought myself of the battlefield of sixty-four squares, and wrote the following stanza on the edge of the board:

> Two armies met and fought, and in the fight
>   Were many slain;
> Yet peace succeeded; and that night
> Each drank success to each,
>   And drank again.

During all this, the perplexity of the King had waxed greater and greater. At length, in order that his wonder might be shared by another, he sent for his only daughter—the Lady of Beauty—in order that she might witness these unheard of doings of an ape. No sooner had she entered the apartment than she hastily adjusted her veil. "Sire," said she, "why dost thou summon me thus into the presence of men?" "Nay, O my daughter," answered the King, "there is none here but myself, a eunnch, a slave, and this ape." Her fingers fastened her veil more closely as she replied, "O my father, this that thou callest an ape is no ape at all. Thou knowest I have the gift against enchantment, and I tell thee this is a man, the son of a king, and his name is Prince Eymar. He hath been transformed into this shape by a son of Iblis. Sire, I know this from the teaching of my old nurse, who instructed me in the seventy rules of magic."

The King was amazed at his daughter's words, and, looking towards me, said, "I can readily believe that thou art Eymar, for none other could beat me twice at chess. What sayest thou?" And I bowed my head, signifying that what had been said was true, and I wept bitterly. Then said the King to the Lady of Beauty, "O my daughter, if thou hast this power of discernment, which I knew not, perchance thou hast the power also to undo the enchantment wrought upon this Prince. If thou canst, I am minded to make him my Grand Vizier, for there is none like him." And she replied, "O my father, I know, and I am able. Witness what I shall do."

The King's daughter then brought forth a large knife, on the blade of which were strange characters engraven.

181

With this she drew a wide circle upon the floor before us, and inscribed within it many magic signs. This done, she stood within the circle, and sang a wild barbaric chant, at which the place began to grow dark, while the roof and walls and floor creaked and groaned with ominous sounds. Suddenly, while fear gat hold on us, there was a blinding flash, and the Efrite appeared within the circle, immense and hideous, his teeth gnashing, and his eyes flashing fire.

"Traitress!" he cried; "did we not swear never to cross one another's path?" "Wretch!" she replied, "I took no oath with thee." At this, the Efrite quickly assumed the form of a lion, and sprang upon her to rend her; but she, being wary, plucked a hair from her head, and breathed upon it, whereupon it was instantly changed into a sharp sword. With this she severed the lion's head from his body, but the head at once became a scorpion. On this the lady became a serpent, and pursued the scorpion, which then took the form of an eagle. But the lady was now a vulture, and the two fought, screaming, in the air. Anon, the eagle changed to a huge black cat, and the vulture, changing to a wolf, fought with it, until at last the cat, finding itself well-nigh vanquished, assumed the form of a pomegranate, and rolled into a pool at one side of the circle. When the wolf dashed in after it, the pomegranate rose up into the air and burst, its grains being scattered over the floor. Quick as lightning, the wolf changed into a cock, which began picking up the grains. And when it had picked up what we thought were all, it began to flap its wings, and run to and fro, looking, as it were, for the last seed. It ran to us with a terrible cry, then, turning, it espied a seed on the brink of the pool, but ere it could reach it, that seed had rolled into the water, and changed itself into a fish. The cock flew screaming to the pool, and assuming the shape of a pike, dived in. Then there was a terrible commotion in the depths. The water foamed and boiled, and the whole place shook as if monsters of the deep were in conflict. Suddenly there was a mighty cry, as the Efrite rose from the pool, encircled with a flame of fire, which continued to issue from his mouth, his nostrils, and eyes. But beside him, in an instant, was the King's daughter, also emitting fire. Then began the most deadly contest between them. From their eyes and mouths darted shafts of fire at one another, until they were enshrouded in a dense smoke. Long the battle raged within this murky canopy, until at last the Efrite was driven forth from it. Pursued by the King's daughter, he rushed at us, and blew fire in our faces, scorching the King's beard, destroying one of my eyes, and killing the eunuch and the slave outright. But, in a moment, the King's daughter was upon him. There was a blinding flash, a cry of victory from her, and we looked, and saw the Efrite reduced to a heap of ashes on the floor at her feet.

"It is done!" she said, panting. "He forced me to the last test of fire, and I conquered. Yet I die, for this fire cannot be quenched, except by my life. Quick! bring me here a bowl of water." I snatched a bowl that stood near by, and ran and dipped some water from the pool. She took it, and having chanted some strange words over the water, sprinkled it upon me, saying: "In the name of Truth, return to thine original form." At this the pang of change rent my flesh and bones, and I became a man again, as I was before, saving the loss of an eye. But lo! as I looked at the

King's daughter, to thank her, I saw a fire come out of her breast, and envelop her head and face. Moans came from within the flame, and she staggered to and fro with muffled cries: "There is no God but Allah! No God but Allah! and Mohammed is——" Suddenly, there was a flash of of fire, and when the flames had disappeared, there, at our feet, lay a second heap of ashes.

I mingled my tears with those of the King, and remorse and bitterness took possession of my soul, for, I reflected, this sweet-faced lady had met her death through me. Yet all is as Allah wills it. The whole realm was cast into mourning over this sad event. The King enshrined his daughter's ashes in a magnificent tomb, and commanded the ashes of the Efrite to be scattered to the four winds. Me he summoned to his presence, and spoke these words: "Would that I had never seen thee, for so I had not lost my daughter. Yet the ways of God are inscrutable, and his will is fulfilled with thee and me. Depart, therefore, O my son, in peace; and think not that I bear thee malice."

So I went out from his presence, and shaved my beard, and left the City. And thus through many regions have I travelled to gain the Abode of Peace, and lay my case before thee, O Prince of the Faithful.

* * * * *

His story being finished, the Khalifeh spoke. "Thy case is extraordinary," he said, "and thou hast done well to bring it before me." And yet, none but Ja'far and Mesrur knew, or even suspected, that he was the Khalifeh. Then, after an interval, the Third Royal Calender rose, and related his story as follows:——

184

THE STORY OF THE THIRD CALENDER.

O KING of the Age, my history is more wonderful than those of my two associates. Their misfortunes were fashioned by the finger of Fate, while mine were the outcome of my own self-will. Yet in the event we are equal, since we each account to thee for the loss of an eye.

Know then, O King, that I, who stand before thee, am a King, and the son of a King. At my father's death, I ascended the throne, and ruled my subjects wisely, as he had done. Yet, unlike him, I was by nature a seafarer, and would often absent myself for the space of a month or more on voyages to parts beyond my kingdom. And it so chanced that from one of these I never returned to my City. And the cause of this I will set before thee.

I had been voyaging for some twenty days with a fleet of ten ships, when we were suddenly becalmed. A few hours later, the master of the vessel I was in came to me in a state of consternation, and told me we were drifting in a rapid current, so wide as to include all the ten ships of the fleet. At this, we signalled to the other ships, and all tried with oars to escape this current; but its width was beyond us; it seemed to flow from all sides to a centre. Then, on a closer scrutiny, we saw that our ships were out-stripping the current, propelled, or attracted, by we knew not what. At this, the master gave a great cry, and plucked his beard, and flung his turban on the deck. "O Sire," he said, "we are doomed! I know now the fate that awaits us. We are speeding towards a great mountain of loadstone, of which I have heard—a great black mountain, which attracteth everything that cometh near it. Soon the very nails of all these ships will be drawn to this mountain, and the ships themselves will fall to pieces."

At this I was dumbfounded. I could not believe that such a thing were possible; and yet there was no denying that we were being drawn by some unseen influence ever more and more rapidly through the water. "Tell me," I said, "what is the history of this mountain?"

"It is black, steep, and inaccessible," he replied. "On its summit is a dome of brass, supported by ten pillars of brass; and on this dome is a brazen horseman, mounted on a brazen horse, bearing in his hand a spear of brass, and on his breast a plate of lead, engraven with mystic signs. Sire, while that horseman sits upon his horse, the spell of the loadstone spares no ship in the surrounding sea, for without iron no ship is built."

The master's words were only too true, for soon the ships were rushing more swiftly through the sea, and it was not long before we sighted the black mountain, of which he had spoken. Our velocity increased. The cleavage of the water rose from our bows. Our ships groaned with the strain, which every moment grew more and more intense. Swifter and swifter we sped on, as nearer loomed the mountain; and we all knew what was before us, and cried out to God for help. At last, our speed was so excessive that no ship could any longer endure the strain. With a creaking and groaning and rending of planks, the nails and ironwork were wrenched away; and every ship fell asunder, and spread itself in wreckage on the sea.

Many were drowned immediately, while some few clung to floating spars. I was one of these, and I know not if others, beside myself, survived, for I could only cling to my plank, and call on God, so great and boisterous were the waves. Hours later I found myself cast up on the strip of shore at the foot of the great black mountain. I praised God for my deliverance, and then, being both hungry and thirsty, I searched for fruit among some trees growing upon the slopes. I soon found some hard by a small stream, and, when I had eaten and drunk, I noticed a pathway by the stream, and followed it. Presently I came to the steep ascent of the hill where the path took the form of rugged steps. Recalling the legend of the horseman, and praying devoutly that I might overthrow him, I toiled up and up the mountain side by this roughest of paths. By the grace of God I at length reached the summit, and found there the great dome surmounted by the horseman. Too fatigued to do more than climb into the dome, I flung myself down there and slept. And, as I slept, a voice spake to me in a dream : "O valiant one, know that in the ground beneath thy feet lie a bow of brass and three arrows of lead, all engraven with talismanic signs. Search for these, and, having found them, shoot the three arrows at the horseman, whereupon thy bow will fall from thy hand, and he and his horse will be hurled down into the midst of the sea. Take thy bow, and bury it again ; and, as soon as thou shalt have done this, the sea will rise swiftly up the mountain sides, until it reaches the foot of the dome. Then, before thee, thou wilt perceive a man in a boat, with an oar in each hand—he being of metal also, but different from the horseman. Embark with him in his boat, and within ten days he will convey thee to a calm sea, and to a ship which will bear thee to thine own land. But beware, O Prince, lest in all these things thou utter the name of God, for, by so doing, thou wilt be in extreme peril."

187

When I awoke, I marvelled at the vividness of this dream, and, remembering all the voice had said, I dug in the ground where my feet had lain. There I discovered the bow and the three arrows, and, taking them forth, I shot at the horseman. Twice my aim failed, but the third arrow struck him, and lo, he and his horse fell headlong down the mountain into the sea. Then, the bow having fallen from my hand, I took it and buried it within the dome. As soon as I had done this, I perceived the sea surging rapidly up the mountain sides. Up and up it came, boiling and seething, until at last it reached the foot of the dome, than which it rose no further. Presently a boat drew near from the midst of the sea, rowed by a man of gleaming metal. Remembering the warning not to utter the name of God, I entered the boat, and the man rowed me away over the sea for many days, until we came in sight of some beautiful islands. When I set eyes on these habitable spots of safety then my heart leapt for joy, and, forgetting the warning of my dream, I cried in my delight, "God be praised!" No sooner had the words escaped my lips than the boat and the man sank in the sea, leaving me upon the surface. My peril was now extreme, for unless I could gain the land I must surely drown. The islands were distant, but they were my only hope, so I swam towards them hour after hour, until night fell. Still I swam on and on in the dark, and at last, when I was spent, and about to sink, I felt a great wave rise beneath me, and hurl me forward. It carried me high up on the shore of an island, where it left me utterly exhausted, but safe from the sea.

The next day, as I was walking along the shore in search of food, I heard voices coming from behind a bend. Thinking not to lose a chance of being taken on board some vessel,

I looked round the bend, and saw ten black slaves of evil aspect, landing from a vessel and bearing spades and axes. I liked not the faces of these men, and feared to expose myself to their view; moreover, being curious as to their mission, I resolved to watch them. Noting the direction they were taking, I ran along the shore for some distance, and then, turning inland, I proceeded until I came to a high tree, into the topmost branches of which I climbed. Presently I saw the slaves pass by and stop at a spot in the middle of the island, where they dug up the ground, until at length they came upon a trap door, which they lifted and set on one side. Then they returned to the vessel, and brought from it loads of provisions, necessaries and even luxuries of every kind. Many times they went and came, and by their loads, it was evident they were preparing some underground dwelling for habitation. At length, after many journeys to and fro, they returned from the vessel laden with beautiful garments of every kind; and with them came an aged sheik, leading by the hand a young man, whose grace and beauty could scarce be expressed in poems. They and the slaves entered the underground abode, and when, two hours later, I counted those who came forth, the young man was not of the number. When they had closed the trap door, and replaced the earth upon it, the slaves conducted the sheik back to the vessel, and sailed away.

These doings caused me great wonder in my tree, and I resolved to see what they meant. I made haste to descend, and, having reached the spot, I ceased not to scrape away the earth until I had found the trap door. I removed this, and descended a flight of wooden steps, which led me to a large apartment, luxuriously furnished; and there, reclining upon

189

a couch, with flowers and fruits before him, was the handsome youth. "Fear me not," I said, when I saw that he had turned pale on observing my sudden intrusion ; "I am a man, like thyself. Destiny hath led me hither, to relieve thy solitude." Then, seeing that he greeted me with delight, I said to him : "O, my brother, tell me how it is that thou art here in this secret place." And he complied with my request, and related to me his history.

"O brother," he said, "my fate has been exceeding strange. My father is a rich dealer in jewels, and his business lies with kings. Many years ago he was wont to grieve that, though God had given him wealth, He had not blest him with a son. Shortly after, he dreamed that a male child would be born to him, but that its life would be cut off at the age of sixteen, and he awoke weeping. His dream was fulfilled, in so far that within a year my mother gave birth to me. Great was his joy at this, but, remembering the further prophecy of his dream, he called in the astrologers, who, by their calculations, confirmed it. 'Thy son's fate,' they said, 'is connected with a great mountain in the sea, called the Mountain of Loadstone, on the summit of which is a horseman of brass, bearing on his breast a tablet of lead, with mystic signs engraven. Sixteen years hence a king, the son of a king, will arise, and hurl that horseman down into the sea, shortly after which he will slay thy son.'

"My father grieved very greatly at this, and ceased not to love me the more throughout my youth. When I was nearing the age of sixteen, he again summoned the astrologers, who told him that the horseman had already been cast down into the sea, and there remained now only ten days of my life. Then my father arose and prepared this place for me, so that

I might dwell here in secret until the completion of the days, for the astrologers had said that if, by the will of God, I passed safely out of my sixteenth year, I should live to a great age. And thus it is that I am here, O my brother."

"What strange thing is this?" said I within myself on hearing his words. "It was I who cast down the horseman, but, by Allah! it will not be I who will slay this gracious youth." Then, turning to him, I said: "Fear nothing, sweet youth! Here, at least, thou art safe. I myself will protect thee, and, when the term is expired, I will go forth with thee to thy father, and he shall restore me to my country, and so reap a great reward." He rejoiced at my words, and was comforted, and so far was I from wishing him harm that I waited upon him, and during the night slept by his side. Once he awoke from dreams, crying: "The horse-man is down! He hath fallen into the sea! Whither, oh! whither shall I flee for safety?" But I quieted him, and comforted him, saying: "Never will such a calamity as thou fearest come to thee while I am by thy side."

For nine days I served him, sparing no trouble for his comfort; and on the tenth I could not conceal my joy, for I knew that, if it rested with me to slay him, he would be alive on the morrow. My happiness infected him, and he begged me to heat some water that he might bathe and array himself in bright garments, and then, with me, celebrate the hour of his release. I prepared all he required, and he bathed, and arrayed himself in costly robes, and reclined upon the couch to rest. It was the hour of sunset: a little while remained till the term expired. "O brother," he said to me, "wilt thou in thy kindness cut me up a water melon, and sprinkle it with sugar?" "O brother mine," I replied, "I see here a melon, but where is the knife?" He pointed to the shelf above his head, saying, "Thou wilt find one there, O my creditor." Then I stepped up on the side of the couch, and found the knife, and drew it from its sheath; but, having done this, my foot slipped, and I fell headlong. The next thing I knew was that the knife was buried in the youth's breast, with my hand upon the haft. I uttered a loud cry, and beat my bosom. Oh! the grief of it! Dead! And by my hand! O God! by what cruel misfortunes dost thou convince mortals that Fate and Destiny are thine instruments!

Long I wept by the side of the youth, imploring pardon from those cold lips; one glance of forgiveness from those glazed eyes. Then, sad and sorrowful, I arose and ascended the steps; and, having replaced and covered the trap door, departed from that place. I remained upon the island, nursing a heavy weight of grief. From a place of hiding I saw them come and take the youth's dead body away. I saw his aged father's sorrow, as he followed weeping, and watched the vessel sail away out of sight. But great as was this calamity, I was destined to further trouble.

In my daily wanderings about the island, I discovered that on one side of it the sea had been gradually receding. When another week had passed, there was a considerable extent of land that had risen above the water. I watched this day by day for a space of some months, at the end of which time dry land stretched into the distance so far that I resolved to set forth upon it, hoping to come at length to an inhabited region. I had proceeded some leagues when I saw before me, in the distance, an upland with a splendid palace upon it, shining all golden in the rays of the sun. When I drew near, almost dazzled at the sight of it, an old man came out to meet

The Prince is taken back to the Golden Palace by the Magic
Black Horse.   Page 197

The Bridge at Baghdad where Abu-l-Hasan awaits strangers

Abu-l-Hasan entertains the strangers with dancing and music

Abu-l-Hasan awakens in the bed of the Khalifeh.   Page 206

me ; and following him were ten young men, each lacking an eye—a thing which caused me great astonishment. They and the old man saluted me, and asked me whence I came, whereupon I told them my story, which they listened to with looks of wonder. Then they invited me into the palace, and one of them said: "Be welcome, O brother, but see to it that thou ask us not respecting our condition, nor yet how it is we each lack an eye." Presently the old man brought food and wine, and we ate and drank together, conversing on many things until it was time to sleep. Then one of them called to the old man to bring the materials for penance, and he arose and placed before each a basin full of ashes and powdered charcoal. One and all then bared their arms and blackened their faces with the mixture, crying continually, "Once we were dwelling in happiness, but now we are wretched ; and this is the result of our idle curiosity." This they kept up till daybreak, when they washed their faces and changed their clothes and slept.

Next day, being unable to cast off my curiosity regarding this strange behaviour, I beseeched them to tell me the reason thereof, and one of them replied : "O young man, ask not what doth not concern thee, lest thou hear what may not please thee." But I was not content with this answer, and continued to entreat them to tell me the reason of their actions, and also the cause of each having lost an eye. "Nay, be silent," said another ; "what the mind doth not know, the heart doth not grieve." Yet I still pestered them with my questions, giving them no peace. At length they lost patience, and, after conversing together awhile, one of them said to me : "O young man, if thou dost above all things desire to know the cause of these things, submit thyself to our hands, and

2 B   193

thou shalt learn." And I answered, "I desire nothing more than to know;" for my curiosity had become a fever.

Then they slaughtered a ram and flayed it, and, placing a knife in my hand, sewed me up in the skin and carried me to a hilltop at a little distance, where they left me. Presently I heard the flapping of giant wings, and then the ram's skin, with me inside it, was seized by the talons of a great bird and borne up and away. After a long flight, the bird set me down upon a high plateau. Remembering the knife they had placed in my hand, I ripped open the skin, and emerged. The gigantic bird, on seeing me, flew off screaming.

Far in the distance, at the side of a hill, I saw a splendid palace, sparkling in the sunlight. It was the only habitation that I could discern, so I made my way towards it. After some hours' journey, I reached its gates, and seeing them open, entered, and soon found myself in a great chamber of indescribable splendour, where forty beautiful damsels, each one like a goddess, welcomed me with cries of joy. "O our Master and Prince," they said, "why hast thou tarried so long? We, thy handmaids, have waited many weeks for thy coming." And they set food and wine before me, and while I ate and drank, some sang and others danced; and they were so wildly beautiful that any one of them would have melted the heart of an anchorite.

Thus suddenly was I launched into a life of pure delight, and I dwelt among these rare and radiant damsels, their sole Lord and Master, in luxury and joy. Thus it continued for a whole year, with never a shadow of dulness in our days; but, on the first morning of the new year, they all came to me weeping, and bidding me farewell, as each in turn clung to me with the sadness of

194

parting. "Wherefore this?" I cried. "Ye will break my heart if ye leave me." And one replied, "Nay, O master; we love thee most of any on earth, but we must leave thee for a time, and we fear to lose thee." And she fell to weeping afresh, and the others added their tears to hers. "Tell me what this means," I said to her. "O my master, if thou wouldst know," she replied, "we are the daughters of kings, and for many years it has been our practice to dwell in this palace, returning only to our fathers for forty days at the beginning of each year. To-day we must go, and we fear that, before we return, thou wilt disregard our directions, in which case thou wilt be lost to us. Here are the keys, a hundred in number, which will unlock a hundred doors for thee, admitting to gardens of various kinds, in which thou wilt find a hundred different delights; but we do entreat thee, open not the door which is fashioned of pure gold, for if thou dost, we shall never see thee again, and that is what we fear."

I took the keys, greatly wondering, and when I had embraced them all, and said farewell, they departed, with sad looks, leaving me alone in the palace. Many times I swore to myself that I would never open the golden door, and even as I swore, the wish to do it came uppermost. But I forced it down, saying: "There are ninety-nine doors without this one: surely it is enough!" And that evening, feeling sad and lonely, and longing for entertainment, I took the keys, and, selecting one engraven with a character corresponding to that on the first door, I opened and entered.

Within lay a garden like paradise, with running streams, and hanging fruits, and birds that sang the praises of their Creator. Every kind of delicate perfume breathed from the

195

rarest of flowers, and the bosom of the dreamy trees moved in the soft wind as if langorous with love. Seeing this wonderful place, I was impelled by curiosity to explore what lay behind the second door. Accordingly, I opened it and entered. Here was a large domain of forest and meadow, watered by a crystal river. Uplands on which the sunlight slept, led up to mountain peaks towering against the sides of heaven. I noted all this with wonder, saying, "I will return, and enjoy this at my leisure; meanwhile, I die to know what fresh joy is concealed by the third door."

When I entered the third place of delight, I found it to be a spacious aviary, containing all the birds of song and of rare plumage that could be found on earth. This vast place was paven with many-coloured marble, and graced with patches of forest and greensward. The birds drank from crystal fountains, and, flying off, sang gloriously. The streams of these fountains were of different colours, and when I drank of one, I found it was pure wine. So I wandered from one to another sipping the rarest vintages I had ever known, until, coming to a soft couch of moss, I reclined, and was lulled to sleep by the songs of countless nightingales.

When I awoke next morning, I opened the fourth door and found beyond it a treasury passing the imagination of kings. Jewels and precious stones there were beyond reckoning. "These," I said, "are mine, and forty priceless damsels are also mine: what Sultan can compare with me?" That day, and on the following days, I opened one door after another, finding within each the strangest and most wonderful things man ever beheld; until, on the thirty-ninth day, I had opened every door except the last,—the one fashioned

196

of pure gold. Long I looked at it, recalling my oath, and fortifying myself against temptation. Many times I turned away from it, with the key in my hand, but always the Devil drove me back again. Then, at last, my curiosity became acute, and I could not refrain.

I opened the door, and passed within. I was met by an odour fragrant beyond conception, which mastered my brain so that I fell in a faint. But I soon recovered, and, rising to my feet, went on, treading on golden tiles spread with saffron, and lighted on my way by golden lamps, from which were wafted the odours of musk and ambergris. I soon saw that the place was, in effect, a stable, though words fail to describe its splendour. There, standing at a crystal manger full of choice sesame, with a trough adjoining filled with rose-water, stood a magnificent steed, as black as night. Never had I seen his equal. He was saddled and bridled, and his trappings were of gold and thread-of-gold, sparkling with gems. "This is the steed of my desire," I said, and then, as I approached him, he turned his head towards me, and neighed. Urged by the Devil, I led him forth and mounted him. But when I jerked the reins, he stood stock still. I persuaded him with my heels, but he did not move. Then I espied a whip deposited in the saddle. I took this and struck him a violent blow. With a neigh like thunder, he rose in the air, and soared up and up to a great height. Then he flew with me over hills and valleys, until at last he alighted on the roof of another palace. There he plunged and reared, and finally shook me off behind him; and, as I fell, a blow from his tail struck out my eye. Leaving me thus, he soared up and away, and was soon lost to sight.

When I descended from the roof, I found I was back in

the Palace of the ten young men. When they beheld me, and saw that my eye was gone, they cried with one voice, "No welcome to thee, O curious one! Thou art now in like case with us, having been chastised for thine impertinent curiosity. For know that we have all opened that golden door and ridden that black horse, and that is why we do nightly penance for our foolishness." I then begged them to receive me into their company, but they refused, saying their number was complete. So I went my way dejected, and wandered as a mendicant, ever on and on towards Baghdad, the Abode of Peace, resolved to seek the Khalifeh of the Lord of all Creatures and set my case before him.

* * * * *

"Verily," exclaimed Harun-er-Rashid as the Third Royal Calender retired to his place, "this is the most astounding tale of all. Hear me now, all of you. These men have suffered greatly, but Fate hath no further trouble in store for them. By Allah! my armies are great, and I will restore each to his throne. As for you, O ladies," he continued, turning to the three sisters, "my Seraglio is dull and lifeless without you. Will you grace it with your presence?" "Yes, O Commander of the Faithful," cried they all, laughing merrily and clapping their hands, for they thought him a perfect impersonator; "we will come to thee." "On the head and the eye?" "Yea, O King, on the head and the eye is our promise given." At this the Khalifeh turned to his two officials. "O Vizier," he said, "I call thee to witness; and thee also, O Mesrur." And they answered smiling, for they liked the pretence of his pretence, "King of the Age, we hear and obey."

Then the Khalifeh approached the porter, who was asleep upon the floor, and stirred him with his foot so that he awoke and sat up. "O thou carrier of goods and vast quantities of wine," said the Khalifeh, "wouldst thou be the Wag of Harun-er-Rashid, Fifth Khalifeh of the House of Abbas?" The porter grinned. "O Prince of the Faithful," said he, "I was born with that ambition, for they say that when the Khalifeh's Wag waggeth his tongue no other tongue may wag." And with this he kissed the ground seven times in mock obeisance. "It is well," said the Khalifeh, "for verily thou art a wag." And they all applauded his seeming royalty and said one among another, "Never have we seen such an excellent impersonation of a king."

The Khalifeh then pointed to the first signs of day in the east, saying, "There was never so pleasant a night but morning ended it." And then, with Ja'far and Mesrur, he set about taking his departure, thanking the ladies for their kind hospitality and bidding them remember the promise they had given. The Three Royal Calenders and the porter also bade the sisters farewell, and, when they were outside the house, the Calenders were directed to a Khan, while the porter took his own way home and the Khalifeh and his two officials returned to the palace.

On the following morning the Khalifeh of Baghdad sat on his throne, and his first thought was to send for the Three Royal Calenders, the three ladies, and the porter. "Lose no time in bringing them hither, O Vizier," said the Khalifeh to Ja'far. The Vizier sent in great haste, and, when the messengers returned with all of them, Er-Rashid received them in private audience.

Not one of them recognised the three merchants of the

former evening, and their faces showed fear and surprise, for they knew not why they had been thus summoned. The Khalifeh spoke. "Know, O ye people, that I, Harun-er-Rashid, of the house of Abbas, do not forget my promises. I promised Three Royal Calenders that I would restore them to their thrones, and, by Allah! this shall be done. Three beautiful ladies of Baghdad promised me that they would come into my Seraglio, which thou didst witness, O Ja'far; and thou, too, O Mesrur." The two officials bowed low, confirming this. "But," continued the Khalifeh, "I have since decided to make them queens by bestowing them in marriage upon these three kings." And he indicated the Calenders. Then, turning towards the porter, he continued: "I also promised that a carrier of goods,—a merry fellow,—should be my Wag. This shall be, and his first duty will be to solve this riddle. Which is easier: for the Khalifeh to play the merchant, or the merchant to play the Khalifeh? Meanwhile, do you all agree to what I have proposed?"

They were all dumbfounded as they realised that their actor of the previous night had played his part so well, because he was indeed the Khalifeh himself. For some moments no one spoke; then they all made obeisance to him and kissed the ground. "O King of the Age," said one of the ladies, "I answer for my sisters and myself. We will obey thy commands willingly and with joy." Then one of the Calenders added, "O Prince of the Faithful, we also hear and obey, with equal willingness and equal joy." "And as for me, O King," said the porter, "I, being a wag, and also a liar of some excellence, knew that indeed thou wert the Khalifeh of the Lord of All Creatures, but I was compelled to dissemble for fear of thine Executioner's sword. Thus I

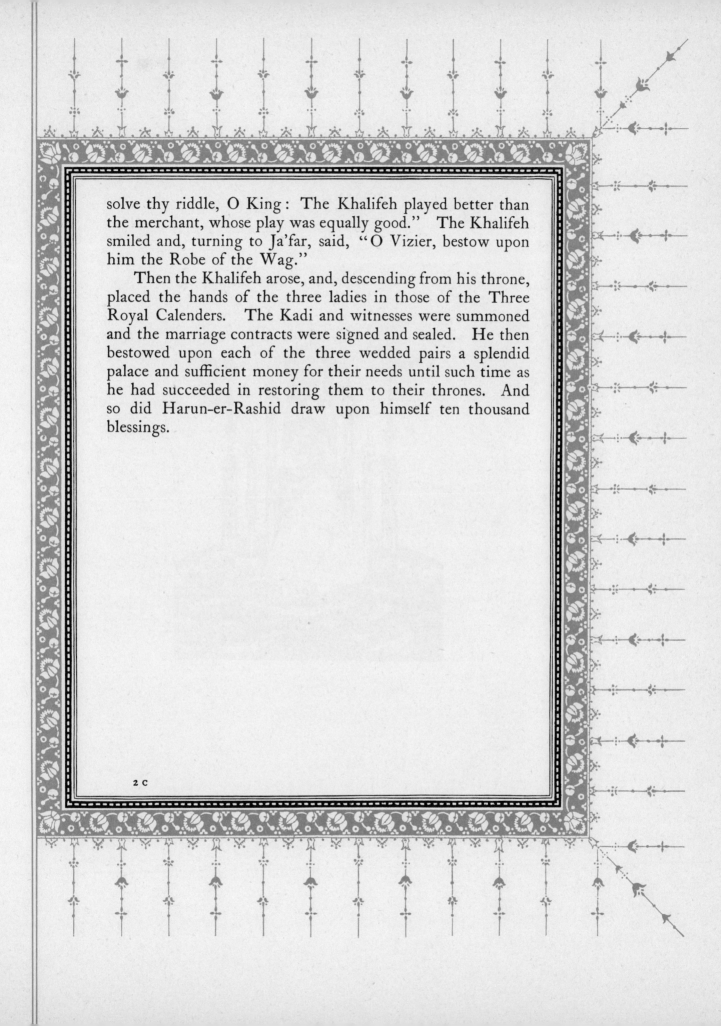

solve thy riddle, O King: The Khalifeh played better than
the merchant, whose play was equally good." The Khalifeh
smiled and, turning to Ja'far, said, "O Vizier, bestow upon
him the Robe of the Wag."

Then the Khalifeh arose, and, descending from his throne,
placed the hands of the three ladies in those of the Three
Royal Calenders. The Kadi and witnesses were summoned
and the marriage contracts were signed and sealed. He then
bestowed upon each of the three wedded pairs a splendid
palace and sufficient money for their needs until such time as
he had succeeded in restoring them to their thrones. And
so did Harun-er-Rashid draw upon himself ten thousand
blessings.

2 C

THE SLEEPER AWAKENED

IN the reign of Harun-er-Rashid, a merchant of the city of Baghdad died, leaving his vast fortune to his son Abu-l-Hasan, the Wag, who at once divided it into two equal parts : one to be set aside, and the other to be spent. Selecting a number of wealthy merchants' sons as his boon companions, he lived a life of extravagance until every fraction of that which was to be spent was exhausted. At this he called his boon companions and laid his case before them, expecting at least sympathy, if not offers of assistance. But one and all treated him with the utmost unconcern and turned their backs on him. Sad at heart he sought comfort of his mother, complaining of the injustice of this treatment. "O, Abu-l-Hasan," said she, "it was ever thus ; when thou wast rich they were thy friends, but now thou art poor they look the other way." And she wept with him, mingling her tears with his.

Then Abu-l-Hasan arose and at once took steps to withdraw the other half of his fortune from the safe-keeping in which he had placed it. Upon this he lived as befitted his condition in life, for he was still a wealthy man. But, remembering the lesson he had bought with the other half of his riches, he took an oath that henceforth he would consort neither with relations nor friends nor acquaintances, but only with strangers ; and, furthermore, that the extent of his association with any one person would be for one night only, the acquaintanceship ceasing entirely at sunrise next morning.

Every evening thereafter, when the purple twilight fell upon Baghdad, Abu-l-Hasan would walk in the ways of the city, saluting none, but at last waylaying a stranger, upon whom he would press an invitation to good food and wine and entertainment at his house. What stranger could refuse? With the guest in the place of honour Abu-l-Hasan drank deep with him till morning, when the guest departed with the understanding that if they ever met again they were not to recognise each other.

This went on night after night for a whole year, until one night an illustrious stranger accepted Abu-l-Hasan's invitation. It was none other than Harun-er-Rashid himself, who had wandered forth in disguise to amuse himself, as was his wont at times. Little dreaming that he was entertaining the Khalifeh unawares, Abu-l-Hasan led his guest into his saloon—a most luxurious apartment where every comfort was provided: streams of water murmuring through silver channels; golden fountains playing in cool grottoes, and, over all, an amber light shed by a wonderful lamp, subduing the richness of the place to a vague and dreaming glamour.

Here they reclined, and Abu-l-Hasan summoned a slave girl, lissom as the willow tendril, and bade her sing to the music of her lute. Sweetly then she sang these verses, inspired by the soft languor of the night :—

> Oh! Love, thy footsteps stray in lands afar,
>   But here within my heart thou dost abide.
> E'en though thou dwelt in yonder distant star
>   No depths of space our spirits could divide.
> Thou art my Love! Thro' all eternity
>   Thou art my soul, and nothing is but thee.

204

Er-Rashid marvelled greatly at the singer and her song, and wondered in his heart what manner of man was Abu-l-Hasan that he could entertain on so magnificent a scale.

"Tell me, young man," he said, "what is thy name, that on a future occasion I may return thy hospitality?"

And Abu-l-Hasan told him, but added with a smile: "Alas! this night must end our acquaintance, for I have so vowed it." Then he set forth the nature and the cause of his vow, at which Er-Rashid laughed heartily and said, "By Allah! brother; I do not blame thee!"

After this came the slave girls and spread a banquet before them, and they partook of it, Abu-l-Hasan giving the choicest portions to the Khalifeh. When they had finished their repast Abu-l-Hasan brought out his oldest and most fragrant wines, laid the wine-cloth himself, and, having lighted some small lamps and candles, filled a goblet and raised it to the Khalifeh. "Best of boon companions," he said, "away with ceremony! Regard me as thy faithful slave and may I never be compelled to grieve thy loss." With this he drained the goblet, and, still acting the part of the Khalifeh's servant, filled another for his master and handed it to him. This pleased the Khalifeh greatly. He appreciated such delicate attention. He took the goblet and drank, saying within himself, "By Allah! a good return will I make him for this." Abu-l-Hasan continued to wait upon his guest in humble fashion, and the Khalifeh enjoyed his hospitality to the full. If his host had known him to be Er-Rashid himself—which he did not—he could not have entertained him better.

At the hour of midnight the Khalifeh spoke to his host in serious tones. "O, Abu-l-Hasan," said he, "tell me what thing thou dost most desire."

"Why, my master," replied Abu-l-Hasan, "if thou wouldst know: my most constant prayer is that I may be rid of the incessant annoyance imposed upon me by the Imam and the four Sheiks of the neighbouring mosque. When they hear the sound of music and revelry at night they inform against me, so that I am harassed by heavy fines. By Allah! if I had my way I would give each of them a thousand lashes."

"May Allah grant thy prayer!" said Er-Rashid, and, unobserved, he dropped a lozenge into his host's wine and handed him the goblet, bidding him drink.

Abu-l-Hasan did so and speedily thereafter fell sound asleep. The Khalifeh at once summoned his servants, who, having followed him at a little distance, were waiting without. He commanded them to place Abu-l-Hasan upon a mule and convey him to the Palace. This was soon done.

Later, when the Khalifeh had rested somewhat, he summoned the most important officials of his Court, and, indicating the sleeping figure of Abu-l-Hasan, said to them, "In the morning you will find this young man upon the royal couch. When he awakes, see to it that you obey his lightest wish as you would my own; salute him as the Khalifeh and make obeisance before him." To his women slaves he gave similar instructions and ordered them to address Abu-l-Hasan as the Prince of the Faithful. Then Er-Rashid retired to another part of the Palace and slept.

In the morning when Abu-l-Hasan awoke upon the royal couch he stared in amazement at the attendants making obeisance before him. "O, Prince of the Faithful! it is the hour of morning prayer," said a beautiful slave girl, stepping forward. Abu-l-Hasan laughed, for he knew not what to make of it. Then he rubbed his eyes and gazed around upon the sumptuous magnificence of the apartment with its gorgeous roof and walls, its rich silk hangings, its vessels of gold and sparkling crystal, its jewelled furniture, ornaments and luxurious carpets. "By Allah!" he gasped; "have I attained to the fragrant Paradise, or do I dream?"

With that he closed his eyes as if to hold the dream in further slumber, but a eunuch advanced and kissed the ground before the royal couch. "O, Prince of the Faithful!" he said, humbly; "bethink thee of thy usual custom." At this Abu-l-Hasan, sorely perplexed, opened his eyes again very slowly, and saw the rich trappings of the couch whereon he lay. Little by little he opened them until at last they were wide with wonder, for this was no dream—the voice of the eunuch who had spoken, the faces and forms of the attendants, the royal splendour of the place—all were as real as he could wish; and yet—yet—he raised his hand to his mouth and bit one of his fingers—hard; then cried out with sudden pain. Angrily he raised himself on one elbow, and, addressing one of the female slaves, "Come here!" he said. "My lord, I am always at thy service," she answered, drawing near. "What is thy will, O Prince of the Faithful?" "Tell me," he said, "who am I, and where am I?" "Thou art the Prince of the Faithful," answered she. "Thou art in thy palace and upon thy royal couch." "Nay, nay," said he; "I sleep. Methinks I dream, or—" he went on, half to himself,—"Can it be? My guest—he bade me drink and—what subtle enchantment is this? Am I now Abu-l-Hasan dreaming I am the Khalifeh, or was I, last night and heretofore for many nights, the Khalifeh dreaming he was Abu-l-Hasan?" And the Khalifeh himself, observing

207

him all the while from a sheltered nook, revelled in the perplexity of his guest.

At last Abu-l-Hasan called one after another to him and questioned each in turn, asking if indeed he were the Prince of the Faithful; and in turn each showed amazement that he should put the question and assured him that indeed he was the Khalifeh of the Lord of all creatures. To the first he said, hotly, "Thou liest!" To the next: "Thou art in error!" To others: "Impossible!" and "It cannot be!" Until at last he was fairly beaten, and had to admit that he indeed was Er-Rashid himself, the Prince of the Faithful. He asked the attendants to withdraw so that he might give himself up to this new-found wonder and perplexity, and accustom himself to the strange position in which he found himself.

The morning wore on and he was aroused from his reverie by a eunuch who approached with a salutation and handed him a pair of shoes of fine spun gold set with precious stones. Abu-l-Hasan put these on. Then came female slaves with a golden basin and a silver jug and they bathed his hands. On this being done, they spread a praying carpet before him. Although he knew not well how to pray, he made many protestations to Allah, earnestly entreating that he might be convinced that this was not a dream. His prayers dispelled the doubt, but it returned when the eunuchs brought him priceless apparel in which to clothe himself, for, when he was arrayed in these magnificent garments, and sat contemplating himself, he muttered, "Surely, 'tis all a dream, and a trick of the Evil One."

This thought was heavy upon him when a memluk entered. "O Prince of the Faithful!" he said, "the

Abu-l-Hasan orders that the Sheiks of the district should be
taken to be impaled on the back of a mangy camel. Page 209

The room of the fruits prepared for Abu-l-Hasan.   Page 210

chamberlain craves speech with thee." "Bid him enter!"
replied Abu-l-Hasan, rousing himself. And presently the
chamberlain was kissing the ground before him and saying,
"Peace be unto thee, O Prince of the Faithful!" Then
Abu-l-Hassan descended from the couch and stood before the
chamberlain. "Allah! Allah!" cried that worthy servitor
in astonishment. "O our Lord! forget not that all men are
thy slaves and it is not fitting that the Prince of the Faithful
should rise to anyone." But Abu-l-Hasan bade him proceed
with his business.

The chamberlain then informed Abu-l-Hasan that certain
high officials and the chief memluks were without, awaiting
his commands. "Let them enter!" said Abu-l-Hasan with
growing authority. So they were summoned, and each as
he advanced kissed the ground before him, saluting him as
the Prince of the Faithful. Abu-l-Hasan was greatly pleased
with this crowning proof of his position, and gave his commands forthwith. To the Wali he said: "Go at once to
the mother of Abu-l-Hasan and give her a hundred gold
pieces, with my blessing." And he named the street where
he would find her. "When you have done this," he continued in tones of severity, "repair to the mosque and bestow
upon the Imam and the four Sheiks, each a thousand lashes.
Then thou shalt bind them upon camels, with their faces to
the beasts' tails, and make a public show of them in the ways
of the city, proclaiming to all, 'Behold the reward of fools
who trouble their neighbours!' When this is done thou
shalt execute a sworn bond expelling them from the mosque.
And see to it that thou carry this out to the very letter."

And the Wali did as he was commanded. And Abu-l-
Hasan continued issuing his commands in like fashion until

2 D
209

the evening, when he felt weary and hungry. Dismissing the officials, he summoned a eunuch and desired food to be brought him. "It is prepared, O Prince of the Faithful!" replied the eunuch. And he led him into the banqueting chamber, where a sumptuous feast was spread. Ten slave-girls waited upon him and he ate with relish of the delicate viands they placed before him. When he had finished they led him to the drinking chamber and danced before him while he drank of the choicest and rarest wines.

"By Allah!" he said in his cups, "this is enchantment—naught but devilry, practised upon me by that guest of mine. Here, girl! why dost thou laugh?" The girl he had called came and kissed the ground before him. "O Prince of the Faithful," she said, "here in thy palace all is thine. I laughed for very gladness to be thy slave." And she whirled away again into the dance. Presently, however, she returned with a cup of wine and handed it to him. He drank, after which another came with another cup of wine, until the last was reached; and she, by order of the Khalifeh, had dropped a drugged lozenge into the cup. Ignorant of this, Abu-l-Hasan took it from her hand, and, saying to himself, "May Allah protect me from the Evil One!" drank the wine; and immediately on this he fell back senseless. The attendants then, in obedience to Er-Rashid's orders, took him back to his own house and laid him on his bed, still unconscious.

When he awoke from his stupor it was dark, and he called loudly for lights; but there was no answer. Where were the slave girls? Angrily he summoned one or two by name. Then it was that his mother, hearing him calling out in this way, came to his couch and asked what ailed him. Had he gone mad? "Darest thou address the Prince of the Faithful so?" he replied. "Who art thou, miserable old woman?" "Canst thou not recognise thy mother?" "Cease, woman! I am the Prince of the Faithful, the lord of the earth and all its treasures; all people are my slaves and—" "Silence!" she broke in, "if thou valuest thy life!" And, guessing that some spell had been laid upon him, she began to mutter charms to drive away the evil spirits. Then, seeking to divert his mind, she told him the good news about the Imam and the Sheiks; how they had been punished, and how she herself had received a hundred gold pieces with the Khalifeh's blessing. When he heard this he started up, shouting: "It was I who gave orders that these things should be done; I, the Khalifeh, the Prince of the Faithful." And thereupon he took a stick and beat his mother till the neighbours flocked in and demanded to know the cause of the trouble. "Wretched old woman!" he was shouting; "am I not the Prince of the Faithful?"

Hearing this the neighbours said among themselves, "He is mad!" And without more ado they fell upon him, and bound him, and took him to the madhouse. There he was beaten every day and treated in such a manner that he feared indeed to lose his reason. After many days of this harsh treatment his mother came to him and asked him what he was doing in such a distressful plight if, indeed, he was the Prince of the Faithful. And he was fain to admit that he had been mistaken—nay, worse still; he had been made the sport of evil spirits and the subject of enchantment. So he repented, and prayed to Allah for forgiveness; and they released him from the madhouse.

Abu-l-Hasan's return to his old life brought with it a desire for a boon companion, and this urged his restless feet through the ways of the city again, searching for one as of old. Now Er-Rashid had kept a watchful eye on Abu-l-Hasan's movements, and thus it happened that one evening the Khalifeh, in the garb of a merchant, stood before him. "Greeting to thee, O master of devils!" cried Abu-l-Hasan, recognising him as soon as he saw him. "Hast thou then suffered at my hands?" asked Er-Rashid. "Suffered! vilest of devil drivers!" returned Abu-l-Hasan with bitter anger. Then, after recounting the many things he had endured, he asked, "Is this the way thou returnest my hospitality, to give thy devils control over me, to make sport of my sufferings? Begone! I wish to see thy face no more."

Er-Rashid then sought to disarm his resentment with courteous explanations. "Nay," he said, "thou art surely in error, brother. Yet I am to blame in some way, for, on parting with thee that night, I neglected to close the door of thy house behind me; and, methinks, the Devil entered to thee after I had gone." And so, with subtle words, Er-Rashid softened the anger of Abu-l-Hasan and drew from him the whole tale of his sufferings, advising him on this point and on that and showing a pitiful countenance at his wrongs. But not until Er-Rashid had sworn on oath that, neither by carelessness nor otherwise, would he let in the Devil upon him again, would Abu-l-Hasan comply with his earnest entreaty to be invited once more to his house that evening. "I swear by Allah," said Er-Rashid, "thou shalt suffer no manner of ill through me."

During the evening Abu-l-Hasan entertained his guest as before, and again, at midnight, the Khalifeh dropped a lozenge into his host's wine, so that as soon as he had drained his cup he fell into a deep slumber. Then once more the

Khalifeh commanded him to be taken to the Palace and placed upon the royal couch and surrounded by slave girls to attend his waking. Towards morning Er-Rashid, from his place of concealment, commanded one the slave girls to strike the cords of her lute above the sleeper's head, so that Abu-l-Hasan awoke to the strains of music. "Mother! Mother!" he called out, but the slave girls answered him, "O Prince of the Faithful! we are here to do thy bidding." At this he gazed about him and immediately threw up his hands and called on Allah to deliver him from the wicked enchantment which the Evil One had a second time imposed upon him. Then he turned to a memluk and bade him bite his ear so that he might know whether or no he was in the flesh, and awake. The memluk at first refused to bite the ear of the Prince of the Faithful, whereupon Abu-l-Hasan would have arisen and hewn off his head, had he not obeyed and bitten the ear till his teeth met. A loud shriek from Abu-l-Hasan brought Er-Rashid to his knees with suppressed laughter. Then Abu-l-Hasan rose in wrath and cursed those who stood around him, calling upon their Master by the most holy passages of the Koran to break the spell which held him in so vile a thrall. At this Er-Rashid, unable to endure it further, called out from his hiding-place, "O Abu-l-Hasan! this is more than I can bear." And he came forth laughing.

Abu-l-Hasan at once recognised him as Er-Rashid, the Khalifeh, and made obeisance to him, praying that he might live for ever. "Rise, Abu-l-Hasan, the Wag!" commanded the Khalifeh then; "and the peace of Allah be with thee." With his own hands Er-Rashid then clothed him in rich apparel; after which he bestowed upon him a thousand gold

213

pieces and raised him to the dignity ot chief of his boon companions.

Abu-l-Hasan quickly grew in favour with the Khalifeh and the Lady Zubeydeh, his wife; and, in the course of time, married Nuzhat-el-Fuad, Zubeydeh's Treasurer. They lived very happily together, tasting every delight, until all their money was spent. Then, Abu-l-Hasan, confronted with poverty and ashamed to beg a further favour from the Khalifeh, belaboured his wits with regard to filling his empty treasure chest. "O, Nuzhat-el-Fuad!" he said at length, "I would play a jest upon the Khalifeh, and I would that thou shouldst play a similar jest upon the Lady Zubeydeh; for so, methinks, we shall receive from them two hundred pieces of gold and two pieces of fine spun silk." "I am at thy service," she replied. "What is thy plan?" And he unfolded it to her.

It was that they should both feign death. He was to die first, and, when she had laid him out with all the proper trappings of a corpse, she was to run dishevelled and in grief to the Lady Zubeydeh, and beat her breast and shriek and moan, and finally acquaint her with the sad cause of her sorrowing. "Then," went on Abu-l-Hasan, "she will weep with thee, for have I not found favour in her eyes? And she will comfort thee and give thee a hundred pieces of gold and a piece of fine spun silk, and bid thee go and prepare my corpse decently for the grave." "It is well, O my lord!" said Nuzhat-el-Fuad, eagerly, "proceed—what then?"

"Then," continued Abu-l-Hasan, "when thou comest to me with the spoil, we will set it by; and thou shalt take my place, and, when I have bestowed on thee the honours of the much-lamented dead, I myself will run to the Khalifeh,

214

distracted with grief, and beat upon my breast and pluck my beard and tear my garments, and prostrate myself in sorrow before him, crying, 'There is no deity but Allah!' And, when he has lifted me up and wiped away my tears, and drawn from me the history of thy death, then will he do by me in like manner as Zubeydeh will have done by thee. He will bestow on me a hundred pieces of gold and a piece of fine spun silk, bidding me go and prepare thy corpse for decent burial. Then I will come to thee and lay my piece of silk by thine, and place my hundred pieces on thy hundred pieces, and thenceforward we shall live in luxury, my Nuzhat-el-Fuad."

His wife laughed with glee and clapped her hands. "Verily, Abu-l-Hasan," she cried, "thou art a wag."

Still laughing, she proceeded to lay him out, directed by her lord and master, who, though dead, failed nothing in his instructions as to the minutest details—even to placing upon his stomach a knife and a pinch of salt. Then she put on the garb of woe and dishevelled her hair, and ran weeping to the Lady Zubeydeh, who, seeing her thus distracted, was filled with pity and questioned her gently as to the cause of so great a grief. But Nuzhat-el-Fuad's sobs and tears rose to shrieks of wild despair before at length she made the matter plain. And, when Zubeydeh knew it, she wept with her and mourned for Abu-l-Hasan the Wag; and she bestowed upon her a hundred pieces of gold and a piece of fine spun silk, bidding her prepare his body for the grave.

When Nuzhat-el-Fuad returned to the house and showed Abu-l-Hasan the first fruits of his plan, he arose and, sharing her delight, danced with glee. Together they took the spoil and laid it by; then they addressed themselves to the second part of their jest. Nuzhat-el-Fuad was speedily disposed according to the first rites of the dead, and Abu-l-Hasan fell to tearing his garments and setting his turban awry, and practising postures of grief. Then he set forth to the Palace, plucking his beard and moaning as he ran. When he arrived there the Khalifeh was in the judgment hall, but Abu-l-Hasan was given immediate audience because of his haste and despair. "What ails thee?" said the Khalifeh, regarding Abu-l-Hasan with dismay, for he was beating his breast and moaning in agony of mind. "Alas! O Prince of the Faithful! Alas! that thy boon companion had ever been born!" At which outburst of grief the Khalifeh took him gently and sought to learn the cause of such overwhelming woe. At length, Abu-l-Hasan told him. Nuzhat-el-Fuad, the half of his life, was dead! "Now, by Allah!" said the Khalifeh, "there is no god but Allah!" And he smote his palms together and raised his eyes to heaven. He condoled with the bereaved man and bade him submit to the will of Allah. It was Abu-l-Hasan's plain duty to do this—especially as he, the Khalifeh, would send him a far fairer woman than the one he had lost. Then he bestowed on Abu-l-Hasan a hundred pieces of gold and a piece of fine silk, and bade him prepare the corpse for burial in a manner befitting one so dear.

Full of suppressed joy, Abu-l-Hasan took the guerdon and hastened back to his house, where he found Nuzhat-el-Fuad ready to dance in her turn. They rejoiced together and presently added the gold pieces and the silk to those already laid by.

Now, the Khalifeh, as soon as he could dismiss his Council, hurried with Mesrur, his executioner, to Zubeydeh to condole with her on the loss of Nuzhat-el-Fuad. But when he came to her he found her weeping and waiting for his coming to condole with him on the loss of Abu-l-Hasan. And when it came to a clear misunderstanding between them as to which was dead—Abu-l-Hasan or Nuzhat-el-Fuad,—or, at the furthest, which had died first, the Khalifeh settled the matter in his own mind by turning to Mesrur, his executioner, and saying, "Truly, there is little sense in a woman."

"Jest not with me," cried Zubeydeh, laughing contemptously. "Is it not enough that Abu-l-Hasan is dead, that thou shouldst seek to bury his wife with him! Cease! Nuzhat-el-Fuad came to me in grief, mourning the death of Abu-l-Hasan."

"Cease to *thee!*" replied Er-Rashid, "for Abu-l-Hasan came since to me, mourning the death of Nuzhat-el-Fuad. Silence, woman! It is Nuzhat-el-Fuad who is dead." Then Zubeydeh recounted all the facts of the case, but the Khalifeh only laughed and reiterated: "It is certainly Nuzhat-el-Fuad who is dead, and not Abu-l-Hasan."

And so they continued to contradict each other until the Khalifeh grew very angry, and, thinking to settle the matter easily, sent Mesrur in all haste to the house of Abu-l-Hasan to ascertain the truth.

The Executioner set forth running at full speed, and no sooner was he gone than the Khalifeh said to Zubeydeh, "Wilt thou make me a wager?" "I will," said she, "for certain am I that Abu-l-Hasan is dead." "And equally certain am I that none but Nuzhat-el-Fuad is dead." So the Khalifeh staked his Garden of Delight against Zubeydeh's Hall of Statues, and, when this was agreed upon, they waited impatiently for Mesrur's return.

Meanwhile, Abu-l-Hasan, seated at the window in his house, beheld the executioner come running in haste, and said to his wife, "Methinks the Khalifeh hath announced thy death to Zubeydeh and she hath contradicted him, saying it is Abu-l-Hasan that is dead. And then, one word giving another, each hath become more obstinate, until the Khalifeh hath proposed a wager and hath now sent his executioner running hither to learn which is dead. I think, therefore, to preserve my honour in the Khalifeh's eyes, it is well that *thou* be the corpse so that Mesrur may see thee and return and inform the Khalifeh, who will then at once believe my assertion and win his wager."

Swiftly Nuzhat-el-Fuad obeyed, and, by the time Mesrur reached the house, she was extended ready for burial, while Abu-l-Hasan sat at her head weeping and beating his breast. And Mesrur advanced and uncovered her face, crying "There is no god but Allah! Alas! Our sister Nuzhat-el-Fuad is taken away!" He hastened back to the Palace and told the Khalifeh and Zubeydeh that Abu-l-Hasan was alive and well, and that Nuzhat-el-Fuad was dead. At this the Khalifeh laughed heartily, saying "Now have I won thy Hall of Statues!" Then he bade Mesrur tell the story again, omitting no smallest point; for he said Zubeydeh was lacking in sense and dull of comprehension. This enraged Zubeydeh and she retorted that it was the one who believed the word of a slave like Mesrur who was lacking in sense. But the more angry she became the more the Khalifeh laughed, until she calmed herself and said, "O Prince of the Faithful! this slave here is lying in order to please thee. Now I will send my messenger, and then the truth of the matter will be clear." The Khalifeh, still laughing, readily consented ; and Zubeydeh summoned an old woman and bade her run with all speed to this house of the quick and the dead and learn for a certainty which was prepared for the grave. And the old woman set forth running as fast as her legs would carry her.

Now, when Nuzhat-el-Fuad, seated at the window, saw her drawing near, she said to Abu-l-Hasan, " Methinks the Lady Zubeydeh hath found fault with Mesrur's report of thy death, and hath sent her messenger to learn the truth. Therefore, to preserve my honour in Zubeydeh's eyes, is it not proper that *thou* be dead ? "

" That is so," said Abu-l-Hasan, and he extended himself on the floor, while his wife prepared his corpse for the grave. When the old woman came in she found Nuzhat-el-Fuad sitting at his head, weeping bitterly and tearing her hair. " O my mother !" she wailed, " there was none like him ! Alas ! I am alone and wretched !" And she fell to moaning and sobbing and rocking herself to and fro in uncontrollable grief.

The old woman comforted her and told her how Mesrur had sought to stir up a quarrel between the Khalifeh and Zubeydeh by a lying report. Nuzhet-el-Fuad, in return, protested that, not long since, she was with the Lady Zubeydeh, who had bestowed upon her a hundred pieces of gold and a piece of fine spun silk, saying, " Go prepare thy husband's body for the grave !" And in a fresh outburst of grief Nuzhet-el-Fuad cried, " Oh ! would that Mesrur's tale were true ! Would that I had died and Abu-l-Hasan had lived, for I am solitary and know not what to do."

After the two had wept together over the body of Abu-l-Hasan the old woman hastened back to the Palace and told her story to the Lady Zubeydeh, who laughed heartily and bade her tell it to the Khalifeh. On hearing it the Khalifeh paused and pondered, but Mesrur cried, "Thou liest, hag! I myself saw Nuzhet-el-Fuad lying dead and Abu-l-Hasan alive."

"It is thou that liest!" retorted the old woman, "and thou hast a reason." And Mesrur would have laid his hands upon her, but Zubeydeh interposed, weeping; whereupon the Khalifeh said, "Nay, nay; it seems we are all liars, and methinks the proper course is that we all go together to the house of Abu-l-Hasan and so see who lieth truly and who lieth falsely." So all four went forth disputing and laying wager on wager as they went.

Now, Abu-l-Hasan, who had said within himself, "The matter cannot end here," had seated himself at the window to watch; and, when he saw the four approaching, he turned to his wife and remarked wisely, "O Nuzhet-el-Fuad! Verily, all is not a pancake that is slippery, and the pitcher that goes often to the fountain will one day be broken. Mesrur and the old woman have brewed trouble with their different tales. See! here come the Khalifeh and *his* messenger, and the Lady Zubeydeh and *her* messenger; and they are contending and disputing among themselves. Now, to save our reputation for veracity, we must *both* be dead."

With great haste they laid themselves out, and, before the babel of contention reached the house, they were lying side by side prepared for burial, and like nothing so much as the silence of the grave. And thus the Khalifeh, and Zubeydeh, and Mesrur, and the old woman, found them when they entered. "Alas!" cried the Lady Zubeydeh, turning to the Khalifeh and Mesrur, "by your repeated tales of her death you have succeeded at last in killing her!" "This is foolish talk," replied the Khalifeh, while Mesrur and the old woman glared at one another, speechless. "Did not Abu-l-Hasan come to me, plucking his beard and smiting his breast, and saying, ' Nuzhet-el-Fuad is dead?' Truly, then, she died first, and he, after we had made our wager, died of grief. I, therefore, have won." But Zubeydeh replied to this in a torrent of words, saying that Nuzhet-el-Fuad came to her, tearing her hair and calling out in sorrow for the death of Abu-l-Hasan. And as this was *before* the wager was made she in her turn claimed to have won. A long dispute ensued in which Mesrur and the old woman joined, but neither side could convince the other; and none knew but the two who lay still as death.

At last the Khalifeh, weary of the wrangle, sat himself down at the heads of the two corpses and said hotly, "By Allah! By the tomb of the Prophet! By the graves of all my ancestors! I would give a thousand pieces of gold to any one who could tell me which of these two died before the other."

No sooner had Abu-l-Hasan heard these words than he, being somewhat quicker in such things than his wife, sprang up crying, " O Prince of the Faithful! it was I who died first. And I have won the thousand pieces according to thine oath." But, when Nuzhet-el-Fuad sat up before them, and the Lady Zubeydeh saw that they had practised a trick to obtain the gold, she chid her gently, reproaching her for not asking for help; and yet she wept all the time with joy that she was alive. And the Khalifeh—he wept with laughter, and, as soon as he could speak, he cried, "O Abu-l-Hasan, truly thou art a wag!" "Nay, O Prince of the Faithful!"

replied Abu-l-Hasan, "I had dispensed the good gifts at thy hands, and, being sore stricken with poverty, could contrive no other way but to play this trick upon thee. When I was alone I used my gold wisely, but since thou hast given me this female slave to wife, all thy wealth would not suffice for our extravagance ; wherefore, if my lord make not haste to bestow upon me the thousand pieces of gold according to his oath, I may not take it, and—"

At this the Khalifeh and the Lady Zubeydeh laughed heartily, and even Mesrur twisted his face into a grin and forgot his threat to bastinade the old woman.

"Come," said the Khalifeh, "I must reward thee for thy victory over death." And, when they had gained the Palace, Er-Rashid gave him the thousand pieces of gold, and assured to him an unstinted plenitude in the future. Zubeydeh also, in token of similar goodwill, bestowed a thousand pieces of gold upon Nuzhet-el-Fuad. And Abu-l-Hasan and Nuzhet-el-Fuad lived happily thereafter, until, in the end, the last cup of joy was drunk, and the Gleaner, who gleans in palaces and the humblest homes, came to gather them in.